~ Note on the Author ~

Julian Lawrence Brooks was born in Bromley in 1967, the eldest of two sons of an architect and a psychotherapist, and grew up in the small Kentish village of Ulcombe. He was educated at Maidstone Grammar School, Liverpool and Greenwich Universities, and Caldecott and Mid-Kent Colleges. He has worked in various forms of therapeutic treatment for children, adults and families. Despite being registered severely visually impaired, he spends most of his free time gallivanting around the high mountains of the British Isles. He lives with his fiancée in Maidstone, and has two children.

Freya's Quest

by

Julian Lawrence Brooks

Grosvenor House
Publishing Limited

This book is published by
Grosvenor House Publishing Ltd
28-30 High Street, Guildford, Surrey, GU1 3HY.
www.grosvenorhousepublishing.co.uk

A CIP record for this book
is available from the British Library

ISBN 978-1-906210-65-6

Dedication

For my family & friends
&
to the memory of all those
I have lost along the way

- I -

2 August, 1987

THE TWIN TOWERS of the Gothic gatehouse stood stark against the darkening sky, their battlements framed by beech trees. Ivy crept over the lower portions of the hewn stonework, invading the lower arrow slits. I shivered at its cold austerity and wondered what might lie beyond the archway, barred by its wrought-iron portcullis.

Heavy clouds rolled in, as I sat in my car and ate the last of my sandwiches. I gazed through the windscreen as forked lightning streaked across the sky between the towers, illuminating the gatehouse further and creating an even greater sense of eeriness. I was startled by the first clap of thunder and dropped my thermos flask, revealing my nervous state.

I knew it was time to go as the heavy downpour began. My Fiat started at the third attempt and it jolted over the ruts of the forestry lay-by as I drove towards the metalled road. The gatehouse was on the brow of the hill, surrounded by dense conifer plantations. I took one last look before driving away, keeping in low gear as the gradient steepened.

The thunderstorm intensified as I went down the hill. The rain came down in torrents. The windscreen wipers fought a losing battle to clear my vision. As I approached a bend in the road, the car's engine began to stutter. Then it cut out completely and I cruised to a halt. I peered through the rain-splattered windscreen. I was still in the middle of the forest. In the loneliest spot imaginable.

I tried the ignition. The engine spluttered back into life. My hopes rose, only for them to fade away when the engine died once more. I crossed my fingers and tried again; then again. But the engine just turned over. And this became more laboured as the battery weakened. I slammed my fists against the steering wheel in frustration.

I sat there in silence, with the rain lashing down onto the car. The vinyl sunroof began to sag under the weight of water. Rivulets flowed across the tarmac in front of me. I was in a hollow in the road. I guessed it would probably flood before the night was out.

I lay my head in my hands and propped up my arms against the steering wheel, thinking about my next move. As the night descended, I decided to look at my map book under torchlight. I calculated I was ten miles from the nearest settlement and public telephone; and the building the gatehouse guarded was now two miles back up the road. I didn't fancy a long walk in this rain, let alone in darkness. I'd left the hotel in such a hurry that I hadn't even had time to bring a sturdy raincoat.

After further contemplation, I climbed out of the car, fighting the wind and the wet. I hugged my leather jacket against my body, knowing I would soon be drenched. I opened the rear engine compartment and shone the torch inside. I squinted at the mechanical components, knowing I'd have to find the distributor and its cables. As I turned to get a better view, I was dazzled by headlights. A vehicle was coming around the bend behind me. It was nearly upon me. And my Fiat was right in the middle of the road, almost blind to the oncoming traffic.

I thought it was about to ram into the back of my car. I would be crushed in between! I dived into the ditch.

The driver of the Land Rover must have seen me only at the last minute. When he finally reacted, he tried to swerve around the Fiat. He would have succeeded, but for a final aquaplaning that sent him crunching into the side of the car. The Land Rover came to rest amidst screeching brakes and exhaust fumes.

The man then reversed, so he could survey the car and its driver through the beam of his headlights. He climbed down from the cab, hunching his shoulders and putting up the hood of his cagoule. He examined the damage he'd caused. He gazed through the windows as if looking for occupants.

I shouted over to him, waving my hand. I had fallen heavily into the ditch, bruising my left side. The large volume of water had saved me from worse injury, but had saturated my clothing.

He came over and hauled me out of the water. 'Are you OK?' he shouted, pushing back my hair and looking into my face.

I nodded feebly.

He guided me over to the back of the Land Rover, lifting me through the rear door and sitting me down on the floor. There were blankets inside. He placed them around me in an attempt to warm me up.

'I broke down....Been here some time,' I mumbled. I was shivering.

He turned on the interior light to assess my condition more closely. Now I could view my rescuer. He was a handsome, clean-shaven man, with a mop of black hair pushed back over his forehead. He looked to be around my age – early to mid-thirties.

'Will you be all right for a moment?'

I nodded.

He left me alone. He went to the front, brought out a torch and proceeded to inspect my car. He returned a few minutes later. 'You won't get that going in a hurry.'

'The electrics've failed, I know.'

'Yeah, you're right. And the accident damage hasn't helped, either. Hope you didn't have far to go?'

I looked at him, speechless, feeling defeated.

'Where're you headed?'

I didn't answer.

'Where've you come from?' he persisted.

'Oh, London. But I've spent a few weeks on the coast of Wales. Now I'm heading north.'

'I see. Long way to be travelling on your own, isn't it? And on such a back route. 'Specially this time of night.'

'Maybe – but I can look after myself.'

He raised an eyebrow and smirked. 'Doesn't look like it!'

I shrugged, too tired and cold to argue with him. 'What can I do now?'

'There's only one thing for it. I'll try to tow your car up to my house. It's only a couple of miles away. You can phone for assistance from there.'

I thanked him for his generosity.

He drove back in front of the Fiat, stopped, brought out a towrope and rigged it up between the two vehicles. He had to do all this in the face of the storm that raged on relentlessly. I felt guilty about causing this stranger so much hassle.

He returned. 'You'll have to steer the car. The wipers won't work, so it'll be difficult. Think you're up to it?'

'Yes.'

'Good. I'll take it slow. Sooner we get there the better, you're looking cold.'

I nodded, thanked him again, then returned to the Fiat. I was appalled by the damage to the nearside. The passenger door and the quarter panel had caved in badly.

We set off at a cautious pace. I had to wind down the window and manually wipe the windscreen as I was travelling along, not an easy task in view of the pounding rain. In the end, I gave up altogether and leant out of the window instead, which numbed my head and sent shivers through the rest of my body.

The road meandered through the forestry plantation. Every now and then, the tops of the swaying conifers were lit up by the lightning and their shadows danced across the glistening tarmac.

The journey seemed endless. Eventually, through the gloom, the twin towers of the fortified gatehouse reappeared. I was astonished when the towing vehicle turned into the driveway. The portcullis began to rise, apparently by remote control. As I passed beneath the archway, I glimpsed a security camera surveying me. I must admit it made me feel uneasy.

He towed me up the driveway, lined on either side with mature beech trees.

Suddenly, a screeching and tearing sound filled the air. Then a great thud. Then silence. Then a light crunch as my car hit the back of the Land Rover.

Within seconds, he was tugging open my door, pulling me roughly from the car.

'What the hell....!'

I choked on my words as he thrust us down the embankment. A large rhododendron bush cushioned our fall.

Then another fearful tearing. Far greater than the first. An awesome shadow flickered past me as I rose to my feet once more. There was a crunching of metal and a shattering of glass.

More lightning filled the sky.

The Fiat lay crushed under the fallen tree.

Not only did I owe this man a tow in foul weather. Now I owed him my very life! A second or more and I'd have been under that uprooted tree myself.

He gripped my shoulders, pulling me away from the wreckage. We hurried up the driveway, through an inner gatehouse and into a courtyard. We rushed over to the entrance, huddling together from the elements whilst he fumbled for the key. Finally he opened the door and we burst across the threshold, dripping wet and shivering. He strained to close the door behind him against the force of the storm.

More thunder boomed around the castle as he guided me through a hallway and into a lounge. The room was dimly lit by candlelight. The furniture was of heavy oak; the walls of bare masonry were lined with paintings and hunting trophies.

He rang a bell on the wall and led me over to the fire. He sat me down on a bearskin rug. The bear's head snarled at me, so I rose again and steadied myself against the marble mantelpiece.

A woman came into the room. She was small in stature, oriental in appearance, her grim face partially masked in the shadows. She had long, dark hair and was wearing a kimono. She nodded at the man, then looked me up and down dismissively. She appeared to be about to question who I was when the man said: 'Please bring me a couple of towels and some dressing gowns.'

The woman nodded and left.

'What am I going to do now?' I mumbled in desperation.

'There's only one thing for it. I'll have to put you up for the night. We can sort things out in the morning.'

I attempted to say thank you, but I was trembling too much.

'Don't worry about it now. Try to warm yourself. We'll have to get out of these clothes pretty damn quick, before we freeze to death.' He began to strip off, revealing a strong physique. 'Shock's probably setting in now, too.'

I huddled by the fire.

Then the woman came back with the things the man had asked for.

He stood half naked before me, towelling himself down. He put on a dressing gown, then said to the woman: 'Yasuko, take our guest upstairs and run a bath.'

She came towards me and draped a towel over my matted hair. I found myself being led upstairs, but it was too dark to make out much of my surroundings. She was carrying a candle to light the way and now I realized the storm must have caused a power cut.

Once inside the bathroom, I shivered as she turned on the taps and poured bubble bath into the filling tub. In normal circumstances I would have insisted on privacy. But I'd been through a lot that night. I was frozen and the damp had weakened me. I knew I had to discard my sodden clothes before I caught pneumonia. She helped me to undress, which wasn't easy, as the fabric clung to my skin and my fingers were too numb to unfasten my bra strap. Once completed, I clutched at my long hair with my right hand and tried to cover what I could of my nakedness with the other.

Then she helped me into the bath, lighting smaller candles and placing them around its enamelled edge. As I sank into the soothing water, and I could hide beneath the bubbles, all embarrassment left me. She stood quietly in the background as I soaked up the warmth, the goose pimples fading as my body slowly came back to life.

When she realized I was all right, she left me to prepare my bed. She returned only after I had risen from the bath, in time to wrap a towel around me and guide me to my room for the night.

Once alone again, I dried myself, then slipped under the covers. As I was edging off into sleep, there was a knock at the door.

'Hope you're OK.' It was my rescuer's voice.

'Yes.'

'I forgot to ask,' he whispered: 'What's your name?'

'Freya.'

'I'm Dylan,' he replied. 'Hope you sleep well. Welcome to Grimshaw Lodge.'

- II -

PEOPLE LAUGHED AT my tiny Fiat 500. But I kept it because it had character and was perfect for the London streets. However, due to faulty electrics, it often broke down in wet conditions. If I'd traded it in for a newer Ford or Vauxhall, as my friends had often suggested, I never would have found my way into Dylan's world.

The Lodge was miles from anywhere. No one would be able to find me. But frankly, this suited me. And John, the man who had sent me, would be pleased. I'd spent three days trying to think up a way of gaining entry through the gatehouse, having quickly realized the walls surrounding the property were too tall and smooth to scale. And now I was here.

Still, I awoke the next morning confused and disorientated, haunted by the power of my nightmares about being crushed under the tree. The unforeseen change of plan had nearly killed me. I hoped that by the end of my quest the results would put this risk back into perspective.

I lay in a double bed and my first sight was a large marble fireplace, above which hung a mirror. All the furniture was pure white, matching the décor of the room and the elaborate ceiling plasterwork. Rustic scenes of Lakeland life filled simple picture frames. A crystal chandelier hung down from above. A semi-circular turret was a feature in one corner.

I pulled back the covers and climbed to my feet. I was naked, but a dressing gown had been left out for me. When I put the garment on, I immediately felt less vulnerable. I walked over to the window. I winced as the powerful sun hit my eyes when I drew back the silk curtains.

The courtyard lay in front of me, hemmed in by a castellated wall, old stabling facilities and the inner gatehouse. Beyond, a gravel road wound downhill, over a bridge unseen last night, to the tree-lined driveway. The outer gatehouse and the fallen tree lay hidden from this viewpoint. The night had made everything appear much bigger than it actually was.

A knock at the door broke my thoughts. I climbed back into bed. 'Come in,' I called.

The oriental woman entered, carrying a full breakfast on a silver tray. She was wearing another kimono, the same design as the night before, but different in colour and embroidered with dragons. Her black hair was tied in a long plait all the way down her back. Her face betrayed no emotion and she had a stern demeanour.

'You shouldn't have!' I said, taking the tray with haste and tucking into the bacon and eggs.

The woman bowed and left, coming back with my clothes which she'd washed and ironed overnight.

'Thanks,' I muttered, my mouth half full. 'Sorry, I can't remember your name.'

The woman didn't answer.

'Are you Dylan's housemaid?'

The woman remained silent, but shrugged her shoulders and held up her hands.

I first found her manners rather rude, then wondered whether there was some cultural etiquette at work.

Then she held up a silver case, which was fastened by a chain around her neck.

I read the word engraved on this: 'Y-a-s-u-k-o?'

The woman nodded, then pulled out a notepad from one side of the case, and a pencil from within the notepad. She licked the tip of the pencil with her tongue, scribbled something onto the pad with her left hand, then ripped off the page and handed it to me.

Cannot talk, but understand.

Now I felt only embarrassment. 'I'm so sorry. I had no idea.'

Yasuko remained impassive.

'How long have you been here with Dylan?'

8 yrs.

I was surprised. 'You must've been very young when you arrived, then?'

Yes. 18.

'And where are you from, originally I mean?'

She gave me a cool stare, then wrote: *Tokyo. But too long ago to talk about.*

'Oh, OK,' I replied, quickly changing the subject. 'Thank you for washing my clothes.'

She nodded and wrote: *Come down in own time.*

She left me to mull over what she had said, or rather written. I was already bemused by this strange household. But I wanted to make the most of my good fortune.

After eating, I soaked in the bathtub again, soothing the bruises down my left side from my tumble down the embankment. The bathroom was now seen in all its luxury, with its marble panelling and gold fittings. Then I dressed and combed my hair, thinking of how I could embellish my cover story before meeting Dylan again.

Eventually, I walked out of the bedroom door and onto the circular landing. This was in two halves, the middle section being solid masonry, the rest dropping over finely turned balustrades to the hallway below. I opened each door in turn, discovering three more bedrooms, similar to the one I'd slept in. Another little door led onto a minstrels' gallery. I caught my breath as I found myself overlooking a baronial dining room.

As I returned to the central landing, Dylan came up the stairs to greet me. 'I hope you slept well.'

'Yes. Thanks for the hospitality.'

'My pleasure,' he replied, smiling.

He was even more good-looking in the daylight. I felt an immediate attraction to his dark, sultry appearance. He was the type of guy I'd fantasized about in my dreams on all those lonely nights back home.

'How are you feeling? You had quite an ordeal last night.'

'I'll mend. Just a few painful bruises.'

He looked concerned.

'Don't worry. None of this was your fault, you know.'

'Yes it was. If I hadn't towed you back here, you wouldn't've nearly been killed....Nor your car destroyed.'

'True. But being stranded out in the storm could've been just as bad. Let's leave it at that, shall we?'

'OK. But let me extend my hospitality further. You can stay a few days, if you like.'

'Really?' I said, trying to disguise my delight.

Dylan smiled again, as if detecting my emotions despite my efforts. 'Yes. Anyway, the phone lines are down, so we can't summon help....And you've no car now, so....'

'OK. Thanks. I accept.'

'Hope there's no one wondering where you are?'

'No. I live alone and tend to travel alone, too. No one will worry till I fail to turn up for work. And I'm on a month's break, so there's plenty of time to play with.'

'That's good. Yet I'm surprised a woman as beautiful as you hasn't a partner or husband to worry about you.' He had taken hold of my left hand and was now rubbing his thumb over my bare ring finger.

I fought off a shyness that had plagued my adolescence and crept back in my adulthood only at moments like these. 'There was someone special once,' I finally plucked up the courage to say. 'His name was John. We're still friends – he's actually my boss now. But we were just too young. I've had a few boyfriends since, but no one who quite measures up.'

This seemed to please him.

'And you?'

'No one special,' he said, without elaborating, as if trying to keep an air of mystery about him.

It was my turn to smile at this growing warmth between us. 'Now, I'm looking forward to the grand tour. What is this place anyway, some kind of medieval castle?'

'No, it's an old hunting lodge, dating from the 1840s, just as the Gothic Revival was gathering pace. Designed by a man named Anthony Salvin. Quite a famous architect in his day.'

'Oh, I see.' I began to survey the landing area again, an excuse to break away from his penetrative gaze. 'I've already taken a look up here,' I said, 'except for this room.' I gripped the handle of the door in the middle of the central area of masonry. I found it to be locked. 'What's behind here?'

'That's out of bounds, I'm afraid. It leads to the tower, where I do all my work. It's my only private space here, so please respect that.' He had taken on a serious tone and an expression to match.

I promptly nodded.

The galleried landing had steps leading down from both sides. These converged at a half landing, where a grander staircase swept down to the hallway. As we descended, I gazed up at the glass dome overhead, the ornate plasterwork etched in gold leaf, and the various paintings adorning the walls. I noticed one picture was a portrait of Dylan himself, dressed in Victorian attire and crouched, quill in hand, over a writing desk.

Dylan strode around his residence with an air of confidence and beaming pride, pointing out the finer architectural details as he went. He took delight in my awe of the building and my attention to his every word. His intense eyes, his brooding looks and the timbre of his husky voice created a magnetism which held me spellbound.

After the tour of the house, he led me around the beautifully landscaped gardens. Mountaintops, shrouded in wispy clouds, could be glimpsed above the green of the forest. A mature deciduous woodland surrounded the edges of the new plantation. The view of lake and mountain must have been spectacular before the conifers had been planted.

Dylan left me to wander around the grounds whilst he began the task of cutting up the tree. After several hours I was bored and decided to find out how he was getting on. As I approached, I could hear a chain saw. Dylan was dressed in goggles and protective gloves, his torso caked in wood chippings. He shut off the chain saw and started stacking logs.

He hadn't seen me, so I weaved around the fallen trunk, and stood on the opposite embankment from the one we'd fallen down the night before. This was a much shorter slope, ending with a wide expanse of lawn that swept across to the perimeter wall.

I realized now the tree had come down because of the wind and the waterlogged nature of the ground, rather than a lightning strike. If Grimshaw Lodge had been built in the 1840s as Dylan had said, then these trees must have been planted around the same time. I was saddened for the uprooted tree nearly as much as for my poor Fiat. Rooks squawked from their nests high up in the branches overhead, sounding as disturbed as I felt.

I grabbed one of the fallen tree's roots and leant against my arm, watching a family of rabbits in the distance. Everything was so quiet, save for the occasional sounds of nature. I'd been an urban girl for so long I'd forgotten how peaceful the countryside of my upbringing could be.

Then the chain saw started up again. As I spun around towards Dylan, I happened to look down into the hole left by the tree where there were signs of old burrows under the roots. Something glinted in the mud. Intrigued, I bent down and disturbed the dirt with my fingers. I gripped the metal object and pulled, astonished that a gold chain rose from the ground in my hand. I dug more, and a medallion was revealed. I rubbed at the grime and saw it was a strange object. Something dark lay in the middle, encrusted with dirt, with a gold disc around the outside. I stood up and the object caught the sunlight.

The next thing I heard was the chain saw approaching, inches from my head! I ducked and felt the juddering blades burying themselves into the trunk above me.

Dylan had been coming towards me, trance-like, transfixed by the medallion.

I quivered in the hole, too shocked to move.

Finally he came to his senses, dropping the chain saw and backing away. 'Jesus! What're you doing! I could've killed you.'

For a brief moment, I'd been sure that had been his intention!

He snatched the medallion out of my hand. 'What've you got there?' he questioned, brushing his hand over its surface. His eyes widened, but he said nothing more and handed it back. He picked up the chain saw again and returned to work.

I walked back up the driveway, my adrenaline still pumping, wanting space to recover. I stood against the parapet of the bridge, breathing hard, before moving on again. As I came through the inner gatehouse, my mood calmed further because the Lodge appeared before me in all its splendour: the mock battlements around the top of the walls; the Gothic arch windows and occasional fake arrow slits; the side turrets on each of the four corners marking the location of the bedrooms; and the dominant central tower, rising three storeys above the roof of the main building.

I found Yasuko in the kitchen. She was on her hands and knees, scrubbing the floor vigorously with a stiff-bristled brush. She rose to her feet when she realized I was there, picking up a pail of dirty water and emptying it into the sink. There was an assortment of cleaning fluids on the draining board and the work surfaces were sparkling.

She looked upset at being distracted from her chores, but when I showed her my discovery she set to work eagerly in cleaning the item. When she handed it back, it was gleaming, as if it had never been buried. The centre was a black stone, carved in the image of a goat's head and around the edge of the gold disc was a series of weird geometric symbols.

Dylan drove back into the courtyard. Yasuko had gone into the dining hall to polish the long oak table, but he sent her off to prepare some sandwiches. Then he led me out through the French doors to the ramparted terrace, which had stunning views of the main garden.

We sat down at a table, shading ourselves beneath the canopy of its large umbrella. Yasuko soon returned with some food and drink, then stood back as if waiting for further instructions. Dylan obliged, sending her off. I watched her as she returned to her cleaning of the dining hall.

'You work her too hard, Dylan.'

'Oh, don't worry about Yasuko Yakamoto – there's poetry in that name, eh? – she's a tough character. Runs in the blood. Her father was an American marine; and her maternal grandfather a kamikaze pilot in the Second World War....And I don't make her clean like that, she chooses to.'

'I see.'

'Helps having an obsessive compulsive around, though, don't you think? Drives you mad after a while, but you get a really clean house!' He chuckled.

'You're wicked, Dylan!'

He started to tuck into his sandwiches and I showed him the medallion again.

'Weird, isn't it?' I said.

'Yeah. Definitely old. Looks Masonic to me. Perhaps we can take it to the local museum. If it's valuable we can share the profits.'

'I couldn't possibly do that.'

He smiled in that seductive way of his again. 'And listen, I'm sorry I startled you earlier.'

I nodded.

After a while he said: 'I reckon I should get most of the drive clear by tonight. If I carry on at the same rate, you should be able to make your escape by tomorrow.'

'Oh.'

'You look surprised. Don't you want to go?'

'Well, it's not that exactly.' Although it was: now I knew his intentions, I would have to formulate a new plan of action. And fast.

'What then?'

'Well, it's going to be difficult without a car.'

'Oh, right. Don't worry. I own a classic car workshop and museum down near Keswick. Once the tree's gone, we can transport your Fiat there. I can lend you one of my cars, so you can get to where you wanna go. Don't want you feeling like I've trapped you here.'

'OK. You're very kind – too kind.'

'Anyway, I've got some guests coming tomorrow afternoon.'

'Well, I wouldn't want to overstay my welcome, then.' I sat back and drank some iced water, smiling on the outside but cursing on the inside.

We finished our lunch in silence.

Later, I decided to help him to chop up some of the smaller logs into fireplace-sized pieces, reassured that the chain saw was no longer in use.

'No, like this,' he said, standing the log back onto the larger circular slice of trunk he had rolled onto the lawn. He raised the axe above his head and brought it down with a crisp thud, shattering the wood into two even pieces.

He made me try again, but I caught the edge, shaving off only a splinter and sending the rest of the log ricocheting into Dylan's legs. He took a step back, clutching his shin.

'Sorry, you OK?'

'Yes,' he replied, rubbing the bruise with one hand and replacing the log with the other. Then he came round behind me and looped his arms under my own and grasped his hands over mine on the shaft of the axe. We lifted it together and he helped me to guide the blade, which embedded itself in the centre of the log.

'That's it, you're getting there slowly,' he said. Then he swung the axe up again with the log still attached and brought it down with a bang, splitting the log in half.

He praised me again, ramming the axe into the slice of trunk. But I was lost in the closeness of our bodies and the beat of his heart against my back. Then he withdrew his hands and gathered up my long hair, giving the strands a twist, before placing the makeshift plait inside my T-shirt. 'That's better. You'll be able to see properly now.'

The touch of his fingers – and now his breath – against my neck, began to arouse me. I knew I wanted him. But he broke away from me and the moment was quickly lost. I resigned myself to continuing with the task in hand.

After another few hours, most of the bigger branches had been sawn into smaller chunks and Dylan could use the winch on the front of the Land Rover to drag the segments free from the driveway. Finally, all that remained was the bulk of the main trunk, cut into two halves. Now we could see how the Fiat had been crushed from the roof to the sills, right across the front seats. I'd have had no chance of survival if I'd remained inside. This confirmation of my lucky escape made me shudder.

Dylan could see my distress. He came over and put his arm around my shoulders. 'Look, why don't you knock it on the head. I can finish up here. Yasuko won't want to be disturbed, but there's a TV in the lounge.'

I turned and gave him a proper hug, whispering my thanks in his ear. Then I headed off towards the main building.

After a quick wash, I sat down in the lounge. I watched the television for an hour, becoming bored by the mediocrity of daytime broadcasting. I yawned, turning off the set.

I went into the library instead, discovering ornate bookshelves from floor to ceiling, except where mullioned arch windows brought in much-needed sunlight.

Dylan had an impressive collection of books. Many were leather-bound and antiquarian; some were important first editions; others were humble paperbacks.

One shelf unit even turned out to be a clever wooden facade, carved and painted to look like real books; created merely to impress or give balance to the room, I supposed.

History, philosophy and psychology were well represented. I flicked through a number of volumes, most of which had been heavily annotated; Dylan was an intellectual, then, not simply displaying books for show.

Yet my attention was drawn to the array of novels. All the classics were here, along with contemporary titles. I was about to pick out *The Picture of Dorian Gray* by Oscar Wilde, when my eyes fell upon five books by Dylan Quest.

I pulled out the one entitled *Friends and Lovers* and looked at the photograph of the author on the back cover. And there he was, looking younger and with shorter hair, but still Dylan: "a contemporary literary giant", if you were to believe the publisher's blurb.

I turned to the first page and began to read. Soon I became lost in the powerful story, full of symbolism and allegory.

I was a quarter of the way through the engrossing novel when Dylan caught up with me again, his hair still wet from a recent bath or shower.

He looked at me, then down at the book I was holding in my hand. His eyes narrowed.

'Why didn't you tell me you were Dylan Quest, the novelist? You must've known I had no idea.' I tried to make my astonishment as plausible as I could.

'It's precisely because I knew you hadn't a clue that so attracted me in the first place. Naturally, circumstances dictated I had to offer you shelter. But I've had too much attention from women lured to me for all the wrong motives.'

'Is this book based on reality?'

'It's not autobiographical, if that's what you mean. Of course, every writer draws on his or her own observations and experiences.' He sat down next to me, putting his arm around me. 'What do you think of the novel, anyway? – out of interest.'

'It's good Dylan, very good. So far, at least.'

This undoubtedly pleased him.

'One thing I did find curious. I notice this novel and the other four are all dedicated to "Seraphina". Who's she?'

I watched Dylan's face crumple. He slouched back on the sofa, raising his head to the ceiling.

'Sera was my wife. We were married when I was only sixteen.'

'Where's she now? Are you hinting it didn't work out because you were too young?'

Dylan remained silent for what seemed like hours.

'She....' he croaked, then coughed, trying to force out the words.

I waited patiently.

'She died shortly after we were married....Seventeen years ago. In fact, almost to the day!'

'I'm sorry, Dylan, I had no idea.'

'It's been a part of my life the papers and my readership have never known about.'

'How....?'

'Car crash,' he interrupted.

There didn't seem to be anything to say after that.

But he was vulnerable. I hugged him tightly and he merged into me. We stayed like this for some minutes. It was difficult to know when my containing gesture began to bring out the sexual undercurrents which had been building between us over the course of the day. But I knew I had to seize my chance. Overcoming my initial shyness, I touched his face with my hand and drew his lips to mine.

This broke his trance-like despair for his dead wife and he began to respond by directing his own affections towards me.

Before too long he was leading me upstairs to bed. And I was left confused, no longer certain whether I was really seducing him, or whether he was actually seducing me.

- III -

I AWOKE THE next morning, still burnt out from Dylan's sexual desires, my petite body swallowed up in his tight embrace. I hadn't quite expected this. John had, no doubt; that's why he had sent me. I could picture him sitting in the shadows behind his desk, clouded in cigarette smoke, smiling. He had thought my "beauty" would lure him. And he was well aware that I'd spent the last year without anyone, with only my cat – since deceased – to ward off the loneliness of my Battersea flat. And all of the teenage John's adequacies – and the five lovers I'd had since then – had been shown up by Dylan's originality.

Dylan stirred and kissed the back of my neck. I turned around to face him and our lips met.

'Last night was good,' he said. 'Looks like you'll be here a little longer than expected.'

'Must be fate,' I replied. My plan had worked and I had found sexual fulfilment for the first time in years. But I had compromised my objectivity. I knew now it would be a battle to resist becoming too emotionally involved.

Yasuko came in with a brunch tray, which shook in her hands when she saw I was in Dylan's bed. She placed the tray on top of the duvet, then began a flurry of hand movements. Dylan replied and I realized they were communicating in sign language.

She left, returned with another tray, then left again.

Dylan smiled.

'Did we shock her?'

'Surprised her, maybe. But it'd take a lot more to shock Yasuko. No, she was concerned you weren't in your own room. Thought you might've done a runner.'

'That would've been a bit difficult.'

'Yeah, I suppose so. Although she says the phone line's been repaired, so you could've ordered a taxi.'

I nodded.

We began to eat our brunch. I finished first, not being able to stomach the cooked food, and picked up the novel I'd left on the bedside cabinet.

Dylan watched as I began to read. 'Still enjoying it?' he said through a mouthful of bacon.

'Yes. Your characters are well tied in to the landscape. Reminds me of the Romantic Poets, the Brontë sisters and Hardy, with the spice provided by a dash of D.H.Lawrence.'

'Very good. You've spotted some of my biggest influences. You've studied Literature, I presume.'

'Only half an A-Level, before I ran away from home with John and went to Art School. But I'm widely read in the classics.'

'I see. Must've been young, then – seventeen, eighteen?'

'Seventeen. And three months pregnant to boot.'

'So, you're a mother?'

'No.' I remained silent for a while, trying to control the rush of emotions welling up inside. '....I had an abortion.'

Dylan dropped his fork onto his plate and put his arm around my shoulder. I cuddled up to him.

'I'm sorry,' he said. 'I'm prying.'

'It all happened a long time ago, Dylan. I was only a naive girl then. I'm thirty-four now.'

'Really? You don't look it.'

I smiled and carried on reading – or at least pretended to read – until he had finished his food. Then we dressed. As we went back down the driveway to finish the last of the clearing up, he said: 'Sometimes I wish I'd kept to the popular fiction I wrote in my youth, before I got published. This literary stuff wins accolades, but it takes a lot out of me.'

A large truck came, with a crane attached. Dylan had called in the reinforcements, four men he evidently knew from the way he greeted them. They had brought heavier cutting gear and they set to work on the thick trunk, under Dylan's instruction. By the afternoon, they were able to crane off the section covering my car. There was a crumpling of metal as the trunk lifted clear and was hauled onto the flatbed of the trailer. Next, they lifted the base of the trunk, but as the remainder of its roots ripped from the ground it started to shift down the opposite embankment. After a dangerous few moments, with men jumping clear in all directions, Dylan decided it was better to release the trunk and let it fall over the edge. There was a rumbling and a tearing as it descended through the rhododendrons, before coming to rest at the bottom.

Some time later, a grey Bentley cruised from the gatehouse and came to a skidding halt in front of the wreck of the Fiat. There was still plenty to finish off, but I was more perturbed about having our space invaded by these guests. It would make my task more difficult.

The passenger door opened and a man climbed out. He was dressed in tweed trousers and a waistcoat that strained against his developing paunch. He must have been in his late forties, but his balding reddish-brown hair, his chubby, pockmarked jowls and his long side-whiskers, made him look a lot older.

He immediately lit up a big cigar. 'Hi, my dear fellow,' he yelled towards Dylan. 'What's all this, then.' He began to walk towards the car wreck. He looked down in disgust as his highly polished shoes became coated in sawdust.

Dylan came over and shook his hand and waved towards a woman, who was now climbing out of the Bentley. She was short and fat, with flowing grey hair. She was probably in her mid-fifties, with a deeply-lined face, still plain despite mountains of cosmetics.

Then the visitor saw me. 'My, my, old man, what have you got here?' He came over and took my hand and kissed it. 'I'm Rupert.'

'Freya,' I replied, coughing as I inhaled some of his cigar smoke.

'Enchanté.'

'That's enough, Rupert. Leave the poor girl alone.' It was the grey-haired woman coming towards us. 'I'm Ronni – Veronica to you, by the way. Can't say I'm pleased to meet you. Is this your little car blocking our way?'

'Yes, it's a long story. I'm Freya.' I extended my hand, but she refused to take it. I took an immediate dislike to her haughty manner.

'You must be Dylan's latest bit of fluff, I take it?'

I flushed in embarrassment.

'Slim, blonde-haired, blue-eyed.' Veronica said. 'You certainly conform to one of his usual types.'

Rupert stepped forward, as if wanting to intervene on my behalf, but he was checked by her piercing stare.

Dylan took over, guiding Veronica back inside the car. He then climbed into the driver's seat and he carefully drove the Bentley around the wreck.

'Let me apologize,' Rupert said. 'It's been a very fraught journey with all the storm damage on the road and we weren't expecting other guests.'

I nodded, but kept my head bowed as we followed the Bentley. Dylan had stopped ahead and was getting out again. He beckoned Rupert into the driver's seat.

'Park up in the courtyard and we'll follow you up. Yasuko'll carry your things inside.'

When they had driven off, Dylan bent down and gave me a kiss, stroking my hair away from my eyes. 'Sorry about that.'

'You're the second man to apologize for her behaviour in as many minutes. Don't defend the indefensible.'

'She's always a bit supercilious upon first meeting.'

'You're doing it again!'

'OK,' he said, putting up his hands.

'How long have you known her?'

'Many years.'

'And Rupert?'

'A few. He helped me put together the financial plan for this place and other Georgian properties I own in Liverpool.'

'You have other houses?'

'Yes. My property portfolio brings in more income than my writing now.'

'I see.'

'Are they a couple?'

Dylan laughed. 'Heaven's no!' We approached the Bentley and found Yasuko struggling with unloading their overnight bags. 'Ronni's trying to pair him off with Janis.'

'Who's Janis?'

'That's me.' I turned to see a woman climbing somewhat timidly out of the rear door. 'I'm Janis Norton. Pleased to meet you.' She was an attractive woman with collar-length jet-black hair. She'd been there all along, unseen.

Later, we all assembled in the drawing room.

'Ah, I see you followed my recommendation, Dylan,' Rupert said. 'What a fine grand piano – even if I do say so myself.'

He sat down on the stool and Yasuko rushed over with an ashtray, just as Rupert was waving his cigar above the keys.

'Careful, Rupert,' Dylan cried. 'You of all people should know how much that's worth.'

Rupert grinned, then launched himself into a series of Noel Coward and Ivor Novello songs. I was surprised how such a melodious voice could spring from such an unlikely source.

'You're on form today,' Dylan said between numbers.

'Give me some of your wonderful wine and I'll entertain you all afternoon.'

'Oh, dear, please don't,' Janis mumbled under her breath, as Yasuko took his hint and poured Rupert a large glass.

'This is such a wonderful room now you've finished it, Dylan,' Veronica said. 'Quite marvellous.' She took a sip of her own white wine.

'But it is a little anachronistic, isn't it,' I chipped in.

'How so?' Veronica raised one of her painted eyebrows.

'Well, it's Regency in style....'

'And?'

Well if you don't butt in all the time I'll tell you, I thought, then wished I'd actually said it out loud. 'Dylan tells me the house dates from the 1840s. This room's decorated circa 1810-20.'

Veronica looked vexed, but said: 'Oh, yes, of course you're right – and let me tell you, I'm steeped in architectural knowledge myself – but it still doesn't take away my earlier comment.'

Janis made a grab for Yasuko's arm as she returned from refilling Rupert's glass. 'Don't give him any more, Yasuko. He's starting on the bawdy ballads already.'

I tuned back in to Rupert for a moment and listened to the suggestive lyrics.

Despite Janis's probably deliberate distraction, Dylan returned to the earlier conversation. 'I agonized over this room for ages. The original fittings had been stripped out and packed off to America after the Great War. I hunted everywhere for the room, and would've paid good money for its return. All to no avail, I'm afraid. Then I heard these fixtures were being auctioned from a mansion demolition in Yorkshire. I bought furniture to match it. But you're right, Freya; it doesn't sit right with the rest of the Lodge, and can only be a temporary solution. The heritage people thought the same. When I find the right interior, I'll redo this room again. Expensive, I know, but I want to keep faith with the original design – eventually.'

Janis frowned. 'I wish you'd stop that crudity, Rups.'

Rupert ignored her and carried on.

Veronica started talking to Dylan about profits from his car museum.

'She does all my accounts,' he explained to me. 'No. I don't want to spend it all on new cars, Ronni. I want to develop the visitor centre so children can appreciate car history. And I want to donate a few thousand so the parish council can build that adventure playground in the village.'

Veronica didn't seem too impressed by his philanthropy. 'Well, I suppose we can get the local MP to open it for you.' Then she turned to me. 'I was dining with him only the other night at the Conservative Club.'

'Well, that's nothing to boast about,' I said loudly. 'The Thatcherites are destroying this country.'

Veronica huffed. 'We've just won another landslide victory. The country doesn't appear to share your view.'

'Calm down,' Dylan intervened sharply. 'Freya, it's understandable that Veronica and Rupert are Tory supporters – one from the landed aristocracy and one from the city.'

'Quite so,' Veronica said.

'But Ronni, I tend to agree with Freya.'

Veronica scowled.

'What are your politics, then?' I asked.

'I'm from the old Radical tradition. Dating back to the Levellers and Diggers of the Civil War, the supporters of the American and French Revolutions, and the Chartist movement. Finds its expression most these days in the left-wing of the Liberals and the Bennite fringe of the Labour Party. But frankly, all today's parties are as bad as each other. And I certainly don't want some Tory upstart making political capital off the back of one of my donations, thank you very much.'

'How can you talk that way, Dylan? Look around you. You should be a Tory. You're a landed gent yourself, now, after all.'

'I'm a self-made man, Ronni, and you know it. I didn't inherit wealth. And all this might be transitory, like it was for you.'

I didn't understand this, but Veronica looked miffed.

'You never can tell. No, I grew up in a mining town, with real working class people. I've sampled their deprivations first hand. And to see how Thatcher used the police to rip through the picket lines, well....words can't express my disgust.'

Veronica looked offended, but said nothing.

Rupert coming to the end of his song helped to divert our attentions.

'Bravo, Rupert,' Dylan cried, with a chuckle.

All except Janis clapped him.

'That's enough of that now, Rupert,' Janis said. 'Let me have a go.'

Rupert relinquished the piano stool and Janis embarked upon a recital of what sounded like a Mozart piece, but she appeared nervous and it was riddled with errors as a result.

Veronica cringed. 'That's awful, darling. I do wish you'd stop trying to pretend you're any good. Your sister was always the musical one. You're never going to be as good, so why bother?'

Janis looked at Dylan, but he said nothing.

'Well, my dear sis. is no longer around! Why can't you just be pleased for *me*!'

'Please don't speak to me like that, dear!' she retorted harshly.

Janis slammed the lid of the piano down, close to tears.

Veronica took no notice of her. 'I know, why don't you play something, Dylan?'

'Yes, old boy. Get your fiddle.' Rupert encouraged.

Dylan reluctantly went over to a cabinet and brought out a violin. He tuned it and then burst into a fast folk reel that had us all stamping our feet to the beat after the first few bars. Janis opened the piano lid again and tried to play some chords, but she couldn't keep up and had to let Rupert take over. Disheartened, she slipped quietly away from the room.

After a while, Dylan slowed and allowed Rupert to play and sing with him. I recognized a few of the folk standards like *Widdecombe Fair* and *The Vicar of Bray*.

Veronica and I watched and I felt a certain charisma emanating from Dylan, in the way he could hold our attention.

'Dylan's multi-talented, isn't he?' I said. 'What with his writing, his musicianship and his architectural knowledge.'

'That's not even the half of it. He has an encyclopaedic mind on many subjects, which he makes good use of in his novels. He's far superior to me. That's why I never debate with him for long.' She paused, and motioned towards Dylan and Rupert in an effort to pretend she was giving them her wholehearted attention.

But she had gripped hold of my arm, hidden from view behind her own, and I could feel her fingernails digging into me. Then she hissed through clenched teeth, whilst smiling towards Dylan. 'Don't you dare show me up like that again!'

I let out a gasp at the pain she'd inflicted and this made Dylan stop.

'Is everything OK?' Dylan said, as Rupert played on. He was looking in my direction, but it was Veronica who rose to her feet.

'I'm getting a headache, darling. I think I need to go to my room and lie down. Will you help me, Dylan?'

Dylan took her by the arm and led her away.

Rupert used their exit to raid Dylan's wine again.

'Don't let on to Veronica, Freya, but I think the Thatcherites are philistines as well. Cutting all that funding for the Arts!' He tutted and swigged down some more red wine. 'I'm a "One Nation" Tory at heart. Don't care for the City, either.' He came and sat down beside me, and sighed. 'My family forced me into joining the bank, as they were dead set against me becoming a professional musician.'

'Shame,' I said. 'You sing and play well.'

'Thank you,' he replied, sipping his drink once more.

An uncomfortable silence filled the room, as we both struggled to sustain the conversation. Finally, I said: 'What do you make of Dylan?'

'Well, I've known him a few years, yet....'

'What?'

'He's a nice enough chap, but....'

'But what?'

He drank some more. 'I don't think I know him at all.'

'What d'you mean?'

'Well, I can't really grasp his true character. He's very defensive. Puts up a brave front....They say he's had a troubled background....That might explain it.'

'Yes, his wife died.'

'Oh.' He gulped, his face blanching. 'Well, he's never said.'

Just then, Janis returned. 'Has she gone?'

I nodded.

'Good,' she said and returned to the piano.

Rupert closed his eyes and drifted off to sleep, snoring loudly.

Janis gave the same recital again, with most of the same mistakes as the last time and a few new ones as well.

When she had finished, I gave her a round of applause and came over to her side. 'That was good.'

'No it wasn't. Mother's right. But I like to play anyway. It winds her up, if nothing else.'

'I see. And how long have you known Dylan?'

'Oh,' she replied, smiling. 'I've known him most of my life. I'm his late wife's elder sister.'

- IV -

THE DINING ROOM was the grandest room in the Lodge, with its dark oak-panelled walls and intricately carved grotesques on the exposed beams of the ceiling. Medieval weaponry hung from the walls and suits of armour guarded the huge fireplace at the far end. Above the sculptured mantelpiece was the stuffed head of a white hart with imperial antlers.

Veronica was out on the terrace beyond the arched French windows, parading herself in front of Rupert. He looked bemused and stubbed out his cigar on the stone balustrade. I watched her for a while, trying to understand her. I was still too disturbed by her earlier behaviour to want to engage with her now.

I felt very inferior when she approached, with Rupert tagging along behind. I was still wearing the same set of clothes I'd arrived in. She had fashioned her hair and was wearing an off-the-shoulder gown, with a fox fur around her neck.

She looked me up and down and muttered under her breath, turning her back on me and taking a large puff from a cigarette through an ebony holder. Then she brushed her hand over Rupert's shoulder to remove the dandruff on his jacket.

'Really Rupert, you need to look after yourself better if you want to claim my daughter.'

'Oh, please do leave off. We're not at one of your charity balls. You're making me more nervous.'

'Why so tetchy? Isn't it going well?'

'She's very off with me and won't say why. Frankly, my dear, I think maybe I should've kept up with Lady Jennifer. I might have better luck with her.... And her father's a banker as well, and seems to like me.'

'Poppycock. You can do a lot better than one of Dylan's cast-offs!'

She turned around and gave me a glare, then wandered over to the fireplace, smoking aggressively.

Dylan entered, and his jovial mood broke the awkward atmosphere. He was dressed only in jeans and a sweatshirt. This casual attire reassured me.

'Hope everyone's getting along OK?'

No one answered, but I came across and hugged him.

'Where's Janis?'

'She'll be along shortly,' Rupert said.

Dylan began to talk, attempting to draw everyone together, as we all stepped out onto the terrace. Before long, his charismatic charm and gift for a good story soon had us all enthralled. Even when Janis meekly arrived she was immediately brought into the conversation and she brightened up at once. Dylan had effortlessly become the centre of attention, and I began to realize this was exactly how he liked it.

'I'm expecting another guest, by the way,' he said.

'Who?' Janis asked.

'Wait and see.'

Veronica turned her nose up, but made no comment.

'That's great, Dylan,' I said.

'Should've been here by now.' He looked at his watch. 'Well, I think we'd better make a start. Can't keep Yasuko waiting any longer.'

As we began to leave the terrace, a distant hum came through the woods, gradually getting louder. A motorcycle scrambled onto the open lawn from a rough track. The rider was dressed in black. Mud spewed behind the rear wheel as the bike churned up the grass. Then it rode up the steps onto the ramparted lawn directly below us.

Even Veronica was lost for words.

The rider braked hard, locking the back wheel, so the bike would skid sideways in order to impress. The rider kicked down the stand and dismounted.

The tinted black visor of the helmet flicked up. 'Hi, Dylan!'

I couldn't believe it was a female voice.

She pulled off the helmet, pushing her long, jet-black hair over her head.

'Oh, it's only Emily,' Janis said.

'My God, Em. Motorbike! Leathers! This isn't you!' Dylan exclaimed.

Veronica stood perplexed and her mouth gaped open.

Emily sat back on the saddle, taking a cigarette packet out of her top pocket. She spat out her gum and placed a cigarette between her lips. 'Well, Dylan, this is the new me.'

'Smoking, too!'

Emily grimaced, flipped her gold-plated lighter, and lit the tip of her cigarette. She took a long drag for maximum effect. She puffed out a couple of smoke rings towards him. 'Yeah. And you lot better start getting used to it! Anyway, you used to smoke thirty a day yourself.'

She bounded up the steps to our level. She kissed Dylan on the cheek. 'Thanks for the invite.' Then she nodded at

Rupert and turned to shake my hand. 'You must be Freya. I'm Emily....Emily Faversham. Nice to meet you.'

Veronica coughed. Emily ignored her so Veronica coughed again, more irritated.

'What's wrong, Mother. Don't you like the new me!' Emily said, mimicking Veronica's pretentious voice.

Veronica glowered at her, but still couldn't find any words. I couldn't suppress my giggles.

Dylan guided us back into the dining room, where candles and fresh flowers decorated the long oak table. Dylan sat at its head, in the only chair with arms. Janis and Rupert sat one side and Veronica the other. Emily and I found ourselves at the other end of the large expanse.

Yasuko came into the room, carrying a silver tray with the starters. She came back some time later with the wine. Rupert was through his first glass before Yasuko had finished serving the rest of us, and beckoned for a refill.

Veronica clicked her fingers. 'Take this away, Yasuko. The avocado's not ripe enough.'

Yasuko bowed and nodded, maintaining her mask-like expression.

'Seems fine to me,' Emily said. The rest of us concurred.

Yasuko took Veronica's dish away anyway and returned to the kitchen to attend to the next course.

Dylan broke the embarrassing silence by changing the subject. 'Why the new image, Em.?– you've always been so strait-laced.'

'Well, I'm fed up with Mum dictating what I can and can't do.'

Veronica tutted and her face grew with anger.

'And you for that matter. I'm eighteen now. I can do what I like.'

'Why the interest in motorbikes all of a sudden? You've always hated them.'

'Mum has, I haven't....Got myself a new biker boyfriend.'

Dylan choked on a prawn. Rupert tried to come to his assistance, but Dylan waved him away.

'I don't think you'll go down too well at Oxford dressed like that,' Janis said.

'Couldn't give a shit!'

'Oh, language please.' Veronica said, trying to remain calm.

'I'm not going. University's for shitheads.'

'Please!' Veronica banged her fist on the table. 'Just you remember. You may be eighteen, but as long as you are living under my roof, I can still bend you over my knee and give you a thrashing! I could do it now and in front of everyone.'

'I'd like to see you try!'

'Really!' Veronica threw down her napkin. 'Can't you do something, Dylan?'

Everyone else sat in silence, although I detected a sly grin appearing on Janis's face.

'Let's all calm down, shall we,' Dylan said. 'Now, Emily, you're being foolish. All that work to win the scholarship. Why don't you take a year out?'

'No! My mind's made up.'

'Not if I have anything to do with it.' Veronica shot her a savage stare.

'You've got no control over me any longer. I'm leaving home.'

Veronica looked dumbstruck.

'Where'll you go?' Dylan asked.

'With my boyfriend and his mates. They're a good crowd.'

'There's always a place for you here, you know.'

'What? With all your fancy women about? – No offence, Freya, but I'm sure you two've already fucked.'

I could feel myself flush.

'That's enough, Emily! Are you doing this to spite me?'

She was taken aback. Her jaw dropped and she clutched at her chest. 'You're so vain, Dylan! The world doesn't just revolve around you, you know, even if you like to think it does.'

This unsettled him. He sat back, deflated.

'Look, Dylan, I'm sorry. You know Mother's riled me up the wrong way for months and you haven't helped me. And if you think I'm changing back to that "cute little girl", think again. You ain't seen nuthin' yet!'

'What *do* you mean?'

'Don't look so worried, Dylan. Just wait and see.' And she burst out in hearty laughter as Yasuko returned to clear the table.

'Oh, this is getting too much.' Veronica shifted in her chair, unsettled.

'Well, you've brought it on yourself,' Emily continued. 'You're still trying to dominate Janis and she's thirty-six. I'm not hanging around that long so you can ruin my life as well.'

'You ungrateful girl. I've given you everything!'

Emily scoffed.

'Yes, Emily, you've certainly had more than I have,' Janis said, a mournful expression passing across her face. 'But I've got my own life now, with my rock-climbing school, thank you very much. Mother has little influence over me now.'

'How can you say that, when she's trying to marry you off to Rupert?'

'Now, now. I've said nothing about marriage,' Rupert muttered, drowning his bashfulness with another swig of wine.

Janis sat in silence, her head bowed.

'What do you know, poppet. They've been getting on fine.'

'No, they haven't, Mother. Janis told me so herself only yesterday.'

Janis looked up, startled, and put her hand up as if begging her sister not to continue.

But Emily carried on regardless. 'I'm sorry, Rupert, but she finds you a drunken fool. And useless in bed. Despite all those silly saucy songs you sing!'

Rupert shuddered, spilling his glass, yet too shocked to pay any attention to the developing stain by his left elbow.

'Get a cloth, Yasuko,' Dylan said, and she scurried away.

Rupert didn't deign to answer Emily directly. 'Really, Dylan, what's happened to her? She used to be such a nice young girl.'

'I'm sure she'll grow out of it soon.'

'Hello, I'm still here, you patronizing bastards!'

'OK, point taken, Em.,' Dylan said, holding up his hands.

Several minutes of silence ensued, everyone using Yasuko's serving of the main course as a useful distraction. Yasuko gave a short bow and retreated to the side of the room as we all began to tuck into the food.

'Oh, Yasuko, this steak's too rare.' Veronica spat out her mouthful in disgust. 'You must know I like it well done by now. I've been here often enough.'

Yasuko had moved forward again and was busy wiping up Rupert's mess.

'Don't keep me waiting.' She held up the plate.

Yasuko took it and marched off to the kitchen. There came a faint sound of breaking crockery.

'Rupert is a gentleman,' Veronica continued, trying to steady herself. 'He has a good income. Just right for Janis.'

Janis continued to say nothing, so Emily intervened again on her behalf. 'If Rupert is that wonderful, maybe you should marry him yourself!'

'Don't jest, Emily!' Veronica retorted angrily. 'You know your father was the only man for me!'

'Oh, I do wish you wouldn't live so much in the past. He's been dead for years! Get over it.'

'Really, Emily, that's too much.'

'Yes, it is, Emily,' Dylan said. 'Stop now, before you create any more damage.'

'Surely, darling, isn't that why you invited me?'

Dylan stared at her in amazement. He dropped his knife, which clattered onto the table.

'Anyway, Dylan, you're just as bad. I'm not prepared to stay living under the shadow of my dead sister any longer, even if you are!'

Dylan's face fell.

'I just can't compete.'

'Nor can I,' Janis said, backing her sister and speaking her own mind for the first time.

'OK, so Sera was special....'

'An artistic genius.' Veronica said, suddenly calming and her face becoming radiant as she remembered her lost daughter.

'So you keep saying....Relentlessly.' Emily frowned. 'And I can take that. And that she was more beautiful. But stop trying to make me follow in her footsteps. I'm not *her*!'

'Yes. A genius and very beautiful. You were too young to know,' Veronica said, glowing more brightly.

Suddenly, it occurred to me that the ghost of Seraphina hung in the room with us. That she, and not Dylan, was the greater influence.

'Maybe,' Emily commented. 'But not any more. She's long dead!'

'That's enough, Emily!' Dylan looked furious.

'Come on, Freya,' Emily said, taking my hand. 'Let's get some fresh air.'

I resisted her tug at first, but Dylan nodded his approval, looking relieved that Emily was going. We left the room, leaving Dylan to remonstrate with Yasuko about the food.

Emily guided me down the steps to her motorcycle. 'Come on, let's have some fun,' she said, straddling her bike and kicking up the stand. 'Here, you better take this,' offering me the helmet.

I was rather anxious.

'Don't worry, I'll look after you.'

Her mischievous smile was enough. I donned the helmet and clambered onto the saddle behind her. The bike was an old Triumph, with discoloured chrome and a skull-and-cross-bones crudely painted on the fuel tank. She kick-started the machine into life. I held on tightly around her slender midriff, buffeted by her flowing hair as we zoomed off. The lawn was wet after the storm, so we churned it up mercilessly in our wake.

'Careful!' I screamed, as she rode over several flowerbeds, but she took no notice.

Then she reached the rough track and we sped through the woods, bouncing over tree roots and loose rocks. Somehow I clung on as we gathered speed along an improving surface. She slowed down only when we reached an old arch. This was set into a high stone wall, a well-built castellated structure which appeared to encircle the whole property. We came to a stop in a sideways skid.

She shrieked like a banshee, flicking up my helmet visor. 'Now, wasn't that something!'

I mumbled 'Wow', trying to get my breath back and feeling giddy.

Seeing my ashen face, she steadied me as I climbed off. She propped the motorbike against the wall and sat down beside me on a tree stump. She put her arm around me.

'You sure know how to ride.'

'Yeah, my boyfriend's a good teacher.'

'You certainly pissed off Dylan. Well, everyone in fact.'

'Yeah, as intended.'

'Thought you'd finish it off by destroying his garden?'

'Yeah. You don't seem to approve.'

'No. And I don't understand.' I paused. 'But the way you handled your mum, well, that was something else!'

'Yeah, the stuck-up bitch. Don't know why Dylan keeps himself tied to her. And I pity Rupert.'

'Me, too.'

'He's just a pawn in Mother's game. Just like Janis. Dylan's probably *comforting* her right now. Or letting Yasuko *comfort* him.'

I looked puzzled.

'You're very naive, aren't you?'

I shrugged.

'I was right. You two have fucked?'

'Made love, yes.'

'Fucked,' she insisted. 'You'll learn, in time....I had to.'

'You mean to say he's been with you?'

She shook her head. 'You really didn't know, did you?'

'No.' I gazed down at the forest floor and kicked at a pinecone, feeling disconsolate.

'Don't worry. Just be careful. Don't expect anything. He's the type of man who's easy to get, but impossible to keep....Enjoy him while it lasts.'

I found her remarks upsetting, but didn't want to show it.

She lifted the left cuff of her leather jacket to consult a diver's watch on the underside of her arm. 'I'll have to go now, before it gets dark.'

I didn't answer. There were scars on her wrist.

She noticed what I was looking at and pulled up her sleeves. Both forearms were a mass of razor-blade cuts.

I averted my eyes.

'I do it when things get too much.' She took out another cigarette, offering one to me, then lighting up when I refused. She didn't care to elaborate further. 'Will you be able to find your way back to the house from here?'

'Yes. I'm sure I can.' I handed back her helmet and watched her mount her motorbike.

She was very beautiful, I thought. Easy to see what Dylan saw in her. And she looked and spoke more maturely than her eighteen years, as if she'd been made to grow up too quickly.

I rose up to say my farewells.

She kissed me on each cheek. 'It's been great to meet you.' She took a few lengthy drags on her cigarette, before stubbing it out on the wall. She put on her helmet. 'Shut the gate after I've gone. 'Bye.'

'Wait. I'm curious. How did you realize Dylan and I are an item?'

'You wouldn't still be here it you hadn't got together. Let's face it, me and my family have seen it all before....Many times.' Her grin disappeared behind the closing visor. Then she gunned the engine and the motorbike roared off through the archway.

I was left to muse over her unsettling comments. But I now knew for certain what I had hoped since seducing him: that being Dylan's girlfriend would provide a perfect cover for my mission.

- V -

I STAGGERED THROUGH the woods as darkness began to envelop the path. I was sure I was going the right way, but there were junctions I hadn't seen on the way in. The call of an owl sent shivers through me. I leant against the nearest tree, clutching my chest and gathering my breath.

After a while I journeyed on, only to trip over a tree root and fall headlong into the undergrowth. I sat up, rubbing my bare arms where nettle stings tingled. I flicked my long hair over my forehead and out of my eyes and rose to my feet once more.

'Lost, are we?'

I jumped back in fright, keeling over onto my bottom again.

A torch flicked on, shining up into the face of a man.

It was all right. It was Dylan.

He laughed.

'That wasn't funny, you scared me.'

'I'm sorry. Where's Emily?'

'Gone. Out the back gate.'

'Oh, she has, has she? Wait till I catch up with her! What were the two of you thinking? My garden's a mess.'

'Sorry.'

'Bit late for that. The damage's been done.'

He gripped my upper arms and pulled me to my feet. We walked back to the house in silence. Guilt overwhelmed me. Maybe this would end his hospitality.

We found Yasuko loading the dishwasher in the kitchen and could hear Janis playing the piano again in the drawing room.

'Put the kettle on please, Yasuko.'

She did as instructed. After he'd gone, I noticed her heavy sigh and the slumping of her shoulders.

'Let me help you with those,' I said, picking up a pile of plates from the counter.

No. My job. I know my place.

I reluctantly left her to finish the task, finding Dylan in the lounge. As I entered the room, I heard Rupert snoring loudly, and turned to find him crashed out on the sofa.

'He's been drinking himself into oblivion because of what Emily said. Probably best to let him sleep it off down here,' Dylan said.

'Where's Veronica?'

'Gone to bed. They're going early tomorrow, so she wanted a good night's sleep.'

'Wanted to get away from Emily more likely.'

'Well....yes. She upset everyone.'

'Sorry, Dylan, if I had any part to play. But Veronica behaved badly, too.'

'I know. She can be hard to like sometimes. She's very needy under the surface.'

'I'm sorry, Dylan. I don't like her very much. I don't know her as well as you, of course, but I'd say she's highly manipulative.' I rubbed at the bruise on my arm, the skin broken in two places by Veronica's fingernails. 'I'd watch her, if I were you.'

He said nothing.

'Emily was great, though. I'm glad you invited her. It would've been dull without her.'

Dylan didn't quite know what to say.

I kissed him and put my arm around him. 'You coming to bed?'

'Later. I've things to do down here first.'

I was beginning to drift off to sleep when I heard a commotion outside. I crept over to the door and opened it a fraction. Through the crack, I could make out Dylan and Janis on the landing. They were speaking in hushed tones.

Then he drew her towards him, but she pushed him away and gave him a slap around his face.

He recoiled, surprised, holding his cheek.

'How dare you! Don't try to comfort me now, it's a little too late for that. Why can't you defend me against Mother? That's all I ask.'

She marched off and I heard her bedroom door slam.

Dylan stood there for a while, still clutching his face. Then he went downstairs.

I tiptoed out onto the landing and leant over the banister. Dylan was down in the hallway, guiding Yasuko towards the front door.

I crept back to my room and watched them walk across the courtyard to the inner gatehouse. Soon a light came on and I saw them moving about inside, before Dylan came to open a window and close the curtains.

Intrigued, I went back onto the landing, down the stairs and into the cool night air. I ran across the courtyard and hid underneath the gatehouse arch. I had hoped to overhear conversation, but all I heard were strange noises and what I thought were mumbled wails from Yasuko.

I hurried back inside. I was soon glad I had retreated when I had, as within a few minutes Dylan returned. He slipped into bed and snuggled up beside me.

Yasuko woke me with an early morning pot of tea. I rubbed the sleep from my eyes and sat up. Dylan was gone.

'Thanks, Yasuko.'

She walked awkwardly towards the door.

'You OK?'

Yes. Just a little cramp. Tired out, she wrote, and came back to hand the paper to me.

'You look it.'

Try telling Dylan that!

She left again, before I could answer.

I showered and dressed quickly, and made my way down to breakfast, passing Rupert with his head over the toilet bowl. Dylan and Veronica were already at the table and relations looked strained between them.

'Morning.' I sat down and poured myself a bowl of cereal. I studied Veronica carefully, embarrassed, before summoning the courage to convey an apology; not because I meant it, but in the hope she would do the same to clear the air for Dylan's sake.

'It's OK. Dylan tells me I was a bit brash myself.'

Lame excuse. No apology. I suppressed my brewing anger.

Yasuko came in with fresh toast and took orders for bacon and eggs.

'Yasuko,' Dylan said. 'Go and change, please.'

Yasuko looked down at her kimono, then back at Dylan, before scurrying off.

'What was all that about?' I said.

Veronica laughed. 'Don't worry. It's all part of the game they play.'

'What? You can't treat employees like that!'

Veronica and Dylan looked at each other, then guffawed together, which broke the tension between them.

I slumped back in my seat, confused, which made their mirth greater.

Only Rupert joining the table curtailed their raillery. His hair was unkempt, his eyes glazed.

'Look at the state of you! No wonder my daughter doesn't want you.' Veronica snorted. 'Well, at least you've changed your clothes now, which is more than I can say for some.' She was looking at me.

I bowed my head. 'This is all I've got, Veronica. But at least I didn't sleep all night in it.' I looked at Rupert, then cast a frozen stare back to her.

She fidgeted with her hair, discomfited.

'Don't worry,' Dylan said, sensing my upset. 'We'll go out this afternoon and buy you a new wardrobe.'

Veronica's eyes narrowed, just as Janis entered the room.

I smiled a wan smile. Then I excused myself.

Dylan drove the Bentley out of the stabling block, where it had been garaged. He parked it on the driveway beyond the inner gatehouse, in front of Veronica, Janis and Rupert. Yasuko struggled with their bags, cramming them into the boot.

Dylan climbed out, handing Rupert the keys.

'Don't give them to him!' Veronica cried.

'Why not?'

'Because, Rups, you're still way over the limit. And if you think I'm letting you drive me about in the state you're in, you've got another think coming!'

He took a step back, in defensive pose. She snatched the keys and climbed into the driver's seat.

Rupert shook Dylan's hand and kissed Yasuko and me. His stubble grated against my cheek and the smell of stale alcohol on his breath was nauseating.

At least he'd deigned to say his farewells properly. Veronica kissed Dylan, but ignored the rest of us. Janis waved meekly and climbed into the back.

When Rupert hopped in and closed the door, Dylan ran on ahead to help guide Veronica around the car wreck. She revved the engine, controlling the clutch so the rear wheels would spin and send gravel up in our faces, before accelerating off down the drive.

Glad she gone, Yasuko scrawled.

'So am I,' I said, relaxing.

- VI -

LATER DYLAN ESCORTED me to the Land Rover and we drove off down the driveway. My Fiat sat precariously on the edge of the embankment.

'Don't worry, we'll move it soon,' he said, noticing my expression as he manoeuvred to within a foot of the wreck.

I tugged at my hair, separating a strand so I could fiddle with it in my fingers. I crouched lower in my seat, not answering. There were other things on my mind.

As we turned out of the outer gatehouse and we gathered speed, I found the courage to confront him. 'Emily reckoned you were going to get comfort from Yasuko last night.'

'What do you think?'

'Don't turn the question back at me.'

My eyes searched his face for clues.

'I'm not going to lie to you. We have a history, certainly,' he said without hesitation or embarrassment.

I folded my arms tightly under my breasts and looked out towards the pine forest, as he opened up the throttle a little more. At least he had been honest.

'What were you doing with her last night?'

'Eh?'

'I saw the two of you going to the gatehouse.'

'Oh, that. Nothing really. I went to her apartment to have a few words with her about what happened at dinner.'

'That all?'

'I think you'd better ask Yasuko.'

I huffed, and drew my arms all the tighter around me.

'Come on, love, don't be annoyed. I've known her a long time. I'm with you now, but I can't just switch off.'

'From now on you better had, or I'm off!' I hoped I hadn't gone too far with my play-acting. Upon reflexion, I realized my forceful response had been fuelled by a genuine anger. I vowed to maintain an emotional distance in future.

He shifted down the gears, which crunched in protest, and pulled the Land Rover over to the side of the road. 'Listen,' he said, undoing his seat belt and edging himself over onto my seat. 'Don't be upset. You're my baby now.'

I felt his arm come around my shoulder and he drew my head into his chest.

He kissed me on the forehead and looked into my eyes. 'Come on, let's go. Let me prove it to you.'

I managed to muster a smile, but my self-esteem had drained away.

We started off again and skirted around the southern shores of Bassenthwaite Lake. Across the waters, the plantations were being felled, leaving denuded wastes over a hill on the lower slopes of Skiddaw.

We didn't talk again until after we'd parked in Keswick.

'Let's see what we can find you, shall we,' he said, before alighting from the Land Rover. He came around to me as I climbed out, gripped my hand in his and kissed me. 'This place isn't very big, but I'm sure we can find something to please you.'

We went into an outdoor retailer, and Dylan kitted me out with walking trousers, socks, shirt and boots. In another shop, he found a fleece jacket, cagoule, overtrousers and a small rucksack. Once we'd taken the bags back to the Land Rover, we returned to seek out conventional clothes stores.

He was making a great effort, and didn't seem troubled about parting with his money. But I wasn't that naive not to know he was probably trying to buy back my affections. Still, something about the way he sat and admired me, as I paraded past him in numerous outfits, gradually thawed my frostiness. And he knew how to exploit a woman's fantasy. I'd only ever glimpsed such fashionable clothes in magazines before, never being able to afford them. When I couldn't decide which ones to pick, he simply bought them all.

'No, you can't.'

'I can and I will. There's no point earning money if you can't spend it. Anyway, I don't want any girlfriend of mine being jeered at over such a silly thing as clothes again.'

I hugged him and kissed him. Underneath, I was cursing that my resolve to remain angry with him had ebbed away so quickly. Although it would ultimately help my cause.

'Now, we can't forget underwear, can we?'

'No, I s'pose not. But I'm not sure how long I'll be wearing it with you around!'

He smirked, then kissed me again, and put his arm around my shoulder as we walked onwards. Once in amongst the racks of lingerie, he watched me intently as I picked out what I considered to be the sexiest numbers.

'Let me try these on.'

'If you do so, madam,' the salesgirl announced, creeping up behind me, 'you'll have to pay for them whether you like them or not.'

I stopped, and stared at the garments, then back at the racks, making sure I had made the right choice.

But Dylan turned around and caught the salesgirl's eye.

'Oh, pardon me, sir, I didn't realize it was you. Same arrangement as before?'

'Yes,' he said, and winked at her.

She blushed so brightly her face soon matched the colour of her reddish hair.

'Stick it all on my account.'

The salesgirl tried to answer, but I was hustling him over towards the changing compartments. 'No peeking till I'm ready.'

He groaned as I pulled the curtains shut on him.

I put on the red stockings, suspenders, panties and bra. I tried to conjure the most seductive pose I could in the mirror, then poked my head through the curtains. 'Come inside.'

Dylan looked around, then slipped into the cramped cubicle, taking no notice of the salesgirl's embarrassment. He admired me intensely, making me spin around for him.

I toyed with the itching bra strap and awaited his reaction.

'It's certainly sexy, darling, but you don't need to impress me with this sort of stuff. By all means I'll buy it for you, but I'd rather you found something more comfortable for everyday use.'

I kissed him, not quite believing his thoughtfulness, and bundled him out again. Before I had fully changed, his hand appeared through the curtains with a selection of other garments, including a skimpy swimming costume. He had even judged the right sizes.

I took so much time choosing one last outfit that he left me to do some of his own shopping. This was a deliberate ploy. I needed some time alone in order to book out of the hotel I'd used as a base before meeting Dylan. They allowed me to leave my luggage in storage until I could collect it at a later date.

We met up again over tea in a café, where I gushed out how thankful I was at the money he'd spent on me. He then handed me another plastic bag.

'What's this?' I said, delving inside to find bottles of shampoo, conditioner, facial cream and deodorant, and even a box of tampons.

'Hope they're the sort you usually use.'

I smiled at his consideration. I'd been too intent on all the luxuries to think about the essentials.

After a while, I said: 'It's such a beautiful place, the Lake District.'

He nodded, but remained silent.

'How long have you lived up here?'

'Since I was ten. I was from Wales originally. My late mother was best friends with Ronni.... We came back here when my brother and father were killed down the pit.'

I was struck by the amount of tragedy in this man's life.

He tailed off. 'Can we talk about something else, please,' he said, taking a sip from his tea.

'Did Seraphina look anything like Emily and Janis? They're beautiful.'

'Yes,' he replied, then realized he'd been drawn again. 'Can we please leave it? It provokes too many bad memories. I'm with you now, let's concentrate on us.'

'OK,' I said, drinking my own tea. I wasn't certain whether Seraphina could still touch such a raw core of feeling seventeen years after the event; or whether he was simply trying to further the air of mystery he seemed to like to shroud himself in.

We walked back to where we'd parked the Land Rover and I loaded the bags into the back after he'd opened the door for me.

'It's a lovely sunny day, now. Fancy a bit of adventure?' he said, as he climbed behind the wheel and turned the ignition.

My expression said it all, which was lucky as he revved the engine so loudly he wasn't likely to hear my response anyway. Perhaps in his arrogance, he knew what my reply would be anyway.

We drove down to an old mill, the site of his car museum and restoration workshops. He waved to a couple of workmen in the nearby garage, who were working on the rear bodywork of a Triumph Vitesse.

Then he put his arm around my waist and pointed upwards. There was a helicopter on the roof. He looked at my astonishment.

'We're going in that!'

'Yes, Freya. Thought you'd like a little more fun.'

'You mean you can fly that thing?'

He grinned, taking out a flying hat and headset from behind his back. 'A friend flew it in for me this morning. But yes, I'm a fully trained pilot.'

Was there no end to his talents? I thought, as we clambered up the stairs. I began to realize I was being seduced as much by his lifestyle as by his sexual and intellectual prowess. But somehow, I could not help myself being drawn in even deeper. Maybe I was thriving on the implicit dangers of getting close to this man.

Soon we were airborne and my thoughts were lost in the general excitement.

We spent the next hour on a grand tour of the Lake District. First came the bleak northern fells: mainly grassy, with the occasional outline of an Iron Age hillfort or old mine workings. Then came the more rugged central region. The glaciated valleys, dramatic combes and barren volcanic crags and cliffs contrasted with the peaceful expanses of lake and tarn. And with the lower, more afforested slopes, where farmsteads appeared as mere specks in the powerful landscape. Lastly, we flew over the verdant meadows and parklands of the southern expanses, before banking away towards the Irish Sea. Only the vulgar structures of coastal industry blotted the spectacular natural environment as we journeyed back again.

We flew inland, coming back across Bassenthwaite Lake and Skiddaw, the only features I could recognize. Dylan drew my attention to a great view of the ridges of Causey and Grisedale Pikes, as the sun began to sink behind their pointed summits.

But I was more interested in a large cliff, shrouded on both sides by plantations. I pointed to it, gaining Dylan's attention. 'What's that white thing?'

'It's called the "Bishop of Barf". It's a statuesque rock that sticks out from the face. They paint it regularly to make it stand out.'

'Oh, interesting.'

'See the hotel at its foot?'

'Yes.'

'Well, I've booked us in for a romantic meal later.'

'Excellent,' I replied, embracing him. Inner relief swept through me. I'd nearly booked myself into this hotel, as it had been the nearest to Grimshaw Lodge. If I had done so, my mission would soon have been exposed.

After our meal, we returned up the road to the Lodge. He surprised me by stopping in a lay-by and pulling me into the forest. He started to make love.

'We can't do this here. Someone might see!'

'That's exactly what makes it so exciting!'

-VII -

THE GARDENS OF the Victorian mansion must have been spectacular in their heyday. Its centrepiece had been the large conservatory. Dylan had restored the intricate glass panelling very faithfully; now it housed a heated swimming pool and sauna.

I found Yasuko swimming in the pool. She was wearing a nightshirt which covered her body and must have been very cumbersome to swim in. She climbed out on the other side of the pool and scurried off towards the changing rooms.

Dylan joined me. We both stripped naked and dived into the soothing waters. We frolicked around for over an hour, swimming, play-fighting and periodically embracing.

After lunch, the truck returned, with the same personnel, to recover the remains of my Fiat. We watched its crane lift the crumpled wreck aboard. It was a sad sight. We followed behind in the Land Rover. Our destination was Dylan's car restoration business. On the outskirts of Keswick, we turned off the main road and drove up a track to the old bobbin mill.

We found Rupert with his head under the bonnet of the Bentley, in discussion with one of the mechanics.

'Still here, Rupert,' Dylan called.

'Yes. Thought I'd get my Bentley serviced before heading to Scotland. I'll pay, of course.'

'Oh, I thought the Bentley belonged to Veronica,' I said.

Rupert grinned wryly.

'Heading up to the MacAlistairs, eh? Ronni said you were keen on Lady Jennifer. She's a bit of a handful. You'll need to keep your wits about you.'

Rupert nodded, then frowned.

'Shame you and Janis haven't worked out.' As he said this, I had the impression he was rather pleased they hadn't.

'No. I can see now it was all her mother's idea. I think I bored her.'

Dylan smiled, then led me away to show me around the four-storey main building. It had been converted into a small museum for British cars from the Fifties and Sixties, which were fast becoming classics. Some were in original condition; others, he told me, had been restored by his small team of mechanics and bodywork specialists. I'd always liked old cars and he smiled at how enthralled I was.

'I notice most are basic models. I see you have some MGs and Triumph TRs here. But I was expecting more high-performance sports cars.'

'Yes. I can understand that,' Dylan replied. 'But there are enough collectors for those already. The more mundane marques and models are being lost as we speak. Take this Humber Super Snipe, for example.' He laid his hand on the bonnet. '85% of all the Rolls Royces ever built still survive. Less than 10% of Humbers do.'

'Really?'

'I suppose I'm also following Sera's example. She had the riches to buy a luxury model. But she chose a humble little car instead. That's why I've dedicated the museum to her memory.' He pointed to a plaque on the wall.

'Come on, let's find Ronni.'

'Veronica? – she's here?' It didn't seem the right sort of environment for her.

'Yes. She manages this place for me.' He chuckled at my astonishment.

He walked me over to the old mill-owner's house, where Veronica lived. She met us at the door. She smiled at Dylan, but gave me a poisonous look. Dylan observed this and rebuked her with a cold stare. She became subdued as she guided us into the living room. A pot of tea was soon provided.

Suddenly, an Old English sheepdog scampered in, jumping up on Dylan's lap and licking his face. This lightened his mood again and the moment was forgotten.

'Hello, boy. Have the mechanics been looking after you OK?'

'He's your dog?'

'Yes. He's been staying here for a few days. Janis unfortunately hates dogs.'

The dog came over to me, sitting down and raising his paw. I cuddled him. 'How could anyone hate you, eh? He's lovely, Dyl., what's his name?'

'Quasimodo. Quasi for short.'

'Oh, surely not. He's too gorgeous for a name like that. Why?'

'My favourite classic novel's *Notre Dame de Paris* by Victor Hugo. I named the dog after the hunchback because I found him abandoned as a puppy, just as unwanted and unloved as Quasimodo.'

'Oh, I see. Is he coming back with us?'

'Yes, of course.'

'I can't get over how Emily was the other night,' Veronica interrupted, looking at Dylan.

'Neither can I.'

Veronica sat down and poured herself a cup of tea. 'She's trying my patience, she really is.'

'She ruined my garden with that bloody machine!'

'Don't talk to me about that confounded motorbike! And what about her uncouth friends? You met them yet?'

'No.'

'I suppose you could euphemistically call them "motorcyclists".'

'What? – A gang?'

'*Hell's Angels*.'

Dylan laughed. 'You exaggerate too often, Ronni, that's your trouble.'

'No. I'm being serious. She's joined them. Giving up the chance of Oxford, to gallivant around the country on that dangerous contraption. She'll get herself killed. Now she's threatening to change her appearance radically, no doubt encouraged by her new friends. Heaven knows what that'll mean….And I think she's self-harming again.' Veronica put her head in her hands and started to sob.

Despite what had transpired between us previously, compassion began to get the better of me. 'She's very young,' I said. 'We all go through a rebel stage. She's got plenty of time to come back to studying.' I already felt an affinity with Emily, having given up my own studies at a similar age, and for similar reasons.

Veronica paused to digest my comments, then said: 'No, she's right. I pushed her too far. Now I've lost her for good.'

Dylan, crestfallen, excused himself. The dog followed him out of the door, wagging its tail.

Once alone with her, silence ensued. After a while she asked a few questions about me. I gave her the same stock answers I'd given Dylan, revealing nothing of any real importance. I managed to draw her onto a discussion about her own family, before her questioning of mine became too difficult.

'I don't know what's gone wrong. Maybe I didn't bring them up right.'

'Don't blame yourself. Sera's death can't've helped.'

Veronica eyed welled up. She paused. 'Anyway, it's "Seraphina". I always hated the shortened form. We chose a very rare name, yet she and her siblings always called her "Sera".' A flash of anger passed over her face. 'Sounds like "Sarah" – too common for my liking.'

'OK. Sorry – "Seraphina".'

An uncomfortable silence followed, until Veronica relaxed her defences again.

'You're probably right. My other children have struggled to cope with Seraphina's death, just as much as I have – Janis a failure, Eric skulked off abroad and now Emily trying to run away, too.'

Emily can't've been very old when her sister died?'

'No, she was only one. An afterthought.' She paused for an intake of tea. 'She never really knew Seraphina. Nor her father. Frederick was heartbroken by her elopement with Dylan. It hastened his death. She died within a few weeks of him.'

'Must've been difficult bringing up your other children on your own.'

'Yes. Well, Janis was nineteen. Two years older than Seraphina. She'd already left home. Eric was only fourteen. He really missed out. I had a complete breakdown, you see. Wasn't really there for him emotionally. He failed his exams and bummed off round the world. He's in Australia now. Doesn't keep in touch.'

'What about Janis?'

'Always had a chip on her shoulder thinking Frederick and I favoured Seraphina. In a way she was right. Seraphina was more beautiful, more intelligent. A genius destined for high achievement. All Janis ever seemed interested in was climbing mountains. A failure, really.'

'Sorry if I seem a little presumptuous, but isn't that being a bit harsh?'

'I don't think so.' Her tone took on a hard edge. 'She's never settled to anything. Got herself engaged to a mountaineer. That soon broke up. He later died on K2. Then she became a single mum. Had loads of jobs. Married and divorced. Now she's got this rock-climbing school. Making a go of that, at least. But she's not strict enough with her daughter. Runs rings round her.'

'And Emily?'

'The baby of the family. My final hope. Emily's made me realize I've tried to put her into Seraphina's shoes too much. As she grew, she looked so like her. It was uncanny. I only hope she doesn't hate me too much.'

'I'm sure she'll come round. How did Dylan meet Seraphina?'

'Really, you're full of questions, aren't you?'

'Sorry.'

'It's OK. But let's make this the last one. Dylan's mother and I were best friends. She lived in Wales. Came up here when Dylan was ten. He was great friends with Eric first. He and Seraphina became childhood sweethearts. But she didn't blossom till she was about fourteen, when she grew into her features and lost her dental braces.'

'I see....And....'

'Enough. Enough. I told you that would be the last question. What is it about Dylan and our family that brings out such fascination in hack journalists and his fancy women? Draws out too many of my own feelings every time. But still you all keep coming! I'm on medication, you know. Nerves and depression.'

'I'm sorry. But that's no excuse for treating me the way you did the other day.'

An awkward silence enveloped us again.

Yet underneath I was happy. Many had come before with probing questions, so I wouldn't look too out of place within Dylan's inner circle if I continued to ask my own.

Then I brought the medallion I had found out of my pocket. 'Found this the other day.'

The change in Veronica was great. Her eyes widened and her interest had been renewed. 'Where?' she asked, eager to hold the object, as if she realized it must be worth something.

As I gave the medallion to her, Rupert came in and immediately took it off her – much to Veronica's annoyance – and sat down in a chair to admire the object.

'Found it under the fallen tree. Up at the Lodge. Dylan thought it might be Masonic.'

Rupert was holding the medallion up to the light and taking a close look at the markings. 'No, he's wrong.'

'How can you tell?'

'I'm a Freemason myself.'

'Oh, that would explain the dodgy handshake,' Veronica said, walking over to Rupert and snatching the medallion back. 'Let me take it to a friend of mine. A local antiquarian. He'll know.'

I was a little reluctant, but she had pocketed the medallion before I had a chance to answer. Upon reflexion, I thought it might help to keep her on more friendly terms. And I reasoned she could be a source of valuable information on Dylan.

The conversation then moved on to more mundane subjects, until Dylan came back into the room. 'Come outside. I've something to show you.'

I was intrigued. I followed him to the car park. We approached a gleaming light-blue Austin-Healey.

'Do you like it?'

'Yes, rather!'

'It's a "Frog-Eye" Sprite.'

'I know – and isn't she a beauty!'

'Good. I'm glad you like it.' He threw me the keys and I caught them. 'It's yours.'

'You must be joking!'

'No. I want you to have it. We've another one in the museum. Shame to sell it, after all our restoration. You keep it.'

'Look. I really can't accept.'

'You can and you will. You'd still have your Fiat if I hadn't towed it back to my place. It's not really a free gift, more a replacement. I feel obliged. And – as I've said before – I don't want you thinking you can't leave whenever you like.'

I embraced him and smothered him with kisses, grateful for his patronage. 'You're too kind.'

'Drive it back to the Lodge. I'll meet you there.' He waved, then walked off towards his workshops.

'You're lucky to've met him,' Veronica said over my shoulder. 'He's a generous man.'

'Too generous.'

'Yes. Though he doesn't give away gifts lightly. This must mean he thinks highly of you. But beware! Affairs rarely last long with Dylan. And anyway, he's not even free. Just be thankful you've lasted beyond the first night.' She paused for a moment. 'I'd make the most of it, if I were you. But be prepared to share him.'

She sniggered when she saw my face. Beneath her sarcasm I could detect the frost of resentment. 'I must go back to work now. It's been nice to talk to you.' She didn't sound convincing.

'Wait. What more can you tell me about Dylan?'

She turned round, angry all of a sudden. 'Stop bothering me. Go ask him yourself!' She must have seen how glum my expression was as I climbed into the Austin-Healey, '....or you could try his scrapbook collection in the library....at the Lodge.'

'Thanks....,' but she was gone, walking off towards the house.

Driving back to the Lodge was unforgettable. Being behind the wheel of such a car, speeding around the twisting bends, with the hood down and hair flowing in the wind, was an experience I never dreamed I'd ever have. I parked in the forecourt, pulling up the roof of the car again.

Then I headed straight for the library. I searched patiently for the scrapbooks. I found them in amongst some ancient books on witchcraft and black magic.

They turned out to be elaborately bound volumes, very similar to those around them. There were ten in all, each one representing a year, starting with the publication of his first book.

Every article and review ever published on Dylan appeared to be here. The good and the bad. His first novel, *Pillar Rock* (1977), named after a real feature above Ennerdale, was a fictionalized account of the beginnings of rock climbing in the 1890s. The sport had indeed started in the Lakes at this time, apparently by people like O.G. Jones, Haskett-Smith and the Abraham Brothers, whom I'd never heard of. It had had good reviews, won awards, but hadn't sold well.

His second book, *The Music Man* (1979), about the rise and fall of a rock star, had secured his future. The book had been developed for film. He had written the screenplay himself. Hollywood had made him a millionaire several times over.

His other books, *The Immigrant* (1982), *Beyond the Raging Sea* (1983) and *Friends and Lovers* (1985) had enhanced his literary reputation, if not his bank balance. He was now seen as a leading figure in a new wave of young writers.

However, increasingly the articles were shifting away from reviews and interviews about his work, towards sensational tabloid exposure of his private life. Highly publicized affairs with a page-three girl, Sheila Delaney; the French cult-film actress, Monique Devereaux; and the pop singer, Amy Morgan, with whom he'd co-written a number of protest songs; had brought the image of Dylan the playboy to life. He'd also been named in the divorce courts twice, and had broken up the marriages of several celebrities. The greatest publicity had surrounded his affair with a cabinet minister's married daughter, which had led to a pregnancy, and then to a scandal.

The articles began to peter out after 1985, with only the occasional story by one of his ex-lovers or one-night-standers, who'd cashed in with pieces like:

MY NIGHT WITH DYLAN QUEST

or

CON-QUEST

I had to laugh. Yet it revealed a very real fear that Dylan was exploiting me as much as all these other women, as Emily and Veronica had warned. What he hadn't expected, though, was that I'd used my pre-knowledge of his womanizing reputation to help me seduce him in the first place.

I put the heavy volumes away and went to the lounge with the copy of *Friends and Lovers* I'd all but finished.

Dylan came back when I was settling myself onto the sofa.

He stormed into the room, his anger all too evident.

I stood up. 'What's wrong Dyl....?'

He shoved me back down with force.

'Shut up and listen! I want you to tell me the truth now. No more lies or you can fuck off!'

I cowered. 'What d'you mean?'

'You know exactly what I mean! You've been lying to me ever since we met! Everything you've told me's probably untrue.'

'Eh?' I struggled to regain some composure.

'Give up, Freya. I went through the wreckage of your car. I found notebooks full of shorthand. Tell me the truth. You're an undercover journalist, aren't you?'

''Course not....' putting on an indignant face. 'I'm really only a secretary. I use shorthand all the time at work.'

I wasn't lying. And whilst John had dabbled with writing in his youth, he was no journalist either.

Dylan sat down, cooling off a little. 'Thank God. Ronni said you'd been asking all these questions. Then I found the notebooks. I came to a logical conclusion, albeit a wrong one. I'm just so fed up with hacks invading my privacy and exploiting my good nature.'

He paused when he saw how upset I was getting.

'I'm sorry. I've overreacted....Just promise me you won't sell your story to the press.'

'I promise,' I mumbled.

He wiped away the feigned tears from my eyes with his hands very delicately.

Then he carried me up the stairs to bed.

- VIII -

WE SPENT THE next couple of days hardly venturing away from the bedchamber. His lovemaking was tender and experimental. The dutiful Yasuko responded to Dylan's bell call with meals in bed at regular intervals. I felt safe, cocooned here in an unreal world. However, the next day he returned to his tower, ostensibly to work on a new novel-in-progress. With Yasuko fixated on all her chores, eager not to receive Dylan's wrath, I felt lonely. And the Lodge had begun to take on a claustrophobic feel which disturbed me.

I decided I had to break free.

I went over to the old stables and opened the double doors. As I was unlocking the car, I spied an ornate gold picture frame poking out of a hessian sack. I went over to it and pulled it out. I choked as a cloud of dust rose into my face. I placed the heavy item onto a workbench and rubbed the grime of a generation off the surface of the painting.

It was a portrait of an old man, with a full head of grey hair and a handlebar moustache. It was well executed. His eyes bore right into me and seemed to follow me as I gazed at the rest of the picture.

I was fascinated, yet unsettled by it.

I licked my right index finger and rubbed at the brass plate at the bottom of the frame. It read:

Sir Frederick Faversham
1890-1970

I nodded in realization: it was Seraphina, Janis and Emily's father. What I couldn't understand was why such an imposing and undoubtedly valuable portrait was hidden away in here. Confused, I replaced it in the sack and made a mental note to ask Dylan later on.

Returning to the car, I climbed in and reversed out into the sunshine. Then I pulled down the roof. Soon I was negotiating the driveway, the Austin-Healey roaring its approval. It only had a small engine, but it gave a good impression of true thoroughbred class.

I journeyed along the narrow country lanes of Lakeland, not taking too much care. I made my way around Bassenthwaite Lake, the shadow of Skiddaw ever present and omnipotent. Then I found myself travelling through the small settlements of Braithwaite and Stair, the mountains rising steeply above me. Onwards through the tranquil Vale of Newlands I drove, with the wind in my hair. Then over the hause for a spectacular view of Buttermere, dwarfed by the high ridge beyond.

I stopped for lunch at an inn, eating chips and sipping vodka. Then I took a short walk southwards, admiring a spur which tapered down to the blue-green water at the other end of the lake. I consulted my map to discover this mountain was Fleetwith Pike.

I returned to the pub and slotted some coins into the payphone. It took a while for John to pick up.

'It's me.'

'Who?' He seemed disgruntled, as if I'd disturbed him in his work.

'Freya.'

'Oh,' he perked up. 'Got anywhere yet?'

'Yes. I'm in. And I'm gaining his trust.'

'Good. Find out as much as you can. But remember what I said. Don't get too involved.'

'Bit late for that....'

I could feel his exasperation on the other end of the line, just as the pips started. But I did not have any more spare change, so I had to hang up.

I set off once more, travelling over Honister Hause, meeting the quarry-scarred Pike at close quarters. A white memorial cross was a conspicuous feature upon its lower slopes. I shuddered at the thought of someone having fallen off. This sobered me up a little and I took extra care with my driving.

However, despite my renewed concentration, I nearly had an accident at Rosthwaite, a small settlement within Borrowdale, on the way back to Keswick. As I was approaching the narrowest point in the road between two ancient cottages, a bunch of motorcyclists roared past, only clearing the wall by inches. If something had been coming the other way, they would've had no chance.

Overwhelmed with shock, I pulled over at the entrance to a farmer's field for a breather. I watched them zoom off into the distance. One skidded to a halt, did a U-turn and returned to where I was parked. The rider flicked up the helmet visor.

It was Emily!

'Hi,' she said, smiling. 'Recognized the car. Didn't think Dylan'd let you drive it, though. Hope we didn't scare you too much!'

I scowled at her.

She lit a cigarette, chuckling.

She was dressed in full leathers, yet they appeared a lot more scuffed and worn than before. There was also a picture of a gremlin's face emblazoned on the back of her jacket. She saw me regarding it and turned her back towards me so I could get a better view. 'Do you like it?'

I shrugged.

'I'm a fully fledged member of the chapter now. I've been earning my right to wear their motif all week. They've been setting me lots of zany stunts. I'm sorry you had to get mixed up in one of them by mistake!'

I shrugged again, lost for words.

'Follow me.' She didn't wait for an answer, simply flicked down her visor, kick-started her machine into life and took off up the road.

When I realized her pace was very sedate, I pulled out and followed along as she'd asked. She made me drive into a car park near the Jaws of Borrowdale. She then assisted me in pulling up the roof of the car. I locked up and we sauntered over to the Bowderstone. Emily told me the huge boulder was an "erratic" dumped by an ancient glacier, and had been a tourist attraction since at least the eighteenth century. We sat down and watched some climbers bouldering on its face. She produced a flask from inside her jacket and we shared her coffee.

'I'm going away soon, Freya.'

'Oh,' I said. 'That'll be sad. I'm only just getting to know you. You're the only potential friend I've got round here.'

'I'm sorry....I like you, too....It's just time for me to move on.'

She wriggled uncomfortably on the rock we were perched on, placing her hand upon her right buttock.

'Are you getting cramp?'

'No, you'll see soon enough. I'm in the middle of a process, you see. The tattoo and piercing parlour's nearly finished work now. One final touch from them and the hairdresser tomorrow. Then I'll be ready for him.'

'Who?'

'Dylan, of course.'

'What!'

'Oh, don't worry,' she quickly added. 'It's not what you think. Anyway, I've got Judd now.'

I was about to ask more, but she was pulling me to my feet. 'Come on, let's go. We've got one last afternoon together. Let's make the most of it.'

I trailed behind her. When I arrived back at the car park, she was already straddling her bike, revving it for effect.

'Come on, on you get,' she called, holding out her helmet for me to put on.

'Oh, no. I'm not getting on that thing with you again.'

'Look, I promise to go slow.'

'What about my car?'

'You can pick it up later.'

Her bewitching smile sealed it. After all, I had nothing else to do. I climbed on board and donned her helmet.

'What about you?'

'I'll be all right. Shouldn't get any cops out here.'

Before I could answer, we were away.

'Hang on tight!'

And I needed to as well. I should've known I couldn't trust her. She picked up speed immediately and we gathered momentum throughout the journey towards Keswick. I gripped her slender waist so tightly I could hear her rasping breath. I kept my eyes shut, feeling her long, silky hair caressing my face. I hadn't had time to pull down the visor. Now I was happy I hadn't, as her hair had a soothing influence upon me. She slowed down only as we approached and went through the town. I was happy for this little respite. Once on the open road again, she gunned the engine and let out one of her banshee cries.

I was frightened, yet exhilarated.

I opened my eyes only when the bike wheels screeched as she did a large turn off to the left. I was jolted out of position. My hands lost their grip. Emily squeezed in her arms to trap me in position again, to make sure I didn't fall off.

I knew where we were now: on the minor road back towards the Lodge. She picked up speed again. I wondered whether my stomach or my bladder was going to give out first with each new twist and turn. I felt glad when she slowed again. We took off up a forest road, dirt thundering up in our wake.

It took me a while to realize we had come to a halt. She let go of my arms and I fell off onto the ground. She was soon standing over me, pulling off my helmet, grinning.

I yanked her down on top of me and we rolled around in the dirt for a while. I cursed her as we playfully wrestled. She held me firmly, then got to her feet. She dusted herself down, before helping me up.

'You bastard, you promised me....'

'To go slow, I know....But you didn't really believe I was going to, did you?'

I smiled nervously and gazed around, not wanting to make eye contact.

She had driven us to the back entrance of the Lodge. There was the high stone wall, with the gated archway bordered by turrets. The sun was doing its best to penetrate the trees, but I still had to squint to recognize my surroundings.

Emily had slumped against the wall, laughing. I shook my head at her, but she continued. Finally, I had to give in to her. I couldn't remain angry for long. Anyway, I was feeling quite queasy, so I sank down beside her.

She did not give me long to recover. She pulled me up with her. 'Give me a leg up,' she said, pointing to the gate. I cupped my hands dutifully for her foot. She launched herself upwards and shimmied over the gate in what looked like a well-practised move. I heard her feet hit the floor on the other side and the drawing of the heavy bolt.

The gate opened and she motioned me forward. 'Come on. I want to show you something.'

Thankfully, she wanted me to walk with her, rather than take to the motorbike again. I followed her along the track we had come down after the dinner party. However, it wasn't long before we had forked off along a tiny trod through a mature passageway of yew trees. I hadn't noticed this on my previous visit. Once it must have been a well-manicured garden feature. Now it was heavily overgrown, with branches flicking into my face and catching on my hair. Each time I became entangled, she delicately extracted me and we sallied further into the darkened tunnel.

The sun pierced my eyes as we came out into a clearing. It took a while for my vision to adjust. I was amazed at what lay before me. It was a folly, built in the same stone as the house: a circular, domed edifice, supported by Corinthian columns, now partly camouflaged by creepers.

She took me by the hand and led me inside. Then she crouched down on the floor and drew me down with her.

'This is my secret little place. Where I come to get away from it all. Meditate even.'

'Right! It is rather romantic, I must say.'

'Dylan and Sera used to come here together to play. When they were children. The main house was still a ruin then. Janis and Eric perhaps came as well, I don't know. I wasn't even born, or maybe only a baby at the time.'

'How did you discover it? It's not exactly easy to find.'

'Dylan brought me. Just the once. He dressed me in white.'

'Why?'

'I don't know. Maybe it was to symbolize my virginity. I *really* don't know.'

She bent over and dusted her hand across the marbled floor. Weird geometric shapes were revealed under the grime, pitted and weathered. They reminded me of those on the medallion. 'Perhaps he got excited by all these old ritualistic markings.'

'I see,' I said, studying the pattern intensely, intrigued.

'No, I don't think you do, Freya. He fucked me that night. I was only fifteen. I wanted to do it with him, don't get me wrong. But not like that. He was rough and unkind. And I was scared.'

I turned away from her and shifted my pose, disconcerted.

'I think he knew he'd done wrong. Couldn't help making it up to me over the years since. He showered me with gifts and was always warm and loving after that. Especially in bed.'

'Why tell me this?'

She could sense my increasing agitation. 'I've never told anybody else. I wanted to get it out of me before I go. So I can move on. I like you, Freya. Maybe I'm also trying to warn you that Dylan has a darker side.'

I scoffed, not taking any of it in.

Emily got up and walked back through the columns. I shifted to follow. She returned before I could leave, carrying some leaves and twigs. She set about making a fire. Once it was lit, she pulled out a tin box from inside her jacket, opened it and took out a spoon. Then she poured powder from a paper wrap onto the spoon and added a little water from a small plastic bottle.

I watched in silence as she heated the spoon over the flame. I hadn't a clue what she was up to, until she pulled out a syringe from the tin box and sucked up the golden-brown contents of the spoon which had now fully liquefied.

She pulled off her jacket and laid it over the fire, stamping on it to extinguish the flames. She was only wearing a T-shirt underneath. I could now see the full devastation of her forearms, a mass of scar tissue and some recent lacerations. There were lots of needle marks in the cavities of her elbows. She was hunting for a vein, tapping her fingers against her skin.

'Bugger,' she said, peeking under her T-shirt to study her breasts instead. 'Nothing doing there either.'

I looked at her in disbelief.

'Care to join me?'

'No, I do not!'

'Sorry about this. Cover your eyes, if you want.' She leaned to one side and pulled down her tight-fitting trousers to reveal the upper part of her thigh and right buttock. I could glimpse the edge of a recently applied tattoo protruding from underneath her panties.

I was transfixed. I couldn't turn away, as she stabbed herself with the needle and pushed down the plunger. Then she discarded the syringe on the stone floor and slumped against the column. She stared towards me, eyes wide and her breath uneven.

'Yes,' was all she said, as the heroin surged through her body.

I thought she'd sunk into unconsciousness or worse. My anxiety rose. I leant over her and put my ear down to her mouth. I couldn't hear her breathing, but I saw her chest rising and falling.

Suddenly I felt her stroking my hair. I looked up at her taut face, her eyes feral. Yet she apparently still comprehended the world around her. She pulled me down against her right breast, stroking my hair.

'Look up, look up,' she whispered. 'This is what I really wanted you to see.'

I lay back against her and gazed up at the domed ceiling.

What I saw was truly awe-inspiring. The dome was covered in a magnificent painting. Its colours were rich and vibrant, protected from the elements unlike the rest of the building. It depicted a devil-like creature, partially enveloped in flames. He was devouring a young black-haired maiden from behind, as she reached out, breasts exposed, to another figure on the other side of the picture. This other side was white and radiant, with a naked long-blonde-haired nymph – or maybe she was an angel? – reaching out a hand towards the stricken woman.

'Beautiful, isn't it?'

'Yes. And remarkably well preserved.'

'It's not as old as you think....Seraphina painted it.'

'Really – now that *is* interesting.'

There was a long pause as we both contemplated the painting. Totally absorbed.

'When I get high, the figures seem to move. Amazing!'

Then Emily floated off into blissful unconsciousness.

- IX -

I HAD FELT VERY relaxed lying upon Emily's breast, absorbed by the sight of the painting on the ceiling. So much so, in fact, that I must have drifted off to sleep. When I awoke, there was a chill in the air and I was alone. I struggled to my feet, trying to concentrate, forgetting where I was for a moment, then worrying where Emily had gone.

I passed through the columns and gazed up at the sky. It looked like late afternoon light, so I couldn't have been alone for very long. Emily must still be around somewhere.

I was about to go back through the tunnel of yew trees, when I saw a flight of steps under the foliage. The plants had been trampled on recently, and as I neared the edge, I could hear a faint thrashing lower down the slope. Perhaps this was what had woken me up.

I stepped tentatively down the first flight of stairs to a landing. There was a carved balustrade on either side, matching the decoration of the ramparted lawns nearer the main house; and the outline of an urn on a small plinth, shrouded, ghost-like, under the greenery.

I continued on, down several more flights of stairs, until I gained a level rampart running at right angles to the stairway. I was about to go along this, when I heard more sounds from below. I peered over the wall and saw Emily lower down, brandishing a stick and thrashing at the stinging nettles. She was climbing out of a hollow onto a steep rise on the other side. Now she had gained an overgrown path that meandered through deciduous trees.

I was going to shout down to her, but decided against it. I sensed she wanted to be alone, otherwise she would have taken me with her in the first place. Intrigued at her clandestine manoeuvres, I brushed away the tree branches which barred my way onwards down the stairs.

I reached the bottom and found myself on a little stone bridge. As I surveyed the hollow around me more closely, I realized I was surrounded by ornamental lakes, clogged up with years of reed-growth and leaves. They stretched out in both directions for over a hundred feet, descending in flights of pools from right to left. I could make out carved fountain heads and one waterfall was still running, albeit only at a trickle.

I would have liked to have lingered longer, but Emily had disappeared and I wanted to see where she had gone.

I followed in her footsteps, up the banks of the hill. As I trod through the trees, the rise seemed conical shaped, perhaps even man-made. After about twenty feet, the trees became thicker and the light faded. I fumbled my way through. This was worse than the yew-tree tunnel, I thought, as my hair, face and clothing tangled on the branches.

And then, unexpectedly, I stumbled through into a large forgotten clearing. Now it was my legs that fought with brambles and burrs.

I stopped, perplexed.

Ahead of me lay more ruins. Yet this edifice was so different. There was a tall tower, with a doorless entrance at its base. To its right, a half-fallen-down wall ran for about seventy feet. Though ruined, the arched windows left me in no doubt this wasn't another folly, but a Gothic chapel. A maturing oak was growing from inside, the canopy spreading skyward where the roof used to be.

The strangest thing of all was the stonework. It was as elegantly dressed as the main house and the folly. But it was of black granite. Dark and lugubrious, with an air of foreboding.

I felt hands upon my shoulders. I jumped backwards.

'What are you doing here?!'

It was only Emily, but I'd nearly burst my bladder in fright.

'I'm sorry, Em.,' I said, recovering gradually. 'I heard you ahead and followed.'

'Spying on me, eh?'

'Well....'

'I didn't want you to come here. Not yet, anyway. I wanted to be alone.'

I apologized again.

'Never mind,' she said. 'I suppose you might as well look around now you're here.'

Relief overtook me. Yet she didn't expand on her motives for coming here so furtively.

She walked me over to the tower. There was a carved head of a horned goat – again reminiscent of the medallion – over the old doorway. As we went inside, a flurry of activity erupted overhead.

I panicked again. I looked above me and gripped Emily tightly. The floors had all rotted away long ago, but I could not see the sky because of a mass of bats.

'Don't worry,' Emily shouted in my ear. 'They're more scared than we are.'

She pushed me through an archway into what had

been the nave. The interior was as black as the exterior, but there were many pillars with amazing twists and carved reliefs, all once awash with colours – monsters, goblins and serpents abounded, some in sexual poses.

This was no ordinary chapel! As we walked upon the floor, I noticed more of the geometric shapes we'd seen in the folly. To the sides were four marble plinths, with black effigies upon them. I moved over to one and looked at the carved lettering, once marked in gold leaf:

BARON SIEGFRIED von ESCHENBACH
1800-89

'A German?'

'Yes, a Bavarian, I think. He commissioned the Lodge in the first place. Or maybe bought it off the first owner, I'm not sure. I read it in this old book in the library. Memory escapes me now, but he was definitely the one who built this chapel.'

I moved along to the next tomb. The effigy was certainly that of a woman, but with the inscription so badly decayed, I could only read the year of her death – 1907.

'I think she was the Baron's daughter. When she died this place fell into rack and ruin. The Lodge lasted a little longer, but had succumbed to the same fate by the 1920s. It would've remained so, if Dylan hadn't renovated it.'

'Why was the Lodge left to rack and ruin?

'Too difficult and expensive to maintain, I suppose. A lot of country mansions suffered a similar fate.'

'There must've been more to it, surely?'

'Well, back in the Fifties, a legend still persisted amongst the locals that the Baron had been in league with the Devil!'

'What rubbish!' I said, yet realizing Sera had obviously taken her inspiration for the folly painting from these rumours.

'Yes, I've always thought so. Especially since his daughter was my grandmother!'

'What?'

'Yes, I only found this out by chance. Mother never tells me anything. Her name was Hildegard. She married an MP called Sir Ernest Faversham.' She pointed to the tomb on the other side of the chapel. 'They only had one son, Frederick, my father.'

I gasped as she led me to the last tomb, which lay half demolished as if by human hand. 'He only lay here for a few years. Dylan had him exhumed and reburied in a churchyard down in the valley, when he acquired this property.'

I didn't know what to say.

We moved forward, skirting the oak tree, whose roots had torn up the floor tiles. Beyond lay the back wall, with its huge, once intricate cinquefoil window. Little remained now. Below this stood a solid black altar, showing a few cracks in its lining.

'The land remained in my family till Mother sold out to the Forestry Commission in 1973. I get the impression Dylan was furious. Anyway, he certainly vowed to buy the Lodge back one day. By the time he achieved it, back in 1980, the building was a derelict shell, ready for demolition. You wouldn't believe it now, would you? He's done such a wonderful restoration.'

'He has. It certainly looks very authentic. What was his motivation? Did he want to recover your family's prestige? Or was it because he always liked the building? You said they all used to play here as children.'

'The second, maybe....But the overriding reason's because Sera's buried here.'

I exhaled deeply.

She guided me back outside and around to the far side, which had been hidden from view on the way in.

Old iron railings, rusted from neglect, ringed an overgrown earthen mound. A simple decaying headstone read:

Seraphina Faversham Jones
1953-1970
Beloved wife of
John Dylan Jones
R.I.P.

'Jones?' I queried.

'Yes, Jones. His mother's name. His parents never married. Quest was a pseudonym for his writing at first. He later changed it officially.'

I stared back at the ill-kept grave, which looked as forgotten as the old chapel itself.

A sense of the finality of death oppressed me.

Seventeen years in the elements, untended, had left her grave in a sorry state. This stark reality told me much more about Dylan than my researches so far had informed me. It was as if Seraphina hadn't existed....No, no....I corrected myself in my thoughts. It was as if Seraphina's death had never happened.

'Dylan hasn't accepted she's dead, has he?'

'No, not really.'

'Mm. Does he visit the grave himself?'

'No. One look at the state of this site should answer that question.'

'What about other people?'

'Only the immediate family know this place exists. And he forbids us all from coming here. That's why I've been so secretive. If news got back to Dylan that I've come here, or more to the point, brought you – an outsider – here, you'd never hear the end of it!'

'But surely you've a right to visit the grave of your own sister?'

'Of course I have the right. But Dylan's too possessive. When he met her, he was bewitched by her beauty and set about possessing her. He succeeded, of course. And he possesses her still, in death.'

I shuddered.

'I'm not going to let him possess me in the same way!' cried Emily, tears welling up in her eyes.

When she'd recovered enough, we left the eerie edifice, for which I was extremely grateful. I had no intention of being caught as night fell in such a haunting place as this.

Once back at the rear entrance, she collected her motorbike. Then she gave me a message that she quickly scrawled on a dirty and creased piece of paper.

'Give this to Dylan.'

I nodded and watched her head off through the archway.

- X -

THE SOUNDS OF a car creeping slowly up the driveway woke me from a fretful sleep. I'd had nightmares about the creepy old chapel, so I was thankful for the fresh morning light streaming through the curtains. I turned to Dylan's side of the bed, but only his compressed outline on the crumpled sheets remained. I sat up and whipped my legs out over the edge of the bed. I clawed my tousled hair away from my face, glad there really were no bats tangled up in it, and walked across to the window.

I could not make out the car at first, only its tinny engine noise. Then a battered Citroën Ami 8 drove through the inner gatehouse and came to a halt in the courtyard below.

Janis climbed out of the car. A girl also alighted, a younger image of her mother, but with longer, dark-brown hair. She ran around in precocious mood, as Dylan's sheepdog bounded out to greet them.

I opened the window and studied them further, as Dylan came into view and called out their names. I watched him embrace Janis. Then he gathered her daughter up in his arms and swung her around. She giggled and began to blurt out an incomprehensible string of sentences.

'Hi,' I finally called down to them, my observations over.

Janis looked up, shielding her eyes from the sun with her right hand. 'Hi, Freya. Good to see you again. This is my daughter, E-J.' She looked around at her daughter, but she was too preoccupied with Dylan's rough-and-tumble games to notice.

I was immediately struck by how much more alive and relaxed Janis looked when not in the presence of her mother.

Dylan eventually stopped and put E-J back down on the cobbles. 'Glad you're awake. Put something on and come on down!'

I needed no further encouragement. I hurriedly dressed, then brushed the tangles out of my hair. Before long I was down at the front door, welcoming the guests over the threshold.

Janis put her hand in mine and gave me a peck on the cheek. 'Hope Dylan's been treating you well?'

I nodded, as E-J raced past between us and sank to the floor, cuddling Quasi and tickling his tummy.

'Calm down a little, E-J! I know you're excited, but there are limits.'

'OK, Mummy,' she answered, yet carried on in the same manner as before.

Yasuko entered the room, carrying a tray.

Dylan looked up. 'Ah, tea. That's great, Yasuko. Let's have it on the terrace.'

We all ventured back outside, Dylan leading the way.

'How's business?' Dylan enquired, sitting down at the garden table and motioning for us to follow suit.

'Booming, Dyl. I've got a full quota for next week and the bookings are well up on last year. I'm rushed off my feet.'

I observed Janis closely as they became absorbed in conversation about her rock-climbing school.

E-J, laughing merrily, ran across the lawn; the dog trailed after her, panting. She threw a Frisbee in a long trajectory through the air and I watched Quasi time his jump to perfection, catching it firmly in his jaws. I applauded and ran over to join them. I'd always had a certain rapport with children, so it didn't take me long to win her trust. I became so lost in merriment that it took Dylan several calls to draw our game to a conclusion when the refreshments were ready to serve.

I collapsed into a chair beside them, mopping the sweat from my brow with the back of my hand. 'Phew,' I said, and guzzled down some lemonade, as Yasuko stooped over us to pour out tea for the others.

'You play well, Freya. Ever thought of working with children?'

'No, Janis. You looking to give me a job?' I chuckled.

'We're always after team leaders to compliment our instructors. They take care of the guests once the rock-climbing sessions are over. But I don't suppose Dylan'll let you go. At least not until he's dumped you."

I flushed.

Dylan glared at Janis and nudged her side with his elbow.

'Sorry,' she murmured, and picked up her teacup, perhaps to hide behind it.

I shifted back in the chair as E-J jumped into my lap.

'Careful, love.'

'It's OK, Janis,' I said, putting an arm around the child. 'How old are you?'

'I'm eight,' she said proudly, wriggling on my legs to find the most comfortable spot.

I felt something in my back pocket. I reached around and pulled out a crumpled piece of paper. 'Oh, Dylan, I almost forgot: this is for you.'

'What is it?'

'It's from Emily.'

'Why didn't you tell me before,' he said, ripping it out of my hand and unfolding it impatiently. He frowned as he read her scrawled words.

'What's she say?' Janis asked.

He passed her the note. 'She's leaving on Saturday. Wants me to come and say goodbye.'

'That's tomorrow,' Janis said. 'It says here she's not coming back. She came to see me yesterday. Said more or less the same thing. She says she's going to change, Dyl. And that you're not going to like it.'

Dylan grabbed back the note and scrunched it up in his fist before pounding the table. This dislodged my drink, which cascaded all over E-J and me. We leapt to our feet, she giggling, me cursing.

'Sorry,' Dylan said, as I picked up a napkin and did my best to soak up the moisture on E-J's summer frock.

Janis put her arm around his shoulder. 'You've got to let her go. We all have. She'll come back eventually.'

'I'm not so sure,' I said, destroying what little comfort Dylan had drawn from Janis's words.

Janis scowled at me and drew herself nearer to Dylan. 'It'll be all right. After all, you've still got me.'

He put on a strained smile.

'It's no good, E-J. This stuff's never going to come out.' I cursed again, more at Janis's over-familiarity with Dylan, than with the stains on our clothing. 'Come on, let's go inside and get changed. Has she got anything else to wear?'

'Yes, she knows where to find it. She's got her own bedroom here.'

We withdrew inside, leaving them to it. I helped E-J to shower, before doing the same myself. She talked the whole time without any let up, about the fun she was going to have now school had broken up for the summer.

When we returned to the garden, Yasuko was clearing away the things from an empty table.

'Where've they gone?'

Down to the bridge.

'The bridge? Why?' I said.

'I know. Mummy's told me all about it, come on.' She took me by the hand and hurried me around the side of the building and down the drive.

'Slow down. Slow down.' I was puffed out.

She took no notice, accelerating away ahead and out of sight.

Dylan was leaning on the parapet of the bridge when I arrived, talking with E-J.

'Where's Janis?'

Dylan simply tapped a rope.

I followed its course over the masonry and peeked over the edge. 'Oh, dear God!' I cried, 'she'll fall!'

'Don't be silly,' E-J retorted.

I stole another look over the edge. Janis was suspended on the rope, attached to a climbing harness, halfway down the wall. Below her lay a sheer drop into the gorge.

'Oh, I can't look!' I said, clutching onto Dylan and burying my head into his chest.

Dylan laughed, shaking his head.

'Why is she being so silly? It's only abseiling. When do I get a turn?'

'When Mummy's ready.'

'You're not letting her go down there!'

'Yes, why not? Once Janis has checked it out. You can have a go, too, if you like.'

'No way!' I clutched him tighter.

'Chicken!' E-J strutted around in a circle, flapping her arms and making clucking noises. She stopped only when Dylan chided her.

'Do you know how far it is to the ground over that edge?' I said, turning to face her.

'Yes. It's only about forty feet, Mummy told me.'

'Only! Phew! What's she doing down there, anyway?'

'She's checking it out as a possible abseiling venue for her school.' Dylan said. 'She uses local rock faces and a couple of artificial towers in her own grounds. But the beauty of this bridge is its archway halfway down. You can bounce out and swing underneath it.'

I plucked up the courage to peer over the edge again and saw Janis whizzing down the rope. I grabbed Dylan by the arm. 'She's falling! She's falling!'

E-J launched herself up onto the parapet. 'You really are a silly billy, aren't you? She's just having some fun.'

I felt sick, cramping in my stomach. But E-J was right. Janis slowed in an arc and landed safely on the bank of the ghyll below. Then she looked up and waved.

I crouched down by the side of the wall. Dylan ruffled my hair and laughed along with E-J. It wasn't long before Janis had clambered up a hidden set of steps through the rhododendrons.

'What do you reckon?' Dylan said, when she returned.

She stood over me, pieces of metal climbing gear clinking on her harness as she took off her gloves. 'There's quite a lot of moss and lichen on the masonry.

We'll have to clean that off. Then there'll have to be a platform up here against the parapet for easier access. Might be a little unsightly.'

'We can work on it.'

'What about your privacy?'

'Well, as long as you tell me in advance, and you don't let any of the party past this point, I reckon I can agree.'

'And what about your fee?'

'I'm sure that can be negotiated in due course,' he said, leaning over as she kissed him and hugged him. I couldn't help noticing the way his hand had crept onto her backside.

E-J saw this and giggled, and they broke away from each other in response to this.

'Mummy, Mummy, when is it my go?'

'Calm down. Dylan has first choice, since he owns the bridge. You can go after him....'

'Goody, goody....'

'But only if you get more sensible.'

'Yes, Mummy, yes Mummy.'

'Good. Then Freya can have a go after you.'

'No way!' I started to back away from the wall.

They were having none of it. They all climbed into a harness and put on a helmet and made me do the same.

'Tie up your hair, like E-J has done,' Janis said. 'We don't want such lovely blonde locks getting caught in the device. Otherwise I'll have to come down beside you on the wall with a pair of pinking shears!'

This seemed to be well-rehearsed banter, but it didn't put me at ease.

Dylan placed his arm around me for reassurance, whilst Janis set up a safety rope.

'You don't have to try it if you don't want to.'

Janis ignored Dylan's comments, and I could sense she saw in me her latest challenge. 'The worst thing is trusting the ropes and leaning back at the start, so you get almost at right angles to the wall. Then you simply walk backwards down the masonry, legs apart for balance. You feed the rope through this figure-of-eight,' she tapped a piece of gear clipped onto my harness, 'keeping your hand firmly by your hip. Don't let it travel up the rope or you may get it caught in the device. Don't fancy mincemeat fingers, do you?'

I gulped.

'Don't worry, I'll have you on this green rope all the time, so I'd stop you before it got to that point. You can control your descent yourself by wrapping the rope around your bum to stop.' She demonstrated. 'And you can pay it out at whatever rate you want. Watch the others first.'

Dylan climbed into position, leant out over the edge and descended steadily. Then he did a small leap, paid out the rope and swung under the arch.

I clutched at my chest, as I began to hyperventilate. I calmed only when Dylan reappeared and sank slowly to the ground safely.

'My go, Mummy! My go!'

E-J was quickly in position. Before I could comprehend what was happening, she'd disappeared over the side with a high-pitched 'Yippee!' By the time I'd braved a glance over the edge, she was swinging in a huge arc under the archway.

'Go, E-J. Go!' Dylan called in admiration, as she eased further down the rope and into his arms at the bottom.

'Christ, she was fast!'

'Yes. Now it's your turn.'

'No way, Janis, no way!' Even as I said these words I knew I had to do it. I didn't want to be shown up by an eight-year-old, even if she'd probably been doing this since she was in nappies. Janis's closeness to Dylan had also awakened a strong competitive streak in me.

I waited until the others had returned. They uttered words of encouragement as Janis guided me into position, facing her, feet wide apart and set half over the parapet.

'Now lean back....slowly....it's all right, I've got you on safety, you can't go anywhere.'

I wasn't convinced. I felt my legs beginning to shake. I gazed at Dylan for inspiration. He winked. It didn't help. Then I made the fatal mistake of looking down between my legs to the raging ghyll below.

I started to panic. 'No. No. I can't do this.' Instinctively, I clutched the rope above the device with both hands.

'Yes, you can.' She placed my hands back into position. 'Ease back slowly....that's it. Keep your hand behind your hip.'

'Thumb up your bum!' E-J called out mischievously, knowing her mother was too busy with me to reprimand her.

I gently fed out the rope and sank down lower.

'That's it, trust the ropes. Sit in your harness. Legs straight and wide apart. I'm sure you've had enough practice at that since being with Dylan.'

I grunted, too panicked to respond. I edged outwards a little more.

'Oh, my God!' I felt myself sinking backwards too fast for comfort.

'No, my name's Janis actually.'

'Oh, funny ha ha!'

'That's it. Start moving slowly backwards. Now look, you're away.'

'You're doing it, you're really doing it!' E-J sounded surprised.

With increasing trepidation, I crept backwards down the wall, feeding the rope out slowly, the others shouting out words of encouragement from above. I didn't dare look up.

'Right, you're at the arch now. Bend your knees in, then spring off and widen your arm so you can pay out lots of rope. When you've got down low enough to clear the top of the arch, bring your rope hand right around your hip again....'

'Thumb up the bum!'

'Yes, all right E-J!'

'Sorry, Mummy.'

I felt myself losing it. My legs were shaking violently. My bowels were loosening as well. And now Janis wasn't even concentrating on me.

'I can't go on any more.'

'Yes, you can.'

Dylan went over to the steps and came down until he was horizontal with my position. 'Come on, be brave.'

'No, I can't.'

'Cowardy custard!'

E-J's teasing was my spur to action. 'I'm going to get you later, Mr. Quest!' I shut my eyes tight, then leapt out from the side of the wall.

I felt a great rush of air and exhilaration. 'Fuckin' 'ell!'

I was so lost I forgot all the instructions about what I was supposed to be doing, until I felt the jerk of the safety rope coming into effect instead. I swung backwards and forwards under the arch, the sounds of the ghyll getting louder in my ears. I wanted the swinging to stop, but I still had around ten feet to go.

'You all right?' Janis yelled down, getting a little concerned.

I managed to mumble a faint affirmative.

'Let out the rope again slowly. That's it, you're nearly there.'

It seemed an eternity before I fell into Dylan's strong arms and he lowered me onto the bank on my back. He kissed me and stroked back my hair.

'You OK?'

'Yes, just about.'

He looked relieved.

'Great one, Freya. Now let's go again. You'll perfect it next time!' came the cry from high above.

'She can't be serious, Dylan. I'm not doing that again!'

He burst out laughing and tried to embrace me. I pushed him away and staggered back towards the steps.

- XI -

A SWIM AND a long steam in the sauna was the only thing I could think of which would relax me after my ordeal with the abseiling. Janis and Dylan's bantering was later replaced by an over-eagerness to reassure me when I struggled to calm myself down. I loathed such mollycoddling. I also loathed their closeness. Pangs of jealousy were set off at each of their interactions. I needed time to myself.

I was roused from my reverie by Yasuko's ringing of the dinner gong. I dressed in fresh clothes and joined everyone at the table. Dylan and Janis came in arm-in-arm. I ignored them, turning to hug E-J when she skipped in as boisterous as ever.

'Where have you been? I've had no one to play with.'

'What d'you mean, E-J? Where was your Mummy?' I asked.

'She was in the bedroom....with Dylan....'

Janis glared at her.

E-J looked all the more mischievous. 'Kissing and cuddling....naughty things.'

'That's quite enough, young lady,' Janis said, whipping the back of E-J's legs with her hand. 'Now go to your room!'

E-J was too stunned to cry at first. Then the pain began to register and she wailed. 'I hate you! I hate you!'

came her forlorn cries as she ran off down the corridor. The dog, who'd been curled up in his basket in the kitchen, got up and scampered after her.

'Was that really necessary?' I said, aghast at her admonishment.

Janis sank into a chair, elbows on the table, head in hands. 'No, probably not. But she's got to learn. She never listens and she's so impolite at times.'

Dylan put his arm on her shoulder and sat down beside her.

I scowled. 'She'll never improve if you mete out punishment so indiscriminately.'

Dylan looked at me hard. 'A slap or two never harmed me.'

'Huh!' I dragged my chair out, its legs screeching on the tiled floor, and sat down. 'Hitting someone because you've been caught out is no way to deal with the guilt.'

Janis looked up and was about to retaliate when my thoughts struck home.

Now I realized I had another rival to contend with.

Yasuko came in with a big bowl of vegetables and returned several more times with the rest of the food. We all sat in silence.

'Are you going to say goodbye to Emily?' I said, as we began to eat.

'Yes, tomorrow morning, I think.'

'Can I come?'

'Yes, by all means, if you want to.' He sounded pleasant enough, but underneath I detected he'd rather have gone alone.

Yasuko came in and, after seeking permission from Dylan, sat down with us at the table. She was dressed in a pink kimono today and was heavily made-up. It made her look tawdry. Her mascara had run a little, as if she'd been crying.

We ate on in silence. Tension building.

Yasuko pulled her notebook from her pouch and scribbled down a message, passing it to me.

Where's the Austin-Healey?

'Oh, God! I was with Emily. I forgot all about the car.'

Dylan didn't look too happy after he'd snatched the note from my grasp and read it. 'Freya, where is it?'

'Don't panic. It's OK. It's in a car park.'

'Where?'

'It's in Borrowdale. At the Bowderstone.'

'Borrowd'l'? That's miles away!'

'It'll be safe enough,' I said, feeling a little worried. 'Won't it?'

'How long's it been sitting there?' Dylan said.

I had to think for a minute. 'Since yesterday afternoon.'

'Oh, how could you!' he fumed.

'I'm sorry. But you said it was my car and I could do what I like with it.'

'True,' he said. 'If there's anything left of it by the time you get around to retrieving it.'

'Oh.' I bowed my head, feeling shamed. 'Might it be stolen?'

'Yes, or broken into,' Janis interjected. 'It's so irresponsible, Freya. Mountain Rescue may even've been called out.'

'I don't understand.'

'Someone might think the owner's lost up the hill!'

'Oh, Janis, right. I didn't think,' I said ruefully.

'I thought you were more sensible than that,' Dylan said.

Janis smirked.

Dylan gave Janis a curt look. 'Maybe it was Emily's influence. Never mind. We can pick it up tonight.'

'OK.'

More silence followed. Time seemed to stand still. Only Yasuko collecting up the dishes and bringing in the dessert gave me any kind of boundary.

Finally, I spoke. 'What's that painting doing in the stables?'

Dylan didn't answer.

'What painting?' Janis was suddenly animated.

'Well, I was getting in the car when I saw this frame poking out of a sack.'

'Oh, no,' Dylan mumbled under his breath.

'And?'

'Well....' I said nervously. 'It was a painting of your father, Sir Frederick.'

'What!' She turned to Dylan in horror. 'You told me you'd got rid of that years ago!'

'Well, you must understand why I couldn't do it, love,' he said, extending his arms to placate her.

'OK, I do. But you could've destroyed it *for me*. Like I asked you to.' She put her head in her hands, rubbing her face wildly until her skin began to redden.

Dylan tried to put his arms around her again.

She pushed him away ferociously, rising from her chair, her face boiling. 'You know how much I hated him!' With nostrils flaring, she seized her fork in a clenched fist and waved it at Dylan. 'You bastard, I hate him!'

Then she thrust the fork down on the table and stormed off.

I looked at the quivering silver, the prongs embedded in the oak.

'Now look what you've done!' He looked resigned, not angry. 'I'd better go 'n' see if she's all right.'

He didn't give me a chance to defend myself. I sat back in my chair, folding my arms tightly and letting out a heavy sigh. 'How was I supposed to know?' I said, turning to Yasuko.

She shrugged her shoulders and set about removing the fork from the table top.

I helped Yasuko with the dishes, despite her body language which suggested Dylan wouldn't like it, and then went off to find E-J, taking her a tray of food.

I could hear Janis ranting on at Dylan in the bedroom next door. I tried to distract E-J, but to little avail. When the noises died away, E-J's anxieties dissipated. Then she was happy to play doll's houses with me until her Mummy came in, dried tears staining her face, to tuck E-J into bed for the night.

Two hours passed before Dylan came and found me in the library. He'd continued to comfort Janis, which escalated my jealousy. I occupied my time by reading the last few pages of Dylan's novel. Its exciting finale gripped me enough to put earlier events and emotions out of mind.

'Come on, find your coat and keys,' he said, ruffling my hair. 'Let's go and get the car.'

We spent the entire journey to the Bowderstone in silence. By the time he pulled the Land Rover up beside the Austin-Healey, dusk was falling. He climbed out and inspected the car.

'All looks well, Freya. You're lucky this time.'

I came up to him and hugged him. 'I'm sorry, it won't happen again.'

'What, leaving the car or upsetting Janis?'

I backed away from him and leant against the side of the Land Rover, folding my arms and looking downcast.

'Hey, cheer up, I was only joking!' He grinned and encouraged me back into his arms. 'Janis'll be all right. She's angry with me, not you. You weren't to know how she felt about her father.'

I snuggled up into his chest and he held me tighter.

'Her raw hatred frightened me.'

He kissed me on the forehead. 'Don't worry yourself about it. She's right. I should've got rid of it years ago. I could never hang it in the house.'

'No?'

'No. I despised the man as much as Janis did.'

'Why didn't you just sell it, then? Or give it to Veronica?'

'Janis would never've allowed that. You saw her reaction. No, I couldn't sell it, nor destroy it.'

'Why ever not? Better than gathering dust.'

'Because, paradoxically, it was one of Sera's greatest works.'

He was back inside the Land Rover before I had fully digested the statement.

He waited for me to climb into the Austin-Healey, then allowed me to head off first. I took my time driving up the narrow roads, watching the moonlight shimmering upon the surface of Derwentwater. I wound down the window to let in a breeze. I was struggling to concentrate. I couldn't stop thinking about Janis. So meek in the presence of her mother. So brave and adventurous on her own. So deeply vulnerable underneath.

Dylan remained firmly on my bumper all the way back, as if impatient with my slow progress. But I wasn't going to be hurried.

Not before time, I drove up the driveway and through the gatehouse to the inner courtyard. Once through the arch, I immediately slammed on the brakes. The car screeched to a halt, skidding on the gravel. I heard the Land Rover doing the same behind me, swerving to the side of my car. He slapped the steering wheel, greatly annoyed, looking straight at me.

I hauled myself through the window and sat on the door. And pointed.

There, in the middle of the courtyard, was a brazier. Janis was standing behind it, pouring an accelerant of some kind over the contents. The moonlight made the gilding glitter.

Dylan frantically fought with his seat belt. By the time he'd opened the door, Janis had struck a match, which illuminated her grief-stricken face.

As Dylan ran towards her, the flames erupted into the night sky. Janis calmly took a step backwards, unperturbed by the sudden heat, eyes widening in wonder.

Dylan tried to pull the painting from the flames, but he was beaten back by the heat. He kicked the brazier over onto the gravel, scattering embers everywhere.

When he extinguished the fire with a hose from the stables, all he could retrieve from the ashes was one charred corner of the frame and the blackened brass plaque.

He sat down on the cobbles, mopping the sweat and the soot from his forehead, allowing the water from the hose he still held to cascade over him. He gazed into space.

And there was nothing I could do to console him.

- XII -

DYLAN DROVE ALONG the road out of Keswick in silence. It was the same route we'd taken last night, but only in daylight could the striking scenery be appreciated. The small road wound around the indented shores of Derwentwater. Pine trees and crags towered above us. Across the water came the occasional sight of a secluded isle. Beyond this lay a green-grey ridge, bathed in the morning sunshine. We crossed an ancient bridge, after the end of the lake but before the Jaws of Borrowdale. The small settlement of Grange was nestled on the other side.

Tourists were out in force everywhere, so it took us some time to drive down the narrow track running parallel to the river. He parked the Land Rover on the edge of a campground. We walked slowly along the track. Tents were pitched everywhere. There were several walled enclosures and other areas cleared beneath the trees, where camps had been set up.

Along with the ordinary walkers one might expect, two more unconventional groups were in evidence. The first was a war-gaming society, and every now and then, we could hear the cries of mock battles. Then, some of them emerged through the trees, authentically dressed in Anglo-Saxon attire and wielding fake axes and swords.

The other group was the band of motorcyclists we sought. Down near the river, there was a meadow of parked Triumphs, Nortons, BSAs and other makes from a bygone age, some sporting weird handlebars and assorted customizations. The men and women who owned and rode these machines must have numbered about thirty. All were dressed in black leathers, the backs of their jackets displaying the gremlin chapter motif Emily had shown me the day before yesterday. Some lay around on the ground, much the worse for drink and drugs. Others were servicing or cleaning their bikes.

'Freya, you sure this is the right group?'

'Don't worry,' I whispered, 'we've definitely come to the right place.'

A giant of a man strode forward, full of purpose, his face mean and battle-scarred. 'Don't wan' anyone 'roun' 'ere. Keep *awfft*!'

'We wouldn't ordinarily intrude on you people, but one of you's expecting us....Emily Faversham?'

The man appeared puzzled at first, tugging at his mammoth-like beard. 'Oh, yea mean Emmy, the one from up road?'

Dylan nodded.

'Well, she's my girl. Be'ave yousself.' He did not wait for a reply, but walked straight over to a weather-beaten tent.

Moments later, a woman appeared.

Dylan was about to ask her where Emily was when the awful truth dawned on him – she was standing right in front of him.

His jaw dropped.

'What's the matter, Dylan? Don't you like the new me?' She stared at him with a vacant smile, posing to show off her new look.

Her lovely jet-black hair had all but gone. Most of her head was shaved to the skin. The remnants of her hair were elevated in a number of long spikes in a fusion of purple and orange. Silver rings ran all the way down the sides of her ears to the lobes. Two silver studs pierced either side of her nose, with connecting chains to her ears. Her eyes were heavily made-up in black, forming patterns which complemented her hairstyle. She wore a cross and chain around her neck; a black miniskirt upon which even more chains were mounted; and a dirty-white T-shirt torn for fashionable effect, and so tight as to suggest piercings to the navel and nipples.

When she realized Dylan was too dazed to speak, she merely took his hand and guided him up the slope and into the trees. They stopped in a blasted-out enclave, an old relic of quarrying.

The giant-man, unimpressed, retreated to his tent.

I was left wondering whether to follow Dylan and Emily, or wait within the camp. I decided on the latter. Before too long Dylan came pounding down the slope. I went up to meet him, but he thrust past me.

'What's the matter?'

He didn't answer.

I went to find Emily. She was lying prone on the ground on her front. Her skirt had risen enough for me to realize she wasn't wearing anything underneath. There were partially revealed tattoos, of what looked like dragons, on each buttock.

She struggled to her feet, brushing off the dust. 'Well, Freya. What do you think?'

Having surveyed her beautiful body, scarred by what she had recently done, I couldn't find the words to answer.

There were also poorly applied tattoos on her upper arms, crude motifs with the name "Judd" appearing on both. Her forearms were a mass of fresh razor-blade cuts.

'What else did you do to upset Dylan so much?'

'I showed him this,' she replied, with a mischievous grin, lifting up the front of her skirt.

I looked between her legs in disbelief. She had several piercings here as well. She had also had her pubic hair dyed bright green; and tattooed on her skin directly above this area was the caption:

KEEP OFF THE GRASS

She pulled her skirt back down and grimaced. 'I had to show him. He was angry. Threw me to the ground.'

'I'm not surprised! You don't do things by halves, do you?'

'No. But it had to be extreme. It was the only way to be free of him.'

'I don't understand?'

'Well, let me put it this way. He's tried to groom me into a new Sera, just like Mum. I can't take it any more. Now I've shattered the image, I can go for good. He won't try to follow me now.'

She kissed me and gave me a hug. 'I wish you well. But be careful.'

I nodded.

'Please go, now. Judd will be waiting.'

I said my farewells. She followed me down the hillside. I turned to see her in the arms of the giant-man, then walked off to find Dylan.

I found him on the riverbank, his eyes cast upon the eddying waters.

He betrayed no hint of emotion.

And he remained reticent as we walked back to the Land Rover.

- XIII -

DYLAN GRIPPED THE steering wheel, staring with intensity, yet his face devoid of all expression. He did not seem to be concentrating on the road. He was lost in his own world. This frightened me, as he had floored the accelerator from the moment he'd pulled away from the Grange bridge and had kept it there ever since, despite the twisting nature of the route.

'Slow down, Dylan. For Christ's sake, slow down!' I screamed, as he veered the Land Rover over to the wrong side of the road.

He did not respond. Instead, he maintained his rigid, zombie-like state.

'Dylan, come on! You're worrying me now.'

Still he continued, even more reckless than before.

I waved my hands in front of his face and tugged at the sleeve of his coat.

He shot a glance at me. A haunted, wild glance. A glance which became a sustained stare that pierced right through me.

I was silenced and he ostensibly returned his attention to the road ahead.

A car, swerving to avoid us, honking its horn in fury, was enough to make me act once more. I unclipped my seat belt and hauled myself into his lap. I rammed my foot down on the brake pedal, and tried to yank up the handbrake.

I felt the whole vehicle shudder, then skew sideways.

Dylan let the steering freewheel.

There was a great thud and the caving in of glass on my side. I was hurled across his lap, then down over his legs into the footwell.

The impact broke Dylan's trance.

He screamed. I could feel his legs struggling to work the pedals under my weight. His hands were also back on the steering wheel, fighting to regain control.

Luckily, the Land Rover was brought to a stop without further damage.

I lay motionless for a while, feeling blood trickling down my face.

'What the fuck's got into you! You could've killed us!' He was yelling at me, as if he had no recollection of his foolhardy behaviour.

He lifted me up and placed me back upon my seat. I clutched at my head, feeling nauseous.

'It was you, you fool. Not me!'

He sat back, gasping for air, his face drained of all colour. 'I don't remember.'

As I recovered, I was filled with anger. I opened the door and stepped outside. I couldn't say what I might've done if I'd stayed in the cab.

I paced up and down, still holding my head, surveying the damage to the vehicle. The panels had received a battering, although the tree in the hedge had come off worse with huge gouges through its bark. I checked all four wheels, then opened the driver's door.

'Budge over. I'm driving.'

Dylan responded meekly, doing as he was told without comment.

I wiped the blood from my face with the front of my T-shirt, collected myself together and started the vehicle. I drove off, slowly at first, listening for any signs of damage. Apart from the passenger door rattling, my confidence rose as there appeared to be nothing else to worry about.

I'm not sure how I managed to navigate the vehicle successfully to the old mill. I can only remember arriving there and stumbling into the arms of one of Dylan's mechanics.

Dylan walked off towards the mill house, oblivious to my plight.

Veronica came out of the door, looking concerned. She extended her arms to greet Dylan, but he simply barged past her. 'Get the fuck out of my way!'

The front door slammed.

As Veronica came over to me instead, the lounge window shattered and a chair clattered over the courtyard cobbles. A few china ornaments soon followed.

Veronica ordered the mechanic to find his workmate and together they headed into the house.

I could hear raised voices from inside.

'Don't worry, pet. He's just having one of his moods.' Veronica's words didn't reassure me.

Dylan stormed out of the house again and ran over to the old waterwheel. 'And we won't be needing this any more!'

'No, Dylan! Not that!'

But it was too late. It wasn't until the object was flying through the air and glinting that I realized it was the medallion. It disappeared with a plop into the millpond.

'No....! Veronica shrieked and ran over to him, but he was making his escape. 'That was valuable!' I thought for a moment she was going to jump in after it. But she slumped against the wall and cried.

I also felt sad for its loss, having been so instrumental in its recovery. At least I'd made a detailed sketch of it, which would help my ongoing research.

I walked over to her, but I felt queasy. She had to steady me as I approached, clutching my head.

'Let's look at you. Ooh, that's nasty!' She brought out a handkerchief, licked it and began to work on a gash near the hairline of my forehead.

I felt my legs buckle and I lost consciousness.

When I awoke, I was in the back of an ambulance on the way to the local hospital. There followed a lengthy wait for an X-ray and various doctors spent the afternoon coming and going from my trolleyside until giving me the all clear. They kept me in overnight, however, to be on the safe side.

This gave me some time to assess where I was on my quest to discover the real Dylan. Yet again, I'd placed myself in danger, this time as a direct result of his strange behaviour. It only intrigued me further. But I wasn't certain I wanted to go on.

Once I'd recovered sufficiently, I took the opportunity to call John. However, I only got the answering machine, so had to leave a message.

Veronica came to collect me the next morning, bringing flowers and fruit from Dylan. She led me downstairs and into the car park. Then she walked me over to an Austin A35 van, its bodywork stripped in readiness for a respray. She helped me inside and soon we were heading back to the mill house.

'How're you feeling?'

'OK. My head's a little sore, but there's no real harm done.'

'Thank goodness.'

She seemed genuine for the first time since I'd met her.

'Can you tell me what happened?'

'Yes. Dylan was driving like a maniac. It was frightening. I tried to reason with him, but he didn't respond. We crashed.'

'I see. I thought you must've been driving.'

'No. Didn't he tell you?'

'He's told me nothing. He rarely does when he gets into this state. Backtrack for me. What was happening before this?'

'We went to see Emily. To say goodbye. She looked very different.'

'Yes, I know. She came to see me yesterday evening. It disturbed me as well, I can tell you. I cried all night. This explains everything.'

I rubbed my head, the stitches in the wound itching. 'That's not all. I found this painting in the stables a few days ago. The one of your husband painted by Seraphina.'

Veronica pulled the Austin over to the side of the road. 'Christ! I thought that'd been lost years ago. I must ask Dylan for it.'

'I'm afraid you can't. When Janis found out he still had it, she burnt it.'

'What!' All her compassion ebbed out of her face. 'Wait till I get my hands on her!'

She manoeuvred the car back out onto the road. She said nothing more until we arrived at the mill. She helped me back inside the house. Workmen were busy reglazing the lounge window. She sat me down on the sofa and laid a blanket over me.

'Some tea, I think,' she said, seeing how disturbed I appeared when I studied my surroundings. There was a large pile of broken pottery and glass shards in one corner, carefully swept up ready for disposal. Books lay strewn across the floor. Pictures had been replaced on the wall, but most had lost their glass.

By the time Veronica returned, I was on my hands and knees, piling up the books and other items.

'You shouldn't be doing that. You need to rest.'

'No, I'd like to. You've helped me. Now let me do the same for you.'

She smiled. 'OK, if you're sure. We can do it together. But make sure you stop if it gets too much.'

'Thanks for your concern. Dylan really went wild, didn't he?'

'Yes. It's rare for him to get into such a state....But when he does, it invariably takes on this destructive form.' When she noticed my mounting concern, she qualified her statement by saying: 'His violence is always taken out on objects, not people.'

I tried to digest this as she poured out the tea. 'Shame about the medallion.'

'Yes.' Veronica looked troubled, but said no more.

I was becoming concerned about the conspiracy of silence between Veronica and Dylan. The goat-head emblem and the symbols on the medallion so closely matched those in the old chapel, and as Sir Frederick and Serapahina were buried there, they must have made the connexion quickly.

We spent the next hour gathering up all the objects that hadn't been damaged and re-shelving the books.

'I'm so sorry he's destroyed so much,' I said.

'Don't apologize for him. Anyway, most of the stuff here is his.'

'Oh, I didn't realize.'

'I lost everything in a house fire in the early Seventies. Not long after Frederick died. The house and furniture was one thing, objects, pictures and photographs quite another. They had a sentimental value – irreplaceable.'

'Is that why you were so keen to know the fate of the painting?'

'Yes. I have little left of him now to rekindle the memories.'

Her face had contorted with a sadness that showed, more than words could've expressed, how much she had loved her husband.

'Of course, the painting you saw has much more significance for Dylan and me. Seraphina completed about twenty-five canvases in her short lifetime. Seven or eight were sold. Dylan has tried to find them and buy them back without much success. I think he recovered one, or maybe two, from this method. He definitely has her self-portrait; an early, but magnificent work, if I may say so. And a couple of others. He never lets anyone see them. All the rest were lost when my house burnt down.'

'How did it happen?'

'No one was really too sure. It was razed to the ground. It used to stand at the base of the hill below the Lodge. The family had it built in the Edwardian era, when the Lodge became too small, primitive and uneconomic to maintain.'

'I see.'

'It was a sad night, seeing that lovely mansion go up in flames. And so soon after my husband and Seraphina had died as well. The last straw. I decided to sell off the land, including the ruined Lodge.'

'Yes. Emily said Dylan bought the Lodge back from the Forestry Commission.'

'Right. The ruin was too complex to demolish, so they simply planted all round it. Some of the outbuildings were used to store vehicles and equipment. I think they were glad when Dylan offered to buy it back. A small group of architectural historians placed a petition to parliament and it gained a Grade II* listing as a result. In time, they would've had to commit capital funds to shore up the ruins.'

'What about the mansion house?'

'Oh, that's entirely under afforestation now. They stripped all the demolition debris away. Even infilled the cellars and blew up the stabling block, the only parts to've survived the fire. If you look carefully from the top of the mountain, you can still see the mature deciduous trees from the gardens amidst all the new forest. Otherwise, all is forgotten.'

Seeing my increased interest, she went over to a bureau and brought out an old folder. She untied the strings after she'd sat down beside me. 'Don't tell Dylan – nor Janis for that matter – that I have these. They're all I have now to remind me. All I could rescue before the flames almost claimed me as well.'

She opened the folder and presented a number of black-and-white photographs, most singed from the fire. The first was obviously pre-war. It showed the great facade of the Edwardian house. I couldn't believe such an imposing building really could have been lost so completely. On the lawn in front stood the unmistakable figure of Sir Frederick, still with a moustache, but much younger looking. Perhaps mid-forties. Another man, much older, with a bald head and a countenance that disturbed me, stood next to him.

'That's Sir Frederick, right?' She nodded. 'Who's the other guy?'

'One of the greatest influences on his life. He was his great spiritual guide. And mountaineering companion.'

'Oh, so that's where Janis's interest stems from.'

She frowned. 'Sort of, though she'd never admit it. Really she found her own way to the hills. Her father spent more time with Dylan and Seraphina in that department. They were both good climbers.'

'Is that where Dylan got the inspiration for his first novel?'

'Yes, I suppose it was. But Janis took things a step further than the others. She did a lot of alpine ascents, then headed for the Himalayas. Her ex-boyfriend's death slowed that down, thank goodness, or she might not be here today. It became an obsession. A dangerous obsession.'

'I take it you never liked it.'

'No.'

'So you didn't like your husband doing it, either?'

'Oh, he'd long-since retired from serious mountaineering when I knew him. He was a lot older than me.'

She pointed to the photograph again. In front of the two men were three little girls, all dark-haired, wearing white summer dresses. 'This picture was taken around 1936. I must have been about four then.' She was tapping her finger against the middle of the three children.

'And the other two?'

'On the left is Agnes Fortescue. On the right is Anne Jones, Dylan's mother.'

I gasped. 'I didn't realize you two went back so far.'

'Oh, yes. Lifelong friends.'

She drew the photograph to the back of the bunch and focused my attention on the next one. It showed a group of twelve young women, grouped together. In the background was the mansion again, with several marquees pitched on the lawns and various people milling around.

'These were all our friends. There's me, look....and Anne....and Agnes.' She pointed to each of them in turn.

'When was this taken?'

'The thirtieth of April, 1950.'

'How can you be so sure?'

'That's easy. It was my wedding day. They were all my bridesmaids and attendants.'

'Oh, I see. So that would've made you and Dylan's mother about....'

'Eighteen.' She looked at me quizzically.

'Rather a large age gap between the two of you, then.'

'Yes, Frederick was sixty-two....I detect your disapproval.'

'Well, each to their own. Wouldn't see me doing it, even for money.'

'I came from the landed class myself. My family had plenty of money. They cut me off when I married him, of course. No, I did it for love.'

She did not care to explain further, but skipped over the remaining pictures. Two of the others were of interest. One showed the Favershams together in a walled garden. It was interesting to see them as a family group. Seraphina was radiant, looking about twelve, her long, dark hair falling over her shoulders and an arm around her father's waist.

It was difficult to distinguish between the two sisters, so similar was their appearance, except for the greater height Janis's two extra years gave her. The elder had a brooding expression, her eyes cast off into the distance as if not wanting her picture taken.

Another child stood on the other side next to a slimmer, but still plain-looking Veronica. It had to be Eric. Only the clothing made me surmise it was a boy, since his head had been burnt out of the picture. The strangest thing was how the hole had burnt in precisely this spot, when the rest of the picture, except for one edge, remained unscathed. It was as if it had been deliberately excised with a match-flame at a later date than the fire damage, but I couldn't be sure. The thought made me shiver.

I think Veronica detected my unease as she flicked the picture away, so I could view the second one of interest. It showed the two sisters again, about three and five, playing in the water at the seaside. A little boy of about two was playing with them.

'Eric?'

'No, Eric had blonde hair. That's Dylan.'

'Really?'

'Yes.'

'I thought they hadn't met until he was ten.'

'No, this was shortly before he and his mother left to go to Wales. My kids never saw them again, till they returned about eight years later.'

I scratched at my brow, trying to gather my thoughts.

'Be careful, you'll pull out your stitches.'

I jumped. It was Dylan's voice. I looked up to find him standing in the doorway.

Veronica quickly slammed the folder shut.

'I hope Ronni hasn't been filling you with too many of her stories.'

Veronica rose, head bowed, and retreated through the other door.

Dylan produced another bouquet of flowers from behind his back.

It put a smile back on my face immediately, before I had a chance to stop myself.

'I'm so sorry, Freya. Are you OK? What must you think of me?'

'I'm not sure I can answer that at the moment.'

'Fair enough.' He didn't care to explain his actions. 'What do you want to do now?'

'Just take me back to the Lodge, please.'

He smiled, reassured that I still wanted to be with him, despite his recent behaviour.

What he couldn't know was that if it wasn't for my covert mission, I'd have been long gone.

He took me back in a Singer Gazelle, as his workmen busied themselves repairing the damage to the Land Rover.

- XIV -

JANIS, E-J AND I were crouched down on the lawn the next day, lazing in the afternoon sun. Dylan was up in the tower, not wanting to be disturbed. He said he wanted to work on his next novel, but I thought he was after some quiet space to reflect after the dramatic departure of Emily. And he'd also had a huge argument with Yasuko.

Janis noticed I was reading *The Music Man*. 'Oh, that's my favourite one of Dylan's books. You enjoying it?'

'Yes. Although I liked the first one I read more.'

'Um....It seems so strange, now, looking back. None of us took Dylan's scribblings very serious when we were growing up. I remember reading his first attempt at a novel. He'd worked on it shortly after Sera's death. It showed promise, but he had a popular-fiction style back then. Nothing like the highly embellished literary works he was later to publish and make his name with. Don't tell Dylan, but I preferred his old style. *The Music Man* is a more commercial book; a halfway house between the two styles. That's probably why it's my favourite.'

Noise from across the lawns broke our conversation, as E-J bantered with Yasuko, who was coming towards us with Quasi. Before Janis could do anything about it, the dog had run over to us and now he jumped upon her crouched form.

E-J laughed.

I was about to join in, but I checked myself when I glimpsed complete terror in Janis's eyes.

She'd been so absorbed in our conversation that she hadn't even noticed the dog approaching. Now its paws were on her back and she looked petrified.

I leaned over and pulled the dog away by his collar.

Janis stood up, shuddering, a damp urine stain appearing in the crotch of her white slacks. Recovering some composure, she kicked out at the dog and walked off towards the veranda.

'Don't hurt him, Mummy, he's only playing!' E-J cried, as the dog yelped. She put her arms around his neck and comforted him.

'That dog should've been on a leash!....Did you untie him?'

'No, Mummy,' E-J whimpered.

'Come with me, before I smack you!' Janis shrieked from the French windows. E-J, confused, obeyed, and ran off to join her mother inside.

What was all that about? Yasuko wrote, after she'd approached.

'I'm not sure. The dog must've scared her.'

Yasuko sat down beside me as Quasi romped off towards a family of rabbits, who darted for the safety of the nearest bushes as the dog came near. I watched him disappear into the undergrowth, save for his wagging tail, as he sniffed out his quarry. He barked, then was lost from sight completely.

I was about to go after him, when Yasuko stopped me.

I waited for her to write: *He all right. Can't go far.*

I sat down again next to Yasuko, who was shifting uncomfortably on the grass.

'He's a lovely dog, isn't he?'

Yes. But Janis hating the dogs. Maybe in mood with Dylan too.

'Or p'haps she's feeling the loss of Emily just as much as he is. Maybe more.'

Yasuko shrugged her shoulders, then leant back to soak up the rays of the sun. She scratched her forehead with her pencil, and scribbled: *Me worried for you.*

'For me? Not Dylan?'

She shook her head.

You play with fire.

I didn't understand and my expression must have conveyed this.

Known him long time. Many like you come. Most leave damaged.

I coughed and shuffled uneasily.

How involved are you emotionally?

'I'm really falling for him.' I hoped I sounded convincing. It would have been the truth a few days ago, but now I was no longer sure.

It looked as though I'd given her the answer she'd expected.

Too bad.

'Why d'you say that?'

Bitter experience. Of others & me.

'Dylan's told me the two of you have slept together.'

Of course. He virtuoso sexual gymnast. And very well endowed! All learn from him.

I laughed. 'Sounds a bit hypocritical, then.'

She became the most animated I'd ever seen her and jabbed her pencil so strongly onto the pad that it ripped a hole through the page. *No laugh. Trying to warn you.*

I drew out a long breath, but let her continue.

Always same pattern. Starts well. Warm & loving. Then hurts you. Never faithful. Loses interest quickly. Look how Emily treated!

'No, I didn't like that. But she provoked him. Gave as good as she got.'

Maybe, but don't you see? His actions drove her to it. No one stays immune to his emotional cruelty for long.

'So you keep saying.'

She didn't look very amused by my facetiousness.

I looked into her face searchingly. 'If it's so bad, why d'you take it?'

She hesitated, giving me a stern glare. *Me his wife.*

I sank back on my elbows. 'Christ, I had no idea! I'm sorry....What must you think of me? I've been here in your house, shagging your husband, and neither of you bothered to tell me!'

She waved her arms around, in an effort to calm me, before returning to her notepad. *Me used to him. Many women. Many years.*

I was too ashamed to speak. Suddenly, Dylan and Veronica's guffawing over my initial perception of Yasuko made sense; it'd been their very private joke. And Veronica's comment about Dylan not being free.

Don't worry. Forgive. You can have him. Me divorcing. Emily leaving give me courage to go.

She climbed awkwardly to her feet, her kimono clinging to the skin of her haunches. *Me show.* She held out her hand to pull me to my feet as well.

She guided me by the hand and led me over to the inner gatehouse. We climbed the spiral staircase and entered her private quarters, located over the archway. There was enough space for a small bedroom, lounge and kitchenette.

She made me a mug of tea and sat down next to me on the bed.

'How did you and Dylan meet?'

He travelling in Far East, on passage to Australia. Young writers' book tour. Picked me up in bar. Married me next day.

'What? You couldn't have loved each other.'

No. Struck deal. Me wanted wealth & citizenship. Me wanted for housework & sex.

'Why would he agree to such an arrangement? Surely not out of pity for your plight? And I don't understand why he needed you for sex, when he was already womanizing back in Britain.'

Many ask. He never tell. Can get rough stuff with me. No one else like Yasuko.

'I'm sorry, I don't follow.'

She rose to her feet and pulled up a long shackle attached to the corner post of the bed. She dropped it on the floor again and walked over to a cabinet on the wall. She opened its twin doors to reveal a varied collection of whips and canes.

I stared at her in utter disbelief. 'He chains you to the bed and beats you for kicks?!'

She nodded and didn't look the least perturbed.

'How can you let him do that to you? Surely not for love?'

Again she nodded.

'Why let him hurt you?'

All I deserve.

I could not speak.

Me enjoy, too. Me grateful.

'But why prostitute yourself out to him?'

Me dumb. Worthless. No job could get. Me prostitute before. Better with one alone than many. He look after me.

'I see,' I blurted out, but really I could not comprehend it all.

She turned around, so that her back faced me, and started to raise the long hem of her kimono.

I gripped her hand to stop her. 'No. You don't have to show me. You can leave some things to the imagination!'

She let her garment fall again. She looked disappointed, as if I'd ruined her chance to shock me.

The awkwardness of her walk at times, her odd noises from the open gatehouse window, and her coy behaviour at the poolside, now made sense as well. How could I have missed what had been so obvious? She was having some of her intended effect. My perception of Dylan had changed further, as Yasuko's revelations now could be paired with Emily's earlier warnings of his darker side.

She sat on the edge of the bed and rubbed her hands, as if she wasn't used to so much writing at once. *He in frenzy last night. Emily upset him bad. Me enjoy beating. Me leave tomorrow. Me have savings & he give payment till divorce settled. Can start new life. Always was plan. Didn't think long as 8 years would take.*

I was becoming overwhelmed with dread. 'Will he want to beat me in due course?'

Yasuko shook her head violently. *Don't worry. Won't beat you.* She paused. *Unless want him to.*

'No, I certainly do not!' This conviction was expressed with such force that her face actually broke into some kind of a smile for the first time since I'd know her.

He treat lovers different, depends on individual desires. That's his secret. But he dangerous. He suck in, then spit out. Like serpent. Leave now.

I tried to quell the chill that shuddered through my body.

'Thanks for the warning, but I'm going to stay. At least for a while longer. With you going as well as Emily, he'll need me all the more now.'

Yasuko sighed disconsolately. She'd tried her best to warn me. Her revelations had certainly disturbed me and made me waver. I wanted to find out more. For my sake as well as John's. But I was worried about whether I could protect myself.

She kissed me lightly on the cheek and guided me to the door. She checked the stairs, as if making sure he wasn't lurking there, before she handed me the last thing she ever wrote to me: *Be careful Freya. Just be careful.*

I returned to my study of Dylan's literature, which continued far into the night. I missed his warmth and couldn't sleep, so simply decided to read on until I'd finished the second of his novels, *The Music Man*. I put it down on the bedside table and glanced at the clock: it was four in the morning.

I climbed out of bed and went over to the window. I parted the curtains and noticed Yasuko's quarters were still lit. Dylan was probably there, exacting his last retribution from his departing wife.

The next day, Dylan was nowhere to be seen as I joined Yasuko in the forecourt. She had loaded all her belongings into a waiting taxi. She kissed her goodbyes, her movements a sure sign she was in a lot of pain. For once, she was dressed in jeans and a baggy jumper, which augured well; she was finally wearing what she wanted to wear, rather than what Dylan had dictated all these years. I sensed in this small way, she was making that first tentative step to finding herself.

She could hardly sit down on the seat. I could only wonder at what kind of welts Dylan had inflicted upon her. I closed the rear door for her. She blew me a kiss from the open window. Then she was off down the driveway. I ran to the archway of the gatehouse and watched her progress until she was out of sight.

Part of me was trying to convince the other half that I should have left the Lodge with her.

Once back inside the Lodge, I hunted for Dylan. As I couldn't find him, I assumed he was still in the tower. I decided to make a surreptitious call to John. I risked discovery, but my mind was frazzled from Yasuko's revelations.

He picked up straight away. ''Bout time. How's it going?'

'Don't you dare say "how's it going" to me!'

'Eh?'

'Well, where do you want me to start? Dylan's nearly killed me in a crash. I find out he's been shagging both his sisters-in-law, one from under-age. And now I discover he's got a Japanese wife who's been his domestic and sex slave for years! What the hell have you got me in to?'

'Calm down. Calm down.'

'No, John. I want out!'

'Listen. Be reasonable. You're close, now. You're close....Hang in there a little longer. Do some research on these old ruins and the medallion. And look into Seraphina more. I think she holds the key....'

The receiver clicked and he was gone before I could answer. As I walked away, I could understand his reasoning as I'd left my latest discoveries on his answering machine whilst at the hospital. But I felt sure I hadn't mentioned his late wife's name.

- XV -

THE LODGE HAD taken on a lugubrious atmosphere, which matched my overriding depression, not helped by the pelting thunderstorm outside. To lose Emily, who was becoming a good friend, and Yasuko, who'd been part of the fabric of this place since my arrival, within the space of two days, had taken away my vibrancy.

I struggled to imagine what this turn of events was doing to Dylan, who'd had them both as an integral part of his life for so long. He wasn't allowing me to understand, as he continued to distance himself by staying up in the tower.

Janis had departed, albeit only temporarily, to prepare her staff for the arrival of a fresh set of clients in a couple of days' time.

So I found myself alone. Strangely displaced. For the first time since I'd met Dylan, I was left to reflect on my own problems, the ones I'd always tried to run away from. I mulled around the house, restless, my anxiety building. I prepared some lunch, but Dylan never came downstairs to collect it, nor to spend any time with me.

The only sanctuary I could find was in the library. Reclining in a comfy leather chair, I could return to the fictional world Dylan had created through his literature. I was on a third novel now, *Beyond the Raging Sea*. I was still struggling to analyse how much of his own experience and emotion might be locked in these pages to the extent it was beginning to ruin my enjoyment of the unravelling story.

I gave up, placing the book on the coffee table. I began to pace around the room, viewing the line of bookcases. I found a large section on psychology, bringing out modern volumes as well as older texts from the likes of Freud, Bleuler and Havelock Ellis. I spent the next few hours browsing through these, searching for some way of defining Dylan's personality. In the end, I was left even more confused than before. However, such a collection did suggest that perhaps Dylan had been doing his own self-analysis.

I rubbed my tiring eyes, leaving the books scattered over the rug, and went to the kitchen for some refreshment. Yet I was soon lured back, mug of tea in hand, for further exploration.

I had always treasured books, and from an early age had mastered the art of escaping from the misery of my own family through the printed page. I felt like a little girl again, as I rooted through this vast collection.

In time, I came across a number of architectural works. I was surprised to discover the ruins of Grimshaw Lodge displayed in the third volume I flicked through, a large tome on the Victorian country house. The cleverly shot photographs, framed by encroaching vegetation, showed the roofless, windowless Gothic ghost. These were juxtaposed with a reprint of a canvas painted when the Lodge had been originally built, and an 1870 photograph of the building in its heyday, as a way of illustrating the author's polemic about its wilful neglect. The work had been published in 1975, and the author ranted on about how the property only had a few more years left before it would be lost. Dylan had succeeded in resurrecting an edifice in its final death throes, then.

Despite the excesses of the author, it still made interesting reading. The Lodge had been designed by Anthony Salvin, as Dylan had told me. He was best known for Harlaxton Manor in Lincolnshire, Peckforton Castle in Cheshire and additions to Alnwick Castle in Northumbria, much vaster projects than Grimshaw Lodge. However, it had still taken seven years to complete, bankrupting Sir Percival Grimshaw in the process; so he had never been able to take pleasure in occupying it for long, before having to sell it.

I was about to flip over the page to discover more, when Janis poked her head around the door.

'Hi yea! I'm back.'

I mumbled a response, but remained fixed on my task. Janis took the hint and left. Shortly, I heard her ringing the old servant's bell in the corridor.

'Where's Yasuko?'

I was in the middle of reading about Baron von Eschenbach's purchase of the Lodge and his bizarre addition in the grounds. I slammed the book shut and rested it on my knees, frustrated.

'She's left.'

'Left?'

'Yes, left!'

'When will she be back?'

'She's not coming back,' I said, raising my voice and opening the book again. 'If you want something to eat or drink, you're going to have to make it yourself.'

'Where's Dylan?' she said, returning to the doorway of the library.

'Up in the tower.'

'Best not disturb him, then.'

'No, he was very angry again last night. And this morning after you left.'

'Mm.' I didn't have to look at her to detect her concern.

I refound my page and continued with the description of the strange black church that left even this erudite author lost for an explanation.

Janis remained standing in the doorway for a long time. Out of the corner of my eye, I could see her regarding the array of psychology books on the floor, before she retreated. Soon I heard her putting on the kettle in the kitchen.

I became lost again in the detailed descriptions of the author's walk around the ruins. The lead from the roof had been stripped off in the Twenties so now all the floors had rotted away. I could recognize the formal rooms, extensively water-damaged, with plasterwork peeling off the walls, fallen beams contorted at odd angles, and floors piled high with masonry debris.

The library still had bookshelves in situ. Something about this particular photograph struck me as strange, but I was distracted by the confusing text. It took me a while to realize several pages of description were missing. I had also expected to see formal plans of the building, included at the end of every other chapter. I felt along the seam of the binding, detecting a roughness which told me the pages hadn't fallen out naturally.

Disappointed, I cast the book aside and delved into further volumes. Two didn't mention the Lodge at all. The third had a picture and description of the Edwardian mansion Veronica had told me about.

The fourth was more interesting. It was a calfskin-bound volume, privately printed before the last world war. One grainy black-and-white photograph showed the Lodge in a less ruinous condition. But the author's sketch of the inside of the chapel was far more intriguing. Emily had been wrong about its history; the chapel had been in perfect order then.

This had also excited the author, as he hypothesized about the bizarre carvings and whether the chapel could be still in use. There were descriptions of his failed approaches to Sir Frederick Faversham, as he'd tried to unravel the mystery. He also told of discussions with locals, who'd remained silent as well. One vignette caught my eye:

> *going into the local public house, I came across an old foot soldier, in his nineties, who'd lost a leg in the Indian Mutiny and had returned to England to work on the von Eschenbach Estate as a servant, until retiring around the turn of the century. He elaborated at great length about the former glory of the house and gardens, but was muted upon the question of his reclusive employer. When I mentioned the chapel, his eyes widened, his pallid countenance paled still further and his hand gripped my wrist. He struggled to speak.*

I cursed aloud when I saw the next few lines had been blacked out by unknown hand.

Suffice it to say, he warned me to stay away for my own good....

I closed the book, keeping it tightly clasped as I pondered its contents. Then I gathered all the volumes together and deposited them back on the shelves.

I found no sign of Janis after leaving the library, so I bounced up the stairs, eager to quiz her on what she knew of the Lodge's history.

All I discovered was a trail of discarded clothing along the landing and through the open doorway of her room. I could hear the sounds of lovemaking, yet I denied their existence, needing further evidence before the truth could sink in. As I craned around the door, Dylan had his back to me, with Janis's head over his shoulder. When she saw me, she carried on regardless, increasing her moans in response to him and never taking her eyes off me.

I stood perplexed for some time.

Then I ran off to the toilet. And I cried genuine tears.

Janis came and found me in my bedroom later on, whilst Dylan prepared the evening meal. I was under the bedcovers, fully clothed, still trying to come to terms with what I'd witnessed.

'Can I come in?'

'No!'

She walked in anyway, holding onto the door.

'Look, I'm....'

'Go away! I don't want to talk to you!'

I threw the clock from the side cabinet at her. She retreated, using the door as a defensive shield. The clock made a large dent in the wood panelling.

I pulled the bedcovers over my head and curled up into a foetal position.

Janis ignored what I'd said and crept over to the bed. She pulled off the duvet and laid her hand upon my shoulder. 'Hey. I'm sorry about before. I acted like a brazen hussy, I know.'

'Leave me alone!'

However much I tried to fight her off, she stayed sat on the bed, waiting for my anger to subside.

I sat up and folded my arms across my chest. I stared ahead, rather than at her, trying to calm myself. I worried about unleashing my fury. Luckily, Janis remained silent, not antagonizing me further. As I regained my senses, I turned to her and was surprised to see tears running down her face.

'I'm the one who should be upset, not you! Why are you crying?'

'You looked so innocent. So vulnerable. You reminded me so much of the first time I caught him screwing someone else.'

'Huh! How old were you when you first had him?'

'Nineteen. Twenty maybe. Not too many months after Dylan'd come out of mourning.'

'And how long after that did he cheat?'

'Not long. A matter of days. A week maybe.'

'Blimey!' I exclaimed. 'So you think that makes it all right to do the same to other people! To women like me? Screwing in secret's one thing. But to milk it in the way you did, well, that just takes the biscuit.'

'You're right. It was despicable. Dylan doesn't think much about anyone other than himself. That can sort of rub off on me. But listen, unlike him, I can empathize. I'm not going to be so arrogant as to presume what you're going through. But I have been there myself.'

'OK....OK....I appreciate you have.'

'And I've seen plenty of other women go through it, too. Or be cajoled into group orgies.'

'Never!'

'Yes. When I told him you'd seen us he even asked me if I'd consider a threesome with you and him.'

I edged further away from her. 'I hope you told him where to get off!' I cried indignantly.

'No, 'course not. He's asked me plenty of times before. And I've complied more often than not, too. But you've given me your answer. And I respect that.'

I was dumbfounded, as I watched her climb out of the bed and move over to the window. She stared out through the gap in the curtains. I thought she looked disappointed.

'Don't worry,' she said, turning back to me when she sensed my increasing agitation. 'The matter won't go any further.'

I sat up, bringing my knees towards my chest and drawing the duvet tighter around me.

'Listen,' she said. 'Let me make it up to you. I've got one last day off tomorrow. Why don't I take you on a mountain walk. I could bring E-J along, too. That'll cheer you up, I'm sure.'

I contemplated this idea for a moment. 'OK. It'll give me a chance to talk to you about all these legends of devil worship I've been hearing about.'

Janis swung her head round sharply.

There was a panic in her eyes.

This was only momentary. Later, I had to question whether or not I had truly witnessed it.

She didn't move for some time. A vacant stare ensued. Only her hands gripping the curtains until her knuckles went white told of her underlying state.

I came over and put my hand on her shoulder, concerned.

This brought her back into the real world and she was suddenly consumed with mirth. 'Oh, not that old chestnut! There's a legend about the old Baron when he lived here. But that was a hundred years ago! The locals are a very superstitious breed. It's been blown out of all proportion.'

'I see.'

'You haven't been delving into Dylan's selection of Gothic novels as well, have you?'

'No.'

Janis was overcome by fits of laughter now. Yet her banter seemed more hysterical than real.

She struggled to calm down. When she did, she changed the subject. She consulted her wristwatch. 'Oh, I must dash. The childminder will be getting worried.'

'Childminder? Can't you get your mother to look after her and save the expense.'

'I'd never let her anywhere near my daughter! Not on her own, anyway.'

'Why ever not?'

'Do you really have to ask? After all the damage she's caused to her own children!' She delivered this with a venom that belied her usual demeanour.

'Sorry. Didn't realize it was such a sore point.'

She composed herself, shoving her hands into the pockets of her jeans. 'Freya, it's me who should be apologizing. You've reminded me how much I hate her.'

'Why?'

'No doubt you'll learn the full truth in the end. But you'll need to find out from her.'

I felt cheated.

'Don't worry. Don't let my issues upset you.... You've got enough to think about....Listen, I'll pick you up about eight?'

'Eh?'

'In the morning. For our fell-walk. I do want so much for us to be friends. This is my way of making amends.'

I hesitated. 'OK.'

She came over to me and kissed me on the cheek. Then she was gone.

A short time afterwards, I heard the distinctive noise of idiosyncratic French engineering, which confirmed her departure.

I climbed out of bed and closed the door, locking it securely and placing the key under my pillow. Then I undressed, turned off the light and slipped under the sheets.

Later still, I heard my bedroom doorknob rattle. Dylan had arrived even earlier than expected, leaving a dinner tray outside the door.

'Please let me in, Freya. We need to talk.'

I didn't respond to him.

He pleaded with me again, but I kept silent.

I heard him cuss, then walk off down the corridor, banging his fists into the wall as he went.

- XVI -

WE SET OUT on our fell-walking adventure early the next morning. E-J was as excited as ever. Janis drove past Keswick, heading southwards towards the idyllic Vale of Borrowdale. She halted in a car park under tall pine trees beside Derwentwater. We boarded the crowded ferryboat and relaxed to admire the picturesque scenery. The boatman piloted the vessel expertly around the shallow reaches of the shoreline, stopping off at a number of jetties dotted along the western bank of the lake.

We disembarked from the boat at Hawes End and walked slowly through the shaded forests of the lakeside. I enjoyed this pleasant walk immensely, although the paths were swarming with tourists. However, I was not expecting the steep open climb up the twisting pathway on the lower slopes of Cat Bells.

As we climbed the long, grassy ridge, over a number of small summits, Janis named all the features we could see: Derwentwater, Keswick and Skiddaw on one side, and Causey Pike, Sail, Robinson, Hindscarth and Dale Head on the other.

I soaked up these panoramic views, happy they provided the excuse to rest every few yards. I was not used to such strenuous climbing! Consequently, I found it extremely difficult to keep pace with my companions. What made matters worse was that every time I thought

I was reaching the summit, and used up all my reserves in a bid to conquer the mountain, I found there were further climbs beyond, hitherto hidden from below.

At last the highest point was reached! I collapsed on the rocky crest, sitting down next to Janis and E-J. 'Christ, that was tough!' I said, breathing laboriously, my face red-hot.

'I can see you've never done any fell-walking before. This is pretty straightforward stuff.'

'What? Even with sheer cliffs either side of the path?'

'This is a wide ridge, Freya, there's plenty of room. Walkers are perfectly safe in this weather. The route is obvious, even in mist. And I wouldn't exactly call that drop a cliff! Now the abseil the other day, that's what I call sheer.'

'Yes.' I gulped, remembering the terror. 'But I was roped for that!'

'When you get a bit more experienced, maybe I'll take you along Striding Edge on Helvellyn in the midst of winter. Then you'll realize how tame this ridge is.'

She chuckled when my expression told her I wouldn't relish such a challenge. I'd never heard of Helvellyn, but the word "Edge" raised my anxiety.

'Having said all that,' she carried on, 'one must never make fun out of any of these mountains. They're not the Alps, but they're still quite capable of killing and they do so every year. I'm involved in my local mountain rescue team. Most deaths are the result of inexperience or lack of equipment.'

Janis removed the rucksack from her back. She showed me all the reserve food supplies, extra clothing, a comprehensive first aid kit and bivouac sacks she had brought with her to protect us in case of an emergency.

'Always be prepared. The weather can change so rapidly.'

We carried on, after taking some refreshment, climbing onto the much bleaker and uninteresting plateau of Maiden Moor. At least the gradient had levelled out now.

E-J ran on ahead, as Janis and I began to talk.

I saw this as another chance to find out more about Dylan and his past life from Janis's perspective. She seemed happy to oblige when I broached the subject.

'What do you wish to know?'

'As much as you can tell me. He wraps himself up in mystery all the time. It's as if he's trying to further a myth that's grown around him, in the eyes of his readership and the media at large. I need to know more about him, if I'm to understand his behaviour and emotions today.'

'You think he's suffering from something?'

'Yes. An insatiable desire to have sex.'

'I think he's very narcissistic. He needs the attention of women to reflect back his own worth.' She paused, rubbing her brow. 'But it's more than that. He lives close to the edge. Maybe he'd've succumbed by now without his writing and creativity.'

'Interesting.' I hadn't expected Janis would echo my concerns quite so strongly.

We walked on in silence for a moment.

'Tell me what you know about him already. What has he told you?'

'Well, let me see....only that he grew up in Wales, in a mining village. His brother and father were killed in pit accidents.'

I noticed Janis's raised eyebrow, and felt disconcerted, but I didn't let this stop me continuing.

'His mother moved up here with Dylan. Your mother and his were friends. He liked it here....spent all his teens here....was friends with your brother, Eric....then fell in love with your sister, Seraphina....They married, but she was killed seventeen years ago in a car crash, some time before he went to university in Liverpool to study architecture.'

'Then he got a book published and became a famous author,' Janis interrupted. 'That's the basic story he usually comes up with, when people get closer to him. I must admit, I wasn't sure you'd fallen for it, too.'

'You telling me it isn't true?!'

'No.'

I gasped, stopped walking abruptly and looked at Janis.

She smiled, as we started to move on again. 'No. He never knew his real father. His mum later had another boyfriend for a few years, but he left when Dylan was ten. Maybe Dylan experienced this loss like a death. He never talks about him. As a teenager, he was very impressionable. He became very close to my father, perhaps seeing him as a substitute dad.'

'Dylan told me he detested him.'

'Oh, yes, that's the truth. But only half the story. They had a big falling out in the last few months of my father's life. But before that, they had a strong bond.'

'What caused the rift?'

'Sera.'

'I see.'

'There may've been more to it, but I could never be sure what. You'd have to ask him.'

'And what about the other facts?'

'More untruths, I'm afraid. They did live in South Wales. But they weren't working-class, but upper-middle-class, his mother having inherited wealth. I think he likes his readership to think he has humbler origins. Self-made man, rising out of poverty, and all that.'

'Mm. And his brother, where's he?'

'He never had a brother; he was an only child. His early childhood loneliness may have produced his later creativity. It certainly helped to fuel his friendship with me and my brother and sister. Although, he was an intensely shy boy when he came here.'

'Really?'

'Yes. You wouldn't think it to look at him now, would you?'

'No, you wouldn't!' I paused. 'What about Seraphina?'

'You know she's dead.'

'Yes. Dylan told me. And at least I know that's true. You and your sister backed it up at the dinner party. And I've seen her grave.'

Janis looked puzzled.

Emily showed me.'

'Oh, I see. I knew Dylan wouldn't've. He forbids us all from visiting to pay our respects.'

She paused when I didn't look surprised. 'Dylan and Sera were lovers, they did elope, she was killed. It's the manner of her death he's concealed.'

'You mean she didn't die in a car crash?'

'No,' she said. 'This is another of Dylan's untruths. He spreads them to keep the enquiring reporters and casual lovers at bay. He finds it highly amusing to mislead such people. He knows such a clichéd death could never appear in one of his novels. It would be too unoriginal for most publishers' editors. Therefore, he weaves it into his own life story. Some intelligent centrefold called Sheila something-or-other – if I remember rightly – has been the only one sharp enough to see through this facade. She questioned Sera's death, believing she either hadn't existed in the first place, or had simply left him and is alive somewhere today.'

'In his mind, I think she is.'

'Maybe. Maybe.' But she'd taken on a more serious tone. 'Such stories don't just halt most enquirers. They also create a safety valve for his own conscience.'

'Eh?'

Janis stopped and pulled me to the side of the path. She turned to face me, making sure E-J couldn't overhear what she was about to say.

'Sera committed suicide in August, 1970, only a few weeks after she and Dylan were secretly married. Dylan's been living with the guilt over somehow having failed her ever since.'

I sank down onto the sparse moor-grass, recovering from the revelation.

'That clarifies a lot! My God....' I remained pensive for a while. 'Perhaps he's relieving his guilt by pretending she's still alive. And he does this through having sex with other women, believing they're actually Seraphina. He moves on quickly when they don't match her standard.'

'An interesting theory, but pure conjecture. And amateurish. I think you've been reading too many of those psychology texts in his library.'

Then she paused, considering what I'd said more objectively. 'Perhaps you may have something there. Certainly I was the first or second person he tried to seduce after her death. And I was the nearest thing to her in looks.'

I didn't want to break Veronica's trust by telling Janis about the photographs of the sisters in their younger days, so simply asked: 'How much like her are you?'

'In personality, intelligence and interests, very different. In appearance, very similar. You must see how much my face resembles Emily's?'

'Yes, very much so.'

'Well, Sera's face was little different. A Faversham trait, if you like. But Sera was a little taller. Fuller in figure. Bigger boobs! Or "assets", as my father often said. She always beat me at everything. Even that!'

I couldn't help laughing and she joined in, even though there'd been a tinge of bitterness to her words.

'Still,' she said, after further reflexion, 'I imagine if she were alive today, she'd look pretty much like me. You must remember, though, she had very long, jet-black hair. Even longer than Emily's, reaching down past her waist.' Looking more melancholy, she added: 'So did I....once.'

Janis's hair, whilst also jet-black and of a vibrant sheen, was cut short around her ears and barely reached her collar.

'What was it like, knowing you were so much alike as sisters?'

'I didn't mind looking like Sera. You can't begrudge being born beautiful. But she was always the favourite. I was devastated by her death. But it did somehow relieve me of my mother's belittling comparisons. Then again, looking like Sera was a nightmare when it came to Dylan. He had such a control over me. He managed to possess me whenever he was back from university. He even drove me away from my fiancé, a local mountaineer, and, much later, my husband as well.'

'Why haven't you left Dylan? Why are you still friends with him?'

'It may sound funny, but I love him. I suppose I was jealous of him falling for Sera, and not me, in the first place. It boosted my self-esteem to have him in my bed. A fantasy come true, I suppose. But there'd been something deeply tragic and unhealthy in their young love, even before she topped herself. And I began to detect his desperation and how much Sera had affected him. You see, in killing herself, Sera had also killed Dylan's child. The autopsy revealed she'd been three months pregnant.'

I swallowed hard, but remained silent.

'Despite my sympathy for him, and our physical and emotional closeness, there was something deeply claustrophobic about our affair. I felt smothered. Almost merged together with him. I needed to escape. So I left abruptly, moving to Glencoe in Scotland to train as a mountain instructor. Once there, I purposely cut my hair short, not so much to spite him, but to dissociate myself from Sera's image. Then I went abroad – first to the Alps, then on Himalayan expeditions. I loved the challenge anyway, but I could also be free from his possessiveness.

'By the time I returned here, Dylan had matured and he was successful. I didn't want to start another sexual relationship with him. But there's always been something about him, which overcomes one's doubts and feelings.'

'I know what you mean. A kind of charismatic charm that unsettles you, hypnotizes you even.'

'Yes, exactly.' She furrowed her brow. 'Looking back, maybe I'd been fooling myself all along. When I came home, I quickly married a postman and became a housewife. But my heart was never in it. It was never going to work out.

'Dylan's magnetism was too great. When he seduced me again, I realized my seven years away had been a facade. I'd always wanted him. I'd been hiding from my own primitive feelings all along. I'd been full of regrets about going away. He'd changed in that time. He'd become a published novelist. His sexual exploits had merely grown, although not into the public domain yet. But I could live with all that. I'd come to expect I'd have to share Dylan with other women. It seems strange to outsiders, I know. You seem to be learning to accept this as well, judging from last night.'

I felt my anger welling up again.

'I apologize for being so blatant when you stumbled in on us. You see, when I'm with him, no one else can get in the way of that. It's my time; there can be no intrusions. It's also a way of coping with his other women.'

I tried to remain calm, but inside I was in turmoil.

'I was like you once. It took me a long time to accept I was never going to have him all to myself. Once I realized I wouldn't, strangely I became much calmer. I know little about you. But you'll either have to accept him for what he is or leave. Otherwise, it'll get too much pretty quickly. As for me, my childhood was so messed up....My family so full of secrets I still don't understand....Or choose to block out....My parents so emotionally denigrating to me....Dylan rebuilt my sense of self, my self-esteem, my confidence. I've sacrificed a lot. But to leave him fills me with unthinkable dread.

'Yet he damages as well. I've felt it. Emily much more so. I should've protected her from him. I could just about cope at twenty. He took advantage of her when she was still under age.'

'Yes, she told me. It's no wonder she's left.'

'She left, and changed her image, for the same reason I cut my hair short. Most of his women seem to love every minute of their relationship with Dylan in the early stages. You seem no different. But I'm not sure Emily ever did.'

She looked at me, but I didn't comment.

'I think it runs deeper with her and me. We're the closest thing he has to Sera. It's as if he puts all the good and tender feelings for Sera into me and all the bad feelings – the anger – for Sera into Emily. At least that's what my therapist thinks.'

She giggled at my surprise, but it felt artificial. 'Yes, I'm not ashamed. I've been seeking help for years. I wish Emily had taken my advice to do so, too. But she's rebelling against authority at the moment – an acting out stage. She's trying to escape from her pain.'

'Maybe that's why she's into drugs.'

'Drugs?'

'Yes. Heroin. Didn't you know?'

'No.' She looked distraught. 'She rarely confided in me. Not since we became love rivals, at any rate. But her feelings'll still be there, haunting her, no matter how many drugs she takes. She'll have to face them one day. I've had to. He's mistreated her. I know she's had two abortions already.'

'At her age!' I could feel my emotions welling up in my eyes again.

'You OK, Freya?'

'Yes,' I said, recovering somewhat. 'Hearing that was a little too close for comfort. You see, I had an abortion myself around the same age.'

'I'm sorry.'

'It's OK, you weren't to know.' I had surprised myself. I'd kept this sordid secret for so many years. Now I'd told two people in a matter of days. It felt cathartic.

We walked on in silence for a time.

'My mother has a lot to do with it as well. She – even more than Dylan – was trying to get Emily to fit into Sera's shoes. Eric and I were the black sheep even before Sera died. It never surprised me when Emily became the focus of all her attention from then on. We all had intelligence, but Sera was a genius, destined for top academic and artistic honours. She'd done her A-Levels by fourteen; could play five musical instruments; spoke three languages fluently; and her paintings were already being exhibited at the time of her death.'

'I'd understood she'd been special.'

'Yes. She was very talented, but ultimately bored. There were very few challenges in the world for her. Part of this disillusion might hold a key to her death. Only Dylan held any excitement for her. Maybe that still wasn't enough.'

'I see. What about Emily?'

'Well, how could she follow in those footsteps? Emily was a practical girl. She always liked to play and explore. Mother made her follow a similar academic path to Sera, but she was never likely to live up to her expectations. I despair now, looking back at the amount of after-school tutoring my mother foisted on her. It doesn't surprise me she ultimately rebelled. I'm worried we won't ever see her again. Just like Eric.'

'Tell me more about him.'

Janis paused and inhaled deeply. 'The family don't really talk much about him. He went off the rails. Got in trouble with the law. Hurried off abroad and never came back.'

'Is that why your mum's so fearful about Emily? That she's following in his footsteps?'

'Maybe. Certainly Emily's departure has tapped into her underlying guilt. But I'm not going to feel sorry for her woes. She deserves it.'

We were interrupted by E-J running back to us for a while and chattering away as incomprehensibly as ever. Together we clambered onto the summit of the next peak, High Spy. We were now over two thousand feet up. We stopped for a short break, sipping tea under expansive skies.

When we resumed, and E-J had walked off ahead again, I strove for refocus. 'You still haven't really told me why you've grown to love Dylan?'

'Why does anyone love? Why him? Because he's like an unexplained part of me. We're like two halves of the same person. When I'm with him, we're emotionally there for each other. He's tender, his lovemaking's superb.'

'Yes. You don't have to tell me that!'

'Savour what he can give you in that department. I've had other lovers, but no one else comes close to him....

'He also gave me independence from my mother. He backed my rock-climbing school financially, in the face of my mother's derision of such a harebrained scheme. It's become very successful. It's my all-consuming interest now. It's made me. I've nearly paid back Dylan's loan completely.'

'But I sense there's something else keeping you tied to Dylan, isn't there?'

'Maybe.' But she did not elucidate.

I left it there. If Janis didn't want to talk about it, then I had the courtesy not to try to drag it out of her. After all, she'd already talked so freely and frankly, to an extent far more reaching than I had ever thought she would.

We were starting to descend steeply off the ridge, through the slag heaps of a neglected nineteenth-century mine. I was exhausted. And the boots Dylan had bought for me were beginning to hurt my feet. After complaining for some time, Janis sat me down and took them off, finding my heels and little toes had blistered badly.

She brought out her first-aid kit. E-J swirled around us impatiently as her mother skilfully plastered over my wounds. 'You poor thing. Dylan should've told you mountain boots take a lot of breaking in.'

She helped me to my feet and stayed near, assisting me to negotiate the descent. E-J skipped on merrily ahead, still full of energy, and grateful to be moving again.

We had started the day's walk at nine o'clock; now it was after three.

'We'll stop by that stream down there in a minute and finish off the rest of our lunch. Looks like you could do with a little more sustenance. Once we're past this bit, it's a much more gentle walk.'

'Good,' I sighed, showing how much I meant it.

'Esmerelda!' Janis screamed suddenly. 'Get away from those mine workings!'

She rushed down to where E-J was located, next to a gaping shaft. Janis gave her three rapid slaps on her bottom, whereupon E-J began to cry.

'Haven't I told you enough times to keep near me and not go wandering off?....Answer me, sweetheart.'

'Yes, Mummy,' E-J whimpered.

'Good. You could've fallen down there, love, and hurt yourself....or worse. Y'know I only want to keep you safe, don't you?'

'Yes, Mummy.'

Janis kissed and cuddled her daughter then, as if to seek her forgiveness for losing her temper.

We sat down to consume the last of the sandwiches, mintcake and orange juice. Then we were off again, joining the old railway which had once served the mine, the tracks long-since removed.

E-J bounced off ahead again, although she did turn around every once in a while to keep an eye on her mother.

I took this moment to say: 'I think I know the overriding reason why you stay with Dylan.'

Janis stared at me, but said nothing.

'E-J is Dylan's daughter, isn't she?'

'How did you guess that?' she said, taken completely unawares.

'Well, I know Dylan's favourite classic novel is *Notre Dame*. He called his dog after one of the principal characters; so it seems natural to assume he might've named his daughter after another of them.'

'Indeed. Clever. You're right, of course....But please don't tell my mum.'

We descended a little further down the slope.

Then Janis said: 'We've talked a lot about Dylan, but you're somewhat of an enigma yourself, aren't you?'

I gave her a puzzled look.

'You intrigue me. You have an intellectual curiosity that reminds me a little of Sera. Maybe that's why he finds you so appealing....But I'm fascinated about what attracts you to him, beyond his obvious sexual prowess.

There's a compulsion in you to go deeper. Is there an ulterior motive?'

My defences came swiftly into action to quell her suspicions. 'No, not really. I only wish to understand him better, that's all,' I said, shrugging my shoulders.

We walked on without further comment.

The track descended through a small gorge. I was stunned by the sight. The mountain had eroded away to leave a small crag of more resistant rock, rising like a sentry all on its own, guarding the Derwent valley. I realized I had seen it several times from differing vantage points over the last few weeks. Only now, at close quarters, did it get my undivided attention.

The path ran directly through this cleft. I looked up at the cliff and the great mass of scree strewn across its slopes.

'This is the most romantic place I've ever seen. What's it called?'

'Castle Crag,' Janis answered politely, but somewhat strained.

I noticed a route to the top, weaving steeply through the scree.

'Can we climb it?'

'No,' Janis said brusquely.

'Oh, come on. It won't take us long.' With that, I began to climb up the path, all thought of my exhaustion and the pain in my feet forgotten for the moment.

Janis was left with no option but to follow with E-J.

The scree turned out to be the waste product of a quarry, located right on the top. The path zigzagged through the heaps of slate, past a ruined house and the hole the quarrymen had left, to the summit.

Stunted trees lined the edges, where rocks sheered away into cliffs. A memorial for local men killed in the Great War elevated the peak a few feet higher.

I reached the top long before the others arrived. No one else was there. For a few moments I had the place to myself.

I was absorbed by the fantastic panorama. I could make out the Skiddaw massif, Keswick and the ferryboat we'd travelled on earlier in the day still chugging its way across the lake. I wished I could wake up every day to such a view.

Presently, Janis approached.

'I'm glad I came up here. For only fifteen minutes of exertion, one couldn't hope for a better summit. It crowns the day for me.'

I swung around and hugged Janis. 'Thank you for a marvellous day.'

She tensed up and pulled away from me. She rushed down the pathway at breakneck speed, gathering up E-J on the way.

I cursed to myself. The friendship I'd been trying to cultivate all day had been jeopardized, but I couldn't understand her reaction.

I followed the Nortons off Castle Crag, down through the gorge and into the forest by the banks of the river.

Surprisingly, we had come out at the very place where Dylan and I had met Emily the other day. But she and her newfound friends had now decamped.

When I caught up with Janis, she was sitting on the riverbank, her back turned towards me, dangling her feet in the clear water.

I came and sat down next to her, not attempting to look at her face.

E-J was paddling in the river with other youngsters. We had caught up with the tourists again.

'I'm sorry, Jan. I'm not sure what I've done, but I'm truly sorry for upsetting you.'

Janis turned her head to face me. She looked as if she'd been crying ever since she'd left Castle Crag.

'Don't worry.'

We set off again, through the campground and along the lane to Grange.

I was expecting Janis to explain what had upset her for every silent second of that walk back to the Citroën. But nothing could prepare me for what she was about to reveal.

Janis stopped in the middle of the Grange bridge, leant against the wall and gazed at the water. Then she lifted her head and looked back towards Castle Crag, now masked by the trees.

'You see, Freya, you were standing on the very spot where Sera threw herself off!'

- XVII -

WHEN I AWOKE the next morning, I shifted uncomfortably on the bed. As I turned over, I felt a strange sensation. I held up the duvet to find the whole of my body covered in freshly cut red roses from the garden. Overcoming my initial surprise, I smelt their sweet fragrance and became caught in the romantic mood Dylan had wanted to induce. I cast off the covers, which sent some of the roses onto the floor, and stood up. As I did so, I stepped on some of the discarded roses and winced as I felt pricks in my feet. I knelt down and clutched my foot, realizing he had left the thorns on the stems. This broke the mood.

I hobbled over to the dressing table and sat down. I began to brush my hair, discovering a tuft of hair sticking out from the rest. At first I thought nothing of it, trying to brush it back into place. This did not succeed, and on further examination, I realized a lock of my hair had been cut off!

I clutched at the side of my head. I was caught in a quandary as to how to react, which symbolized my growing ambivalence towards my lover. I'd wanted to spend this second consecutive night on my own. I could live with knowing he had invaded my privacy to make a romantic – and perhaps a conciliatory – gesture. But in cutting my hair, I felt he had abused my trust. Something about this behaviour disturbed me, and I wondered about his motivation.

I stared into the mirror and could not move for at least five minutes. I carried on brushing out the tangles in my hair, steadying my nerves. I heard the mingled voices of Emily, Yasuko and Janis rumbling away in my thoughts.

Leave now, or be further embroiled….Leave now, or be prepared to share him….Be careful, he has a darker side….Easy to get, impossible to keep….

I debated whether it was the time to go. I had stayed with Dylan longer than most. I could have left long before now. In remaining, I'd begun to discover deeper layers of his complex character. This held out a fascination for me. But something lay beyond even this – a strange compulsion to keep close to Dylan, utterly beyond all reason and self-preservation.

To depart now would leave my task incomplete. An oddly disappointing scenario. Not just for John, but for me.

Instead, I put some of my new clothes into my rucksack, together with the spare set of Austin-Healey keys. This would facilitate a fast escape at a later time, if need be.

Dylan's approaching footsteps in the corridor made me bundle the rucksack back inside the wardrobe. Then I dived onto the bed and flipped myself over onto the floor on the other side. I climbed to my feet, running back to the dressing table and sitting down in the chair, just in time for Dylan to appear.

I fiddled with my hair as Dylan came up behind me. He nestled his head against mine, laid his hands upon my shoulders, and whispered into my ear. 'I hope you liked the roses. Peace offering. I'm sorry I upset you so much.'

He kissed my cheek and his right hand crept under my gown and encircled my left breast before I could answer.

'It was a nice thought.' I felt myself succumbing to his roaming fingers on my nipple and fought hard mentally to resist it.

I turned and gave him a perfunctory kiss on his lips, then tried to rise to my feet. He withdrew his hand, disappointed.

'Look, I just need a little more time, Dylan.'

He sat down on the bed, but did not respond.

'I can't get my head around the concept of sharing you with others.'

'I see.' He bowed his head to the floor and fidgeted with his fingers. 'You're not the only one to've said that, of course. That's why few stay for long.'

'It doesn't help when you hide things from me. Why didn't you tell me Yasuko was your wife?'

'Well....you never asked.'

I shook my head at his facetious reply and ignored his grin. 'You'll need to give me more time to process it all. Otherwise you'll lose me for good as well.'

Dylan became distressed, slapped his hands on his thighs and cast his arms skyward. He climbed to his feet and paced the room in manic fashion. Then he became more pensive as he propped himself against the windowsill.

'Well, I've said all along you can leave when you like. I'm not stopping you. Everyone else seems to be doing so, so why not join the crowd, eh?'

I came over to him, compassion returning, draping myself over him and kissing him again. 'I'm still here, aren't I?'

'Don't tease me, Freya. Make up your mind.'

He pushed me to one side and made for the door.

Seeing my forlorn expression as he turned back to face me, he said: 'I've got a novel to write, so you'll have plenty of time to think things through.'

He closed the door and my composure broke. It was getting increasingly difficult to maintain my false facade.

Suddenly, the door reopened and he saw me slumped against the wall. He ignored this, and said: 'I'm expecting a postal delivery. Please see to it, so I don't have to be disturbed. Thanks.'

He left and I heard the door to the tower being opened, closed, then locked.

I'd made my choice, at least for now.

I dressed and went down to the kitchen, trying to cheer myself up with a full fried breakfast. Despite this, I found myself moping around the Lodge with increasing lassitude. I returned to Dylan's novel, which provided some escape, finishing it and falling asleep on the sofa in the drawing room.

The shrill sound of the entrance buzzer awoke me. I wearily climbed to my feet, and went into the front hallway to find a red light flashing on the video link. I picked up the telephone, seeing the postal truck on the monitor, and buzzed him through when he confirmed his details.

I went out to meet him at the front door. A short, grey-haired man in a cap climbed down from the cab.

''Ello, deliv'ry for Mr. Quest.' He held out a clipboard with the paperwork to sign. 'Ain't seen you before?'

'No,' I said, signing the form for him.

'Dyl'n not around?'

'No, he's busy writing. Told me to deal with you.'

'OK. I need key to outer gate'ouse. I'll jus' ge' it.' He walked towards the door.

'Hold on,' I said, trying to block his way.

''Ey, don't worry. 'E knows me well. I'm 'is ex-brother-in-law.'

'Oh.'

He held out his hand for me to shake. 'I'm Norton, Paul Norton. Go'n' find Dyl'n if you ain't believin' me.'

'No, let's not disturb him,' I answered. 'So you're Janis's old man?' It was a slip of the tongue in response to my realization that he must have been about twenty years older than her.

He nodded. 'But we ain't b'n together for years.'

I eyed him curiously, but let him go into the hallway and pick a huge brass key off the hook on the wall.

He returned to the cab of his van, then wound down the window. 'Yea c'n join me if yea wan', if yea still ain't certain. Could do wi' an extra pair of 'ands, any'ow.'

I paused for a moment. With nothing much better to do, I was soon in the cab alongside him and we were driving down to the front gates. He parked up and opened the back doors and climbed inside.

As I alighted, I heard the rooks' cries echoing across the grounds, where morning mist still clung to the dewy lawns.

Paul hauled a large sack to the edge and let it fall onto the driveway.

'This all for him?'

'That's jus' one. There's more back there,' he said, pointing over his shoulder. Sure enough, he retrieved four more sacks. Then he jumped out and pulled down the rear shutter, making sure it was securely fastened.

He walked over to the arched oak door and twisted the key in the lock. I tried to pull one of the sacks towards him.

'Whoa! Yea'll break yea' back, lady.'

He went inside and returned with a trolley. Then we loaded the first and made separate trips until all the sacks were inside.

The ground-floor chamber was full of gardening implements and machinery. I stared around the cobwebbed walls, whilst he climbed the spiral staircase and opened up a trapdoor overhead. A rope with a large hook on the end was lowered by pulleys. I placed each sack on the end of the hook and watched them rise into the roof one at a time.

Then I joined him upstairs. The upper chamber had bare floorboards, fake arrow slits and the portcullis mechanism. Over half the room, from floor to ceiling, was filled with postal sacks.

He looked at my incredulity. 'It's all the fan mail 'e gets. Comes through a PO Box Number, so they can't discover 'is address. 'S'ad a number of stalkers and fanatics, yea see. We store it up at depot and deliver't once a month. '

'He gets all this?'

'Yeah. Can't be bother'd to 'ire secret'ries no more. Jus' got too much, innit? Stores 'em 'ere, then builds big bonfire on Guy Fawkes 'n' invites local children up t'watch.'

'He burns them unread?'

'Oh, yeah.' He started towards the stairs. 'Look, I mus' be off. Yea c'n leave place unlocked. I'll be back after end of me rounds to do garden. Somethin' 'bout motorbike damage to sort ou'.' He gave me a wry look, as if he knew I'd been partly to blame for this, then he was gone.

I heard the van move off and caught a glimpse of it through an arrow slit, which had been glazed to keep out the elements. Then I jumped as the portcullis descended automatically in response to the vehicle passing through.

The urge to take a peek at some of the mail was too tempting to ignore. I undid one of the sacks and let a stack of letters pour out onto the floor. According to Paul, Dylan wasn't even going to open them. So, even though I was breaking a trust, I justified it to myself quite easily.

Once I'd opened one, I was drawn into another, then another, and so on, until well over three hundred letters lay discarded around my feet. And several hours had gone by without me really noticing.

The mail could be placed into four main categories. A small proportion of them were from academics, distilling the literary qualities of Dylan's novels, sometimes with requests for a meeting or a lecture. The second lot were conventional fan letters from readers who'd taken pleasure from his books. A lesser amount were from would-be writers, inspired by his work, questioning where he got his ideas from and seeking other advice. Sometimes they even enclosed unsolicited manuscripts for him to read and make suggestions.

But by far the greater majority of letters were from female fans wanting to meet him, the prose ranging from the rather restrained to the gushingly amorous. Most had sent in accompanying photographs of themselves, from the conventional to the downright pornographic. The fans ranged in age from early teens to past retirement. Dangerously, almost without fail they'd left their contact details; one or two of these were from ladies famous in their own right, who should've known better.

The great majority of this sample were lost deep within their own fantasy worlds, sometimes detailing these graphically. However, I counted at least ten who'd had some kind of sexual relation with the author. Some appeared contented with a one-night stand, knowing to expect nothing more. Others were enraged by Dylan's lack of contact after the deed, one or two of these sounding deeply disturbed.

I stuffed the letters back into the sack, which was harder than imagined now the seal was broken. Then I followed the staircase upwards, drawing the bolt on the heavy door and finding myself out on the battlements. I could see part of the main Lodge, but most of the view was lost by the ever-encroaching trees.

As I descended to the ground floor, a white Bedford minivan appeared in the entrance. Paul Norton got out and I had to run back to the main house in order to activate the portcullis again. I returned to find him putting on overalls and selecting a few tools and placing them in a wheelbarrow.

'B'n 'ere all this time, 'ave yea?'

'Yes.'

'B'n nosing, 'ave yea?'

'No!'

''Course yea 'ave, but don't worry. Discreet's name o' game wi' me.'

I thanked him, but was still wracked by guilt.

'Well, don't jus' stand there. Either 'elp or bugger off, there's work to do!'

Somewhat taken aback, I decided on the former, and I was soon carting tools over to the back of his van. Then he locked up the gatehouse and drove us back to the inner courtyard.

He took off his cap and scratched his bald head as he surveyed the churned-up lawn and the two damaged flowerbeds. He had a gaunt and craggy face, as if he'd spent all his life halfway up a fellside. I still couldn't envisage him and Janis together; even supposing she'd been seeking a stabilizing father figure, and allowing for the passing years since the break-up of their marriage.

He sank to his knees and began to dig about in the flowerbed with a trowel, endeavouring to rescue what he could.

''Ow long yea b'n 'ere, then?'

I did a mental calculation, using my fingers to count which amused him. I came up with a figure of eighteen days. 'Nearly three weeks.'

'Mus' be 'is latest, I take it.'

'Yes, hasn't Janis told you?'

'Oh, no. Ain't spoke to 'er in years.'

'Why's that?'

'Well, 'twos acrimonious split. For me, at least. Never lasted beyon' six months. Frigid cow only let me shaft 'er few times. Old Questy cuckolded me pretty damn quick, if yea mus' know.'

'Why be his gardener, then?'

'Well, jobs're 'ard to come by round 'ere. Post Office don't pay enough. Really down on me luck, I wos, when 'e 'ired me as workman when 'e restor'd this place. Despite diff'culties, I's a loyal man. Dyl'n don't trus' many, no' wi' reporters sniffin' 'round, so I's done odd jobs for 'im 'bout place ever since.'

'Is that how you and Janis met?'

'Aw no, watch'd 'ole fam'ly grow up, I did. Me Dad wos 'ead gardener at Faversham 'Ouse for many a year; follow'd in 'is footsteps, I did.'

'Faversham House? The Edwardian mansion that burnt down?'

'Yeah.' He looked surprised that I knew. 'That's it. Mysterious episode, it wos. Me Dad wos badly burnt rescuing Lady Faversham. Both lost our liveli'oods after tha'.'

'I'm sorry. So you watched the children grow up?'

'Yeah, from distance, at least. Ser'phina was a beauty. 'Ad plenty of fantasies 'bout 'er, I c'n tell yea.' He gave me a leer, before returning his attention to the plants. 'Janis was a tomboy. Used to come into green'ouse an' 'elp ou' sometimes.'

'So that's how you two got to know each other, then?'

'Yeah, but she wos jus' a littl' girl then. Wasn't till she lost all 'er money an' property, tha' she wos brough' down to my level. All tha' death didn't 'elp, neither. Well, Sir Fred'rick was an ol' man, 'is time'd come. But Ser'phina, well tha' wos jus' tragic.'

'Yes.... What happened to all their wealth?'

'When 'ouse burnt down, insurance didn't cover't. Lost a lot there. Then there wos lots o' legal wranglin' when Eric in'erited title 'n' estate as male heir.'

'Title?'

'Yeah, Sir Fred'rick wos a baronet. That's why 'e wos called "Sir"; yea stupid or somethin'?'

His patronizing tone rankled, but I let it pass.

'Lady V'ronica challenged 'im in court, once 'e came of age. There wos two diff'rent wills. 'Is paternity wos also questioned....'

'Eh?'

'V'ronica couldn't be sure Eric wos Sir Fred'rick's child. 'Ad an affair, or so she said. Made some sense, too.'E wos blond-'aired. All rest of 'em 'ad black 'air. 'Is face wos diff'rent, too. 'E might've suspect'd 'isself, cos 'e wos a righ' tearaway.'

'Really?'

'Yeah. 'E wos in nick when will case came t'court. Righ' delinquent, 'e wos – vandalism, thieving, arson. Ev'ryone 'round 'ere knew 'e'd burnt down mansion 'ouse.'

'Really. Now that is interesting.'

'Wos talk o' ev'n more serious stuff.'

'Like what?'

'I's only knows wha' I knows. Wouldn't wanna commen' further. None of them do. 'E's serving time over in Oz now 'n' all.'

'I see.' A missing segment was coming together in my mind.

'Decid'd in Eric's favour, them judges did. But most o' money wos lost to them lawyers. Only thing Sir Fred'rick'd bequeath'd 'er wos this godforsak'n Lodge, 'n' she'd 'ad t'sell it jus' t'cover 'er own costs. Janis wos left wi' nothin'. 'N' Em'ly 'ad t'grow up like one of us, not all 'oity-toity like Ser'phina.'

'Well, Janis seems very down to earth.'

'Yeah, Janis wos always treat'd like dirt. Never quite treat'd us as equals, but us servants gave 'er 'lot more attention than 'er own folks, 'n' she 'preciated tha'. As for m'Lady, she wos common as mud 'erself.'

'She told me she came from a wealthy family?'

'Aw, don't believe tha'. No, she wos part o' scheme Faversham fam'ly 'ad f'r givin' schol'ships t'bright young girls wi'out own means. Ended up marrying one o' them, Sir Fred'rick did. 'Twos weird if yea ask me. Cradle-snatching, local's called it. Couldn't've b'n more'n eighteen when they 'itched up.'

'Was Dylan's mother one of those girls given a scholarship as well?'

He thought for a moment. 'Yeah, now yea come t'mention't, believe she wos. There wos twelve in all. Think the ol' Baron instigated scheme back in them Victor'n days. 'Bout ev'ry twen'y years a new lot wos given't.'

'What did these scholarships entail?'

'Believe they wos tak'n 'way from families 'n' giv'n places at posh schools. Came 'n' stay'd at big 'ouse in 'olidays. Pretty girls they wos, too.' He gave me another leer.

'I see.'

'I basic'lly grew up wi' their comin's 'n' goin's.'

He had completed work on the first flowerbed and we meandered over to the second, carrying the tools. He began rearranging the flowers, showing a lot of patient nurture. Every now and then, he tutted at the damage.

'Lots o' weird goin's-on, there wos.'

'How d'you mean?'

He looked about furtively, as if making sure no one was about to overhear. 'Well, I tried t'come up 'ere as a kid wi' me mates once. 'Twas a ruin then. Got scared off by dogs.'

'Dogs?'

'Yeah. Only thing Sir Fred'rick ever kept upkeep of wos outer walls 'n' gates, jus' t'keep them dogs in. Dobermans they wos. Fierce buggers 'n' all!'

I nodded, gripped.

'Me mate manag'd to get 'isself over wall, then got 'is arse all bitt'n off. Badly mauled, 'e wos. Story wen' 'round village 'n' none o' me gen'ration ever came up 'ere no more after tha', I c'n tell yea.'

'Emily said Janis, Dylan and Eric played up here as children.'

'Maybe so, but tha' wos twen'y year after my time.'

'OK, I see. So you never came back here till Dylan bought it?'

'No, I didn't quite say tha', now did I?'

I didn't reply, puzzled.

'As a kid, never. Too terr'fied, I wos. But as a young man, yeah.'

'Go on.'

He was getting pleasure from my rapt attention. 'Me girlie, as a dare, got me to take 'er up 'ere after dark. Must've b'n 'bout twen'y-two, twen'y three, somethin' like tha'. No sign of any dogs then, but we wos both scar'd jus' gettin' up drive! We crept into upper storey of inner gate'ouse. I wos jus' gettin' me 'and down 'er knickers, I wos' – another leer – 'when we 'eard cars approachin'. Posh cars they wos, too. Blew ou' candle, we did, 'n' sat 'n' watch'd. Weird, it wos. Wearin' black cloaks, they wos. Dis'pear'd 't'middl' o' ruin. Set up lanterns all o'er place.'

'You must've been terrified!'

'Ay, we wos. Spent hours up there, we did. Didn't dare move till mornin'. Once we wos sure they'd all gone off.'

'What did you do?'

'Never talked t'no one 'bout it, 'part from two friends. Even then, tha' wos years later. Thought I'd made it all up, they did.'

That thought had crossed my mind, too.

''Twos only when one o' 'em wos wi' me when we dismantl'd old church over yonder for Dyl'n. Stripp'd off all roofin' slates 'n' winder lead t'use on main buildin'.

Tha' wos righ' weird, tha' place. All them carvings 'n' stuff inside. Pristine condition, it wos, too.'

'Really?'

'Yeah. Made 'im believe me then, I c'n tell yea.' He chuckled as he relived the event. 'Scarper'd off job nex' day, 'e did, too!'

'And you?'

'No. Need'd money too much, didn't I.'

He looked at his watch and began to pack up the tools. ''Ave t'come back 'n' finish this some other time. B'n nice talkin' t'yea.'

He stood in front of me a while longer and I began to wilt under the heat of his gaze. I followed the line of his vision and it dawned on me that he was probably becoming excited by the way my nipples were poking through the fabric of my T-shirt.

I couldn't be certain, of course, but I felt very uncomfortable all the same. I persevered however, as I wanted to ask one last question before he left: 'So the stories about devil worship in the ruins are true, then?'

'Now, I didn't say tha', now did I? Don't go quotin' me none. Draw y'own conclusions if yea mus', but keep me ou' of it.'

He left me to contemplate his recollections as I observed him crossing the lawn towards the inner courtyard.

- XVIII -

THAT NIGHT I let Dylan back into my bed, against my better judgement.

I suppose it started when I became lost in the pages of *Pillar Rock* after Norton had left. Dylan had been up in the tower. I had hours to fill. Soon I was enthralled by the quality of the writing and the story at the heart of the book. It was very accomplished for a first novel. The tension was built around a number of pioneer climbing episodes and the love the central character had for the innkeeper's daughter. What struck me was the intensity of their love. And how the heroine matched many of the qualities of Seraphina. When I came to the climax – where the hero fell to his death off a cliff whilst the heroine watched – I became convinced he'd been at his most autobiographical in this novel.

I lay on my front on the bed, the book propped up on a pillow. I became absorbed into the small hours before I finished its two hundred pages. Only then, with my head splitting and exhaustion evident, did I realize everything had stopped still. I hadn't eaten; my bladder was full; and my body ached from lying prone in one position for so long. And Dylan was sat in a chair across the other side of the room.

I let out a cry when I noticed him there in the shadows.

'I didn't mean to frighten you. Didn't want to disturb you, that's all.'

I climbed off the bed, stretching in pain, and went to the toilet. Then I returned and lay back on the bed in the same position as before, with my back to him. I picked up the book again.

'Don't be upset. It was fascinating to watch. I rarely get a chance to see how a reader enjoys one of my books. OK, the critics wrote rave reviews and it was awarded three different prizes. But they pale into insignificance against what I just witnessed.'

He came over and lay down next to me. I didn't stop him from caressing my naked back and bottom.

'It was very powerful. It triggered the whole gamut of my emotions at various times. The story was simple, but the characterization magnificent. I was willing Percy to succeed in that final climb, right up to the last moment. With its setting in the late Victorian era, you expect the classic Victorian ending. But you get only tragedy.'

'I'm glad you said that. That's precisely what I was trying to evoke.'

'I love it. I really love it. I've only read four of the five, but this is my favourite by far.'

'It's my favourite, too. There's a rawness of emotion, reflected also in that of the landscape. I've struggled to recapture its essence ever since.'

His hands had continued to work on my body. From the way I was physically responding to his attentions, I knew I was going to give myself to him again.

Only now, in the morning light, did I have second thoughts. I'd sobered up from the novel's intoxication and Dylan's rough lovemaking. All I was left with now was a thudding pain down below and a feeling of dread at my lack of resistance. Lust had ruled over reason and sense. I'd begun to break away from his influence. Now I was even more deeply embroiled and corrupted.

When I went downstairs to the kitchen for breakfast, I found Dylan already at the table, munching on a slice of toast. He poured out some tea as I sat down and he smiled warmly.

'I thought we could go out somewhere together today.'

'Oh,' he said, knotting his brow. 'You gave me so much inspiration last night. All I want to do now is write.'

I slouched back in my chair.

He could sense my disappointment. 'I'm sorry. But if you want to be a novelist's girlfriend, you're gonna have to get used to me cloistering myself away for long periods.'

'But I've hardly seen you for days!....It's as if you're losing interest in me.'

'Have you forgotten about last night already?' he retorted, sarcastically.

'You're satisfying me physically at night. You know that. But a relationship's got to be more than that.'

'Indeed. But the creative process stops for no one. Not even someone as beautiful as you.' He chuckled, and slurped his tea.

'Bullshit!'

Dylan was stunned and froze.

'I think going up in that ivory tower of yours is just a ruse to avoid deeper emotional engagement.'

'What's that supposed to mean!' he said, hurt.

'It needs no further explanation. I've learnt more about yourself from everybody else, than I have done from you!'

Dylan banged the teacup back into its saucer and stood up. 'I'll see you later.' He kicked the chair out of his way and stormed into the hall.

I followed behind him as he strode upstairs. He slammed the door to the tower behind him as I arrived on the landing. I reached for the doorknob, but could hear him locking it from the other side. I listened through the door and could make out his footsteps trailing away up a further set of stairs on the other side.

I pounded with my fists on the door and screamed for him to return, surprised by the strength of my emotion.

Eventually I stopped and walked down the stairs, feeling rejected. I sat on the lowest step and looked up at the portrait of Dylan the writer in Victorian attire. I stuck my finger up at his image and swore. Then I returned to the kitchen.

As I was finishing breakfast, I was disturbed by the entrance buzzer. I went over to see who was at the outer gates, thinking Paul Norton must be returning to complete the garden repairs. However, it was Rupert's Bentley pictured on the video link. I let him in and walked out to the courtyard to meet him.

He arrived and climbed out of the car, giving his over-exaggerated welcome. He looked to be in an excitable mood. I was about to tell him Dylan was not available, when I realized he appeared to have come to see me.

'How did it go with Lady Jennifer?'

'Oh, good. Very good. Much more marriageable material than Janis. Although Lady Veronica was cross when I said this to her earlier.... Anyway, enough of that. I've got some news on the medallion....Can I see it?'

I led him inside and told him that Dylan had thrown it into the millpond.

'Oh,' he replied, looking disappointed. 'Well, that might explain why Lady Veronica's hired a frogman. Found him diving into the millpond earlier, but she wouldn't tell me why.' He sat himself down in a lounge armchair and unwrapped and lit up a cigar.

'I drew a copy of it, though.'

I was about to run to the library and retrieve the drawing when he brought out a photograph from his jacket pocket. 'No need. I took this before I left for Scotland.'

He passed it to me and I viewed the medallion again.

'There is no doubt it has a satanic purpose.'

I drew in a deep breath. 'How can you be so certain?'

'Well, the Viscount, Lady Jennifer's father, is quite an authority, apparently. He studied this photo in detail and realized straight away. The goat's head is an old pagan fertility god. The Catholic Church demonized this competing religious symbol by portraying the Devil as having horns. Later satanic cults then subsumed the emblem for their own use, along with some of these other symbols from ancient Hebrew, Greek and Egyptian origin.' He pointed to smaller engravings around the outside of the gold disc. 'He reckons the medallion itself is late eighteenth century in date.... Of German or Austrian origin probably.'

'That would fit with the facts I've learnt.'

He took on a curious countenance, as if disappointed that his news wasn't as revelatory as he might have imagined, but eager to find out more about my own discoveries.

I told him about the ruined chapel and the folly, the

local satanic legends and my researches in Dylan's library, and finished with Norton's colourful reflexions.

'Well, my word! Who'd've believed all that.' He scratched his balding head. 'And the old Baron was a German, you don't say....Now that would fit.'

'Perhaps the medallion was his.'

'I doubt it. The Viscount's sure it was meant to be worn by a woman.'

'How so?'

'See this larger symbol around the gold disc, surrounding the goat's head.' He traced its outline with his finger on the photograph. 'The pentogram. A motif known in many ancient religions and perhaps the best known symbol in satanic cults. Nothing too out of the ordinary in this context, you might think. But this is where it gets more esoteric. The pentogram originally signified the passage of the planet Venus across the sky. Hence it came to represent the goddess Venus. The Viscount believes the underlying meaning for those in the know was that the medallion was meant to be wore by a woman for an ancient rite – her union with the goat or devil.'

I gasped.

Rupert seemed pleased now to have imparted some important fact not previously known to me.

I was equally intrigued. I couldn't help remembering the image on the fresco in the folly.

Rupert stayed for tea and cake and we talked some more about the possible darker side of Grimshaw Lodge's history, amidst clouds of cigar smoke. He encouraged me to research further into the mystery.

Then he took on a more concerned demeanour. 'The Viscount warned me too, you know. There are plenty of stories about aristos in the eighteenth and nineteenth centuries forming weird clubs as an excuse to prance naked around their country estates and have sexual orgies. (Sir Francis Dashwood and his "Hellfire Club" is perhaps the most infamous of these.) But a small percentage really did dabble in the black arts and were more sinister. It's difficult to know which category the old Baron fitted into!' He started to laugh, but the sound choked in his mouth.

We sat in an uncomfortable silence for some time.

Eventually, he took his fob watch out of his waistcoat. 'Gosh! Is that the time. I must dash off, I'm afraid.' He took out a bundle of papers from his briefcase. 'Some financial details Dylan asked me to look over. He needs to sign and return them to me at my London office.'

'Don't you want to see him yourself?'

'No,' he said, chuckling. He stubbed out his latest cigar in the ashtray and took a swig from a hip flask. 'I've learnt the hard way over the years not to disturb him when he's writing!'

We bid our farewells and soon he was cruising off down the driveway.

I stayed outside for a while in pensive mood.

When I returned I made sure Dylan was still in the tower before calling John again. He seemed agitated when he answered, but listened carefully to all my revelations about Satanism in times past at the Lodge.

'This is all very well, Freya, and it's all relevant, no doubt. But what of his late wife?'

'Her sister, Janis, told me she committed suicide.'

There was a long intake of breath at the other end of the line. 'I knew it was no accident!'

Suddenly it dawned on me that he'd sent me on this

mission of discovery without telling me he already had some of the facts.

'Look, John. What's going on? You've sent me into this thing blind. You must have known all along that getting close to Dylan could be dangerous for my emotional well-being. Why d'you want to know all this about him?'

There was silence from his end of the line.

'You better tell me, or that's it....I'm off!

'No!' he barked.

'Tell me, then!'

He hesitated. 'Well....'

'Tell me!'

'All right! All right!....It's simple: I used to know Sera. And I'm certain he's responsible for her death!'

He slammed down the phone before I could answer.

I hardly had a chance to recover before I heard Dylan hurrying down the stairs. I replaced the receiver and jumped into a chair. He came into the room, but made for the servant's stairs to the basement. He didn't give me a second glance, mumbling 'Bitch!' under his breath as he went.

I followed after him, into the basement, past the wine cellar and then the larder, each with vaulted-brick roofs. I found him in a further pantry, opening a reinforced steel cabinet and producing a shotgun. He broke the weapon open and put a box of cartridges into his pocket.

I edged backwards, scared by what he might do.

He knew I was there, but ignored me. He fumbled with the door, then ran up a flight of stairs that ended with an archway into the courtyard. I followed at a discreet distance as he marched off down the driveway.

By the time I reached the bridge, two shots rang out in quick succession and the sound echoed around the grounds. The rooks squawked and rose from their nests in the beech trees. I rushed down the driveway, then the embankment onto the outer lawn. I was consumed by a feeling of dread that Dylan may have done himself some harm.

But then I saw him, breaking open the shotgun and struggling to reload as rabbits scattered in disarray in front of him. As I approached, he pulled the trigger again. One of the shots hit the hind quarters of a retreating rabbit, cartwheeling it into the air and onto its back. It had failed to reach the safety of its burrow by only a yard. It then rived in agony on the ground until Dylan went over and put it out of its misery by thrusting the butt of the gun down onto its head.

I heard the skull crack, and recoiled in disgust.

I sat down on the banking, which rose into a tree-covered mound where the rabbits had made their burrows. I watched Dylan pick up three bodies and tie them to a cane from their back legs. He then hoisted the cane onto his shoulder and came over to me.

'How could you! Poor little creatures. Why take it out on them, just because you're angry. They've done nothing to you!'

'That's the trouble with you urbanites,' he replied, laying the cane over a nearby branch. 'You have a very naive view of the countryside. They're a cursed nuisance and need to be culled from time to time to keep the numbers down. They can damage the garden if not controlled properly.'

'It's still cruel.'

'Shooting's more humane than poisoning or gassing. Anyway, they're bred to be killed.

'Explain,' I said, unconvinced.

'Well, these mounds here are coney beds. Deliberately built to provide an extra source of food; and fur for clothing. The Normans introduced the idea, and the rabbits themselves. We only had hares in this country before that. You'll find many country estates had them. The old Baron, who originally owned the Lodge, was keeping up with a dying tradition.'

'I see.'

'The rabbits had overrun the place when I bought the estate. I thought about killing them off for good, but decided to save the blighters for the sake of authenticity. Been cursing that sentimental decision ever since. I hate shooting them, despite what you think!'

I apologized.

'But I suppose it gets rid of my pent-up anger. Some of what you said earlier hit home.'

'Really?'

'Yes. And anyway, I've been suffering from writer's block these past few days. I can't quite get at the heart of my central character's motivation. It's been very frustrating. Maybe a day or so off with you will give me some perspective and clear my thoughts.'

I smiled. At last I appeared to have influenced his decision-making.

'You would've noticed, I'm sure, from your reading of my novels, that they turn on two or three main characters. But I feel my writing's regressing. If I don't get this right, the whole book's going to fail and I'll have to put it in the bottom drawer. I already have two junk manuscripts in there; I don't really want a third.'

'Ah. That could explain the greater gap between the publication of your second and third novels.'

'You're very intuitive, aren't you?'

'I suppose I am.' Hadn't that been another reason why John had chosen me over other possible candidates?

'But no, you aren't right on this occasion. Both were written before the publication of *Pillar Rock*.'

'Ah. So that was not actually your first true novel?' As I said this, I remembered my conversation with Janis about unpublished works.

'No. The others were a way of learning the craft. It's probably the same for most successful novelists.'

'So what explains the gap?'

'This place. I spent three years out here in the garden in a caravan, spending the proceeds of *The Music Man* film rights on rebuilding the Lodge. It was in an almost irredeemable state. Trying to write a third novel and project manage the builders and subcontractors at the same time was exhausting. I can still remember all those nights returning from the site, particularly those winter months with limited heating. Then I'd type *The Immigrant* into the small hours, resting the typewriter across my knees.'

'But you must be pleased with the result.'

'Yes. On both counts. The novel was critically acclaimed. It sold disappointingly at first, but sales rose due to my tabloid exposure. And while there are still outer areas of the garden to reclaim, I'm very satisfied with the transformation of the Lodge as well. Not many people can see an adolescent fantasy come to life in the way I've realized this.'

'No.'

'It was all carefully planned. I deliberately wrote *The Music Man* as a more commercial book, together with an accompanying film script, hoping it might generate enough capital to save the Lodge. I succeeded beyond all my hopes.'

'Yes. That book is much less literary than the others; though no less interesting as a result.'

'Thank you. I wish more of my former girlfriends – and the tabloids for that matter – had taken as much of an interest in my writing as you appear to be doing.'

'You're certainly a lot more complex a character than the "ruthless philanderer" usually painted. Even the people you surround yourself with seem to have dwelt on the sexual angle to the detriment of everything else.'

'Indeed,' he said, smirking. He took out a cloth from his pocket and began to wipe down the butt of the shotgun. 'So what's keeping you here if I'm this sexual ogre?'

'Well, many a philanderer has settled down eventually.'

Although he smirked again, his wiping of the gun became more vigorous and his face became more lined and intense. 'I can't promise you anything, you know, Freya. I don't want to hurt you.'

'I know. But promise me this one thing. Spend the next couple of days with me.'

'OK. So long as you allow me to return to my writing after that.'

'Agreed....And I know Janis has been in your life for a long time, but can you just concentrate on me for the next few weeks without her intruding. Or anyone else, for that matter. Only then will we know whether we have a future or not.'

I already knew there wouldn't be. But I had to keep making Dylan believe there might be in order to complete my mission. And getting Dylan on his own could only help John's cause.

'I can go with that.'

'I hope so.'

'Let's go on a two-day expedition.'

'Oh no, not more mountain walking,' I moaned. 'My feet couldn't take any more of that at the moment.'

'No. Something a little more sedate, but still in the outdoors.'

'Surprise me.'

'OK,' he said and kissed me, taking me unawares.

We made love right there on the bank.

When we had finished, I rolled over and found myself staring into the eye of one of the dead rabbits. I wondered whether I might share a similar fate, now I'd renewed my commitment to Dylan. And to John's quest for knowledge.

- XIX -

WE SET OFF later that day on Dylan's surprise trip, taking Quasi the dog along with us. We drove first to the museum and exchanged the Singer Gazelle for a sturdier Rover P5 Coupé. Then we travelled into the heart of the district, through St John's Vale, over Dunmail Raise for a view of "The Lion and the Lamb", then down through Grasmere and Ambleside and thence, on narrower roads, to Coniston. Dylan took delight in pointing out the sights on route, whilst Quasi stuck his head out of the back window all the way there. We parked at the northern end of the lake. It was a perfect day. The tranquil waters, catching the sunlight, were framed against the sylvan shoreline.

Dylan opened the boot and took out two waterproof canisters. Then we packed all the gear we'd brought into these and made our way over to a boathouse.

'Great. What are we going to be doing?'

He had kept the surprise well, and wasn't about to reveal it quite yet. Only when he pulled out the open canoe from inside the building did I realize what he had in mind. He spent some time strapping the canisters against the bar in the middle of the canoe, then searched for further gear. He returned with two paddles and a tarpaulin, whilst Quasi sniffed around the bushes, piddling regularly.

Dylan went through the procedures of how to paddle and told me I was to sit in the bow, as the person at the stern needed to steer.

'You own the boathouse?'

'Yes. But most of it's rented out to a local outdoor pursuits company.... Damn!'

'What's the matter?'

'This paddle's developing a crack.' He went back inside and brought out a roll of waterproof tape and proceeded to bind up the paddle blade. 'That should do it.'

Then he handed the faulty paddle to me, along with a buoyancy aid.

'No wetsuit, then?'

'No. I'm not planning on getting us wet if we can help it. But we've packed spare clothes in any case. Now, help me drag it over to the water. Come on Quasi, here boy, here boy.'

He held the canoe against the side and showed me how to get in safely. Once inside, he clambered in himself and whistled for Quasi to follow. The dog jumped in the middle and lay down with his head on one of the canisters and felt immediately at home.

Before long, we were off and he continued his instruction as we hugged the western shoreline. I soon mastered the basics and we found a rhythm quickly. The Coniston fells dominated the scene, but the smaller hills to the east showed we had come to the very fringes of the mountains.

'How long have you canoed for?'

'Oh, since childhood. Sera and I would come here often and camp out where we're going today.'

He went very quiet after this. I turned around and found him staring vacantly into the far distance.

'It must've been hard, finding someone so special, yet losing her so tragically after such a short time.' This sounded a little crass, but I wanted to provoke a deeper level of emotional response in him.

It was a long time before he replied, as we paddled onwards. 'You never get over something as traumatic as that....You never do....A dream died with her. And so much talent, too. Such a waste. I've never been the same since.'

Dylan went through a series of deft paddle strokes to steer us away from the bank to round a jetty. We were passing a number of exclusive properties and I admired their opulence.

'Nearly bought one of those,' he said, noting my interest. 'But in the end, the Lodge was the only place for me. I owed it to Sera's memory to restore it. And in doing so, it restored me.'

'Perhaps the experience of her death also led you to write? Writing the emotions out of your system, and all that.'

'You're probably right. I think it was Georges Simenon, the Belgian detective novelist, who said: "Writing isn't a profession, it's a vocation of unhappiness". But my motivation can be traced back to my childhood. I'd wanted to be a writer for as long as I can remember.'

'So was it the Lakeland scenery that inspired you?'

'Certainly. But again that was a later addition. I didn't come here till I was ten. Or, at least, that's what I initially thought. Mother told me a few years later that she'd known the Favershams previously. I'd even played with Sera and her siblings as a baby and toddler. That lost association formed a bond that had unwittingly drawn us back together. My mother never approved of our closeness, nor the subsequent marriage.'

'Why?'

'I could never be entirely sure. There'd been some rift between her and Faversham and she fought hard to keep me from his influence.'

'No one's told me much about your mother. Janis said she'd come from an upper class family.'

'No. She was of pure working-class mining stock. She heralded from Ebbw Vale, the third of seven children. She gained greater status through her education, funded by a Faversham scholarship. After the rift, we returned to her roots. But the community couldn't easily re-assimilate her; she'd become so divorced from their world. It was a difficult seven years for her. Only a deep religious fervour kept her going through these years....Although I felt suffocated by it.

'But this tightknit community was the real shaping of me as a writer, with its library and pithead both seen from our cottage window. I used to watch all the dust-ridden miners walking past at the end of each shift. Much of the detail of *Friends and Lovers* is lifted straight from these experiences, although I transferred them to the Coniston copper mines in the story.'

'Oh, right. Those passages are very evocative.'

'Thanks.'

'So your mother was a great influence in your writing?'

'Heaven's no! She only had time for the Lord's book and found novels sacrilegious.'

'And your father?'

'I never had a father.'

'But you told me he'd been killed down the pit. And your brother, too.' I turned around to face him. He had reddened, as if he'd forgotten he'd spun me this falsehood.

'I'm sorry. I weave stories about myself, it's easier that way. No one likes to admit they haven't a father.'

'I see.'

'But Geraint, a mining manager and lay preacher, married my mother. He had a great love of literature and used to take me down the library every night after school. He encouraged me to read. He was my true inspiration.'

'Janis thought he was just her boyfriend.'

'Oh, no. You had to do things properly down there. And he gave us extra security, as Mother's savings had run out. It may simply have been a marriage of convenience for her. I never felt her heart had been truly in it.'

'What happened? Did he die?'

'No. Mother ran back up here. She'd confided in him about her past and he could have nothing to do with her after that. He tried to explain things to me when we left, but she never mentioned anything about it ever again.'

There was a silence for a long time, with only the sounds of the paddle blades knifing through the water and the gentle lapping against the side of the canoe for company.

'Where're we headed?' I finally said.

'Over to that isle in the distance.'

My arms and back were beginning to ache from the effort and our destination still looked a long way off.

As the canoe edged towards the shore, Quasi jumped into the water and began to drink. Then he grabbed the bow-rope in his jaws and carried it ashore. I soon followed, leaping clear of the water and landing on the gravelly shore. I threw the paddle in front of me and there was a splintering of wood as it hit on a rock. I went over and found the blade had broken in half where the earlier crack had been.

Dylan didn't look amused as he passed by, carrying the containers into the wood that covered the isle.

'Go and find some dead wood for a fire,' he said.

I went off obediently. Quasi came close on my heels, sniffing new smells as he went. By the time I returned with an armful of sticks, Dylan had already rigged the tarpaulin between two trees, creating a tent-like canopy. He was placing blankets underneath as I approached.

He put his arm around my back and kissed me. 'This'll make a cosy retreat tonight.' He winked.

He guided me back to the shore and told me to dump the sticks. He pulled out rocks from the water and buried them into the gravel to act as a hearth for a fire. Then he shaved off some bark to act as kindling, with a knife he'd unsheathed from his belt. He lit it by striking the edge of the blade against a special stone he'd brought with him. He held the bark in his hand and blew carefully into it until flames took hold. Then he returned it to the hearth and added other smaller sticks. A fire was soon blazing.

I became more amazed at his bushcraft. He started by fashioning a tripod using sticks bound together with twine made from strips of bark. He used this to hang a saucepan of water over the flames to brew some tea. He made me tend this, whilst he went off into the wood. He returned later with a log he'd scavenged and sat down beside me. He took out a saw, whose blade folded out from its handle, and made a number of cuts. He asked me to sort out the potatoes and fish he'd placed into tinfoil before we'd left. When I came back, he was hacking away at the log with a hatchet.

He suspended his carving so we could eat dinner. As we munched away, our eyes were cast out across the water as the sun sank lower in the sky.

'So, it must have been difficult without a father and not being very close to your mother,' I finally said.

'You survive. She was a very angst-ridden woman, too, which didn't help. I sank into my own imagination as a way of escaping her and all her religious mumbo jumbo. She even hung a large crucifix from the ceiling above my bed. So Jesus's pain would be the last thing I saw every night before going to sleep. Gave me many a nightmare. Often thought I was hanging up there with him.'

There was silence for a while. He picked up the log again and returned to his carving. 'Meeting the Favershams took me away from all that....I was able to distance myself further from my mother's influence. Veronica and Faversham were more like parents in those six years before I ran off with Sera.'

'Running off caused the rift?'

'Yes.'

'Was there more to it?'

He didn't answer, but cut away at the log more vigorously again.

I sat and watched his skill as minutes trickled over the hour, like the water lapping back and forth against the shore at our feet. Gradually, a familiar shape became discernible.

'You're making a new paddle!' I cried in amazement.

'Well, yes. Since you've finished off the old one through your clumsy actions. How else do you expect us to get back tomorrow?'

'I'm sorry. Who taught you all this?'

'Faversham. It's a dying art.' He continued to chip away at the log whilst he spoke. 'I could live in the wilds for weeks if I wished, living off the land and using these survival skills. I could've made us catch a fish for dinner, but thought that might've stretched things a little too far for a first outing!'

Quasi lay down beside me, with his head in my lap, as I continued to marvel at Dylan. He was using a small rasping tool now, to shape it further and give it a smooth finish.

'What was Seraphina like?'

Dylan carried on with his work and didn't look like he was about to answer.

'I'm sorry. If it's too painful, don't worry.'

'Of course it's painful!' He dropped the rasp on the ground and climbed to his feet. He filled a bucket from the lake and threw the water over the fire. He watched to ensure the embers were properly extinguished, before retreating into the woods.

I stood and spent time aimlessly skimming peddles across the water. Eventually, I followed Dylan back to the camp.

I expected him still to be angry, but he allowed me to snuggle up close. I fell asleep almost immediately. It was the first night I'd spent together with Dylan without us making love. But there was poignancy in the closeness we achieved that night, heightened by a sense of communing with nature.

We awoke early to a chilly morning and hurriedly packed up the camp. We put on warmer clothes and huddled against a rock, eating cereal. He took out a camping stove this time to brew some tea, boiling two eggs with the same water.

The cold stiffened my joints and made my movements slow. But Dylan jostled me along, wanting to make an early start. Soon we were in the canoe and heading back. But Dylan added interest by following the eastern shore for our return leg.

We had been confined to small talk for much of the journey until I suddenly said: 'Sorry if I upset you last night.'

'It's OK. The harm dates from years back. It's nothing you've done.'

This reassured me. 'What was she like, then?' I said, continuing to paddle, glad my back was to him, so he couldn't see the air of expectation on my face.

'Sera was very aloof. Her intellectual abilities put her far ahead of her peers and she felt alienated from them, as they did from her. She was just as arrogant in the early years with me, too. And she had another boyfriend at that time....Some older, more mature guy from Keswick. Fancied himself as a would-be man of letters. But Sera said all he wrote was puerile junk....Now, what was his name....Jason, Jacob, Jeremy....no, something beginning with "J" anyway....'

John! I thought. His motivation for my mission was finally making sense.

'But she dumped him eventually....And gradually, as I lost interest in Eric, the bond with Sera grew. Underneath her cold exterior, there was a passion burning. Ready for me to unleash it. Her accident first melted the facade. She clung to me desperately after that.'

'Accident?'

'Yeah. She had taken her father's boat out on the water. Must've been nearly thirteen. She was very adventurous and could handle herself well. Just a freak accident, that's all.'

'What happened?'

'She had very long hair – that's what crowned her beauty, for me – but the wind splayed it out over the end of the boat and it got caught in the propeller of the outboard motor. The engine cut out, but it jolted her off into the water. If I hadn't seen it as it happened, and sent Faversham to her rescue, she would've drowned.'

He paused, as I swung around to face him.

'She was traumatized and began to cling to me after that.'

'Did she suffer injury?'

'No. Not physically, at least. Only to her hair – they had to cut a lot off to free her.'

'Oh.'

'Sometimes I wonder, with hindsight, whether it might've been better if she'd drowned after all.'

'Before you got so heavily involved with her emotionally, you mean.'

He did not reply.

I was still facing him, resting from my paddling. 'So you wouldn't have to've faced up to her committing suicide later?'

Dylan's face fell. His eyes narrowed. 'Who told you that?!'

The force of his response was so strong I nearly fell off my seat.

'Janis,' I said.

His face reddened under his growing rage. He thrust his paddle back into the water and trebled the speed of his movement. 'Come on. Start paddling!' he shouted.

I turned, and did as he said.

'Faster, damn you!'

I could feel the heat of him burning into my back. And the anxiety he'd also instilled into Quasi, who was cowering up against me.

I wanted to apologize again, but found I daren't open my mouth, for fear of reprisal.

Luckily, we only had another half an hour before we regained the northern shore. Dylan kept up his relentless paddling pace throughout, then jumped in as we approached. He hurried past me, walking shin-deep in the water. When he reached the shore, he smashed his hand-made paddle over the nearest rock, repeating the action again and again until it had shattered.

I was left behind in the canoe, bewildered at the force of his pent-up rage. And guilty at being responsible for provoking it.

- XX -

IT HAD TAKEN a long time for Dylan to calm down. We ate lunch at a pub in the town, surrounded by old photographs of Donald Campbell's ill-fated attempts on the water-speed record. The long drive back to the Lodge was undertaken with an awkward atmosphere inside the Rover throughout. Once back, Dylan retreated to the tower, and left me alone.

I took a walk with the dog around the grounds, then had a swim. Later, I strode into the library and picked up Dylan's final novel, *The Immigrant*. After the first few chapters, however, I was drawn away by nagging thoughts. Recent events had drawn out a compassion which now threatened to compromise my quest: going deeper might upset Dylan further. But Dylan's reaction had stopped me from pressing him about what Paul Norton had said. Now I had to follow my instincts and find out more myself. And John expected it, too.

I scoured the shelves again, remembering ancient tomes I'd fleetingly glanced at when hunting out Dylan's scrapbooks. I found one elaborately bound book and pulled it out. It was large, about two foot by one, and I almost buckled under its weight. I steadied myself and lifted it over to the coffee table. The binding was old and battered, edged with gold plates. I noticed some fire damage. Perhaps it had once been in the library at Faversham House.

I opened it and felt and smelt the dust and odour of past ages. The frontispiece, much foxed around the edges, gave a publishing date of 1779 and a title in elegant Gothic calligraphy. As I carefully turned over the first few pages, I realized it had been handwritten. Each chapter started with a highly decorous letter, depicting goblins and serpents and other mythological creatures – half man, half beast.

The text was in Latin. This was disappointing, as I had no knowledge of the language. However, every now and then, there were detailed sketches which left little doubt what the book was about. There were depictions of geometric shapes on walls and floors of unusual temple structures. Some – like the pentagram – were not unlike those I'd seen in the folly and the ruined chapel.

There were various ceremonies and detailed hierarchies of where people should stand. Differing costumes appeared to indicate differing ranks. There was also a list of eight dates: 2 February, 21 March, 30 April, 21 June, 1 August, 21 September, 31 October and 21 December. I construed these to be possible times of the main ceremonies, as some marked the equinoxes and solstices. This was followed by extraordinary representations of sexual acts and orgies.

The final section appeared to show codes of practice, each sentence prefixed with Roman numerals. The last page was an image of the Devil, executed to perfection. But ultimately chilling. I struggled to replace the book.

There were two more, smaller volumes, one with a hobgoblin embossed on its spine. These dated from the early nineteenth century and were in German, again a language I couldn't understand. They contained long lists of procedures in tight Gothic print, but with no pictures to conjure with, it was difficult to connect them to black magic with any certainty.

The middle pages of one of these works began to crumble and part from the binding. I hastily shut it again and put it back on the shelf, lest Dylan find out I had damaged it.

In the back of the other book, I found a handwritten sequence of names and dates, most written in differing hands. Wolfram von Kloeppendorf was the first name, with a date of 1721. I searched down the list. Most of the rest were von Eschenbachs. The last name was Sir Ernest Faversham, with a date of 1889. I recalled this was the date when the Baron had died. There was no more space at the end of the page for additional names. I studied the binding closely. It was the final page.

I put the book away and went into the kitchen for some refreshment. As I sat at the table with a mug of tea, I was left with more nagging questions, and no answers.

I returned to the library and Dylan's novel. Then I was hit by another thought: what was it about that old photograph of this room, when the building was a ruin, that wasn't quite right?

I retrieved the book and flicked through the pages, needing several attempts to rediscover the photograph. I looked at it long and hard. Then I stood up and orientated the photograph to the room. Some of the old panelling and shelving had been reused, or very good copies made. But the photograph showed a dark hole between two of the bookcases. There was no wall. It was an opening of some kind. And now my gaze was being drawn towards its location in the modern room.

I was led to the fake bookcase I'd discovered on my first visit, seemingly months ago. Now what had always been the obvious finally entered my mind: it had to be a secret door!

I walked over to it and began a detailed examination. The carving of the books had been expertly rendered, the overlay of different paints crowning the effect. I ran my fingers across the surface, searching for some kind of mechanism which might open it. But I found none.

I stepped back, viewing the unit in its entirety. I noticed one book was sloping to one side, on the middle shelf, when all the others were upright. I felt into the space between this carved book and the next. My fingers touched a metal ring. I pulled on this and heard a clunk.

I stepped back, with bated breath, then thrust my outstretched hands against the bookcase. And the whole unit, hinged on one side, moved outwards. It was indeed a hidden entrance.

I ran back to the main library door, checking for any signs of Dylan. There were none, so I returned and stepped over the dark threshold. I found myself in a small chamber. Light was coming in from the left. As I walked into this space, I found myself looking back into the library. The glass must have been the backing of the mirror.

I felt around the edges of the room at this end, but found no way forward. I returned to the entrance, opening the doorway further to cast in extra light. A narrow staircase swept up into the shadows.

I started to ascend. After two full twists of the spiral, I was met by a solid oak door. I found a handle, and grabbed it. It opened stiffly. I was suddenly bathed in light. I was on a well-decorated landing, with a wider staircase heading upwards. I saw another door on my right, unlocked the latch and found myself out on the bedroom landing.

Realizing I had to be inside the tower, I immediately shut the door and headed back whence I'd come. I knew Dylan was up there. There was no telling what might happen if he discovered me.

Once back in the library, I was about to close the bookcase door, when I looked down. There was a trapdoor in the floor, directly under the first step. I brushed my hands over its wooden surface, discovering a brass-ringed handle and pulled. It was very heavy and I had to strain hard to lift it over the perpendicular. Its hinges creaked, which suggested no one had opened it for quite some time. I dusted my hands off against the top of my jeans and gazed down through the opening. The spiral staircase appeared to descend further into the depths.

I'd never been very brave in the dark, so I wasn't encouraged to venture forward. Instead, I rushed out of the Lodge and over to the stabling block. I remembered seeing various torches in amongst the tools. I leant against the side of the Austin-Healey and rifled through various boxes. I picked out two large torches and a box of matches and returned to the library.

I tested them both out down the hole and picked the one with the stronger bulb. I crept down the stairs, with increasing trepidation. I counted twenty steps before I hit another level surface. I shone the torch down at my feet to be met by black-and-white tiling similar to the flooring in the ruined chapel. Then I scanned upwards to a superb vaulted-brick ceiling.

I edged forward, along a small passageway and through a pillared archway. The torchlight didn't hit on anything but blackness at first. Then I realized I had entered a large open space. I turned and followed the side on the wall with my fingers, directing the torch beam along the hewn stonework.

I was becoming increasingly disappointed. While large, it appeared to be no more than a storage cellar.

I was about to give up on any further exploration, when my hand felt something metallic. The torchlight confirmed it to be an ornate structure, housing an old beacon. I pulled up the old wooden handle and it came away quite easily. There was a cloth wick still in the top, surrounded by metal gauze. I placed the torch at my feet and drew out the matchbox. I lit the beacon. I coughed as a foul-smelling odour filled my nostrils. When this had subsided, I realized the beacon was producing a lot more light than the torch.

I swayed the beacon above my head. Now I could see I was in a large man-made cavern. A vaulted ceiling, supported by serried rows of pillars, ran for over a hundred feet. There were other beacon holders along both walls. There were also rusting iron chains and shackles mounted at regular intervals. On closer inspection, the shackles appeared to be dog collars.

As I stepped through the pillars, I was met by a pentagram within a circle on the floor tiles. I moved into the middle. Then my right foot gave way, and I keeled over. I felt my ankle throb with pain and clutched at it, writhing in agony. Once back to my senses, I realized I'd not done any lasting damage. I picked up the flaming beacon again. I'd fallen into a hole about two feet deep. It appeared to be in the centre of the floor pattern and was perfectly round. A closer inspection showed signs of burning inside. I looked upwards and could make out a tapering chimney in the ceiling.

I climbed to my feet again, testing the ankle and finding it could still take my weight. Then I crept further forward. Ten feet past the end of the pattern, I came across a raised stone dais. I thrust the beacon forward.

I began to make out a carving of exquisite quality on marble. I staggered back when glimpsing scenes of a sexual nature on this frieze. It formed one side of a plinth, some six foot by two. All the other sides were similarly carved. I expected the top to be smooth, but there was a deep impression in the marble. As I traced its outline, it was as if someone had lain flat on a lump of wet concrete to create an indentation of human form. But this effect had all been achieved by the skill of a stonemason.

I leant against the plinth and peered further into the gloom. The light cast by the beacon was ebbing away as the wick burnt down. I could see enough to safely negotiate the edge of the dais on the other side and walked slowly onwards.

Then I recoiled in fright!

There was a horned head staring at me from the far wall. It was like the centrepiece of the medallion and the gargoyle above the entrance to the ruined chapel. But this was a much larger carving, with a diameter of at least five feet.

I fell backwards on the floor, jarring my back. The torch exploded into pieces to my left and the beacon rolled off across the floor and was soon extinguished.

I was left in utter darkness. Scared. With only my thudding heartbeat for company.

Eventually, I recovered enough to feel around on the floor for the beacon. This took longer than envisaged. When I traced the outline of its handle, I picked it up and fiddled with the matchbox. Once I'd relit it, I braved another look at the horned head, stepping closer. The eyes had red-coloured glass in them. Traces of wax, which had dripped down over the cheeks, gave the impression the face was crying. It looked as if the lenses could be opened and candles placed inside to add to the effect.

Underneath the head, there was a sunken archway. Another flight of stairs led down from the dais to give access to this. I descended and found my way into another anteroom. The concave shape of the horned head was visible on this side. There were a number of stone plinths in niches along both sides of the walls. Ahead was another passageway.

I began to sense the beacon was coming to the end of its life. I needed to retrace my footsteps. As I was about to climb back up the stairs to the dais, I saw a torch beam arcing through the cavern.

It had to be Dylan! I was going to be discovered!

I hastily sat down, using my bottom to extinguish the flame. I felt the denim scorch and pulled the beacon away before it could burn my flesh. I heard it rattle off down the stairs.

I crouched in a state of mounting fear. The beam of light was getting closer, but there were no sounds of a human voice. Yet I was convinced he must have seen my own light source.

He was going to be angry. I didn't want to face his wrath. Nor another of his destructive moods.

I bum-slid down the stairs, then carefully stood. I felt around the floor, but could not find the beacon. The torch had been broken, so there was no sense in retrieving it. And the beam of light was getting closer still. Soon he would be upon me!

I stumbled forward, trying to use my outstretched arms to guide me through the archway. I must have achieved this, as my shin slammed into one of the plinths in the anteroom beyond. I fell to the floor, rubbing my leg furiously, cursing aloud.

I crawled on all fours, touching each plinth in turn and counting them as I went. There'd been six of them in all on each side. Beyond lay the narrower passageway. By extending my arms full length, I could feel the walls on both sides, so I knew I had negotiated my way into the only possible escape route.

I began to walk, then run along the lengthening corridor. I tripped and fell several times, due to slight rock falls from the ceiling or sides of the structure. The walls were getting slimier with moisture the further I travelled.

I was going deeper into the labyrinth. And I appeared to be descending.

I must have gone a couple of hundred feet before I had to stop. At least, it seemed that far. It may have been much more, or a lot less. I was getting more confused with every step.

I leant against the wall, gasping for breath, clutching at my chest. The air was stale and unventilated, which added to my discomfort.

Then I saw the flicker of light. He'd entered the passageway!

This was enough to spur me into action once more. I tried to quicken my pace. I stumbled, did a half somersault, then stood up again and continued. My knees and the palms of my hands had been grazed. One knee of my jeans had torn and I felt blood oozing down my leg.

I couldn't let that bother me. He'd soon be on top of me if I didn't hurry up!

But the passageway went on and on. Then it began to flatten out. I wanted to halt again. My lungs were at bursting point. My ankle was throbbing. But the light was approaching, beginning to illuminate the darkness behind me.

He was gaining on me!

I persevered without let up. Within another ten paces, I stumbled and fell, landing awkwardly. I shook off the fuzziness in my head. I was sprawled out against a flight of spiral stairs. I must have tripped on the first step.

I gathered myself together for one last effort. I crawled on all fours ever upward. On and on and on and on. Was there to be no end to my torture? I'd counted over fifty steps before I rammed into a solid wall. I crumpled against it.

I'd expected there to be a way out. But it was a dead end! I was trapped! Panic gripped me. I began to claw at the masonry. All reason gone.

A light flickered up from below. He was mounting the stairs himself now. Soon he'd catch me! All hell could break loose. I'd abused his trust.

I could sense the beginnings of hyperventilation. I sat back and tried to calm myself, clasping my hands around my mouth in a cup-shape and breathing deeply into it.

I could hear footsteps below. Getting closer.

Then I became aware of fresh air cooling my face. I had to be near the surface! I climbed to my feet once more and felt around the wall. High above my head, my outstretched arms were detecting the source of the air. My fingers passed through a small crack. I pulled down on this, but to no avail. I stood on tiptoe and ran my hands down from the crack.

I sensed I was slipping before I fell backwards. I thought I was going to career back down the stairs. And headfirst at that.

One hand became lodged in a metal structure embedded in the wall. I hung from this one arm. Crying out in pain. Feet dangling over the steps. I fought hard to recover my footing. As I did so, my hand gave way and I sank backwards onto the small landing. Or rather, the metal had moved, suddenly releasing my wrist from its bondage.

There was a tremendous sound of grating masonry, like rotating quernstones in a mill. Rock dust flew into the enclosed space. I looked up, rubbing my eyes, feeling the dust choking my lungs. A slab of masonry above me had fallen down into a concealed slot. Now a window of light was cascading through the open gap.

I pulled myself upwards and crawled through the opening. I collapsed on the other side. I lay on my back, looking up into the sky, breathing hard.

I had come out through the altar in the ruined chapel!

I staggered to my feet, aghast at the state of my clothing. My blouse was torn. My jeans had a hole in the knee, and the right buttock where the beacon had burnt. My trainers wouldn't see another wearing. My nails were all broken. My hair was filled with dust. I stood up as best I could and brushed myself down.

A head poked through the opening.

I collapsed to the ground once more. Overwrought.

'That was really cool, Auntie Freya. Can we do it all again!'

I turned to see E-J's grime-ridden smile framed in the altar.

She checked herself in response to my panic. 'You OK?'

'Yes. But you nearly gave me a heart attack!' I rose to a sitting position again.

She threw me the torch. It was the one I'd left by the trapdoor. Then she clambered out and pulled me to my feet. She looked nearly as dishevelled as I did.

'What's your mum going to say about the state of your lovely dress?'

'I'm more worried about going down there in the first place. She told me not to.'

'Is she down there, too?'

'No, she was too chicken.'

'We better get you back to the Lodge pretty quick. She must be going spare!' I took her by the hand.

'Please don't let Mummy spank me.'

'I'll do my best. But I can't promise.'

I led her away quickly, knowing her inquisitive mind would be riveted by the interior decoration of the chapel. Once outside, she tried to discuss the "naughty monsters", but I diverted her attention. It was clear she'd never been here before.

I was glad I knew the route back to the safety of the gardens. It would not have been at all clear which way to proceed if I'd come across this haunting place for the first time. E-J was too caught up in the adventure of it all, and what her mother's reaction might be, to be scared about the surroundings.

It took us a good fifteen minutes to return to the Lodge. We found Janis in the library. She was pacing up and down, clawing at her face and hair, tears streaming down her face. She had worked herself into a frenzy of worry. She was so lost from reality that it took her a while to register her daughter had safely returned.

E-J ran over to her, clutching her waist. 'It's OK, Mummy. I'm all right!'

'All right! All right!' Janis screamed. 'I was worried sick!' She looked at me with hatred. 'How could you leave that door open? She could've been hurt!'

'I'm sorry. I had no idea you were coming. I wasn't expecting you.'

But she'd turned her attention back to her daughter. She pulled her away. 'Go and bend over the arm of that chair.'

Horror swept across E-J's face. 'Oh, please Mummy. Don't hurt me.'

'Do as I say.'

She complied, reluctantly, bending herself over the leather chair I'd spent so many happy hours reclining in. Her unkempt, dust-ridden hair cascaded over the cushion.

E-J's pleading face looked in my direction, as her mother came up behind her.

'Now, look, Janis. I'm to blame for this. Please don't punish her.'

Janis pulled up E-J's dress and folded it over her back. 'You're right. You are to blame,' she said, pulling down her daughter's knickers. 'But I called and called. Didn't I, E-J?'

E-J didn't answer. Mounting dread passed across her face. She stared at me.

'Didn't I?'

'Yes, Mummy.'

'You should've listened.'

'Yes, Mummy.'

Before I knew what was happening, Janis delivered a blow onto her daughter's naked buttocks.

I flinched at the ferocious slap, as the sound reverberated around the room.

E-J carried on staring at me as she cried out in pain.

'Please, Janis!' I shouted.

'No, she must learn!' she shrieked, delivering a second blow. 'Now go to the car, you naughty little girl!'

E-J ran out of the room in floods of tears, tugging her knickers back into position as she went.

'That was completely uncalled for!'

Janis was sweating from her exertions. 'Please don't presume to tell me how to deal with my own daughter. If she'd come back when told, none of this would've happened.'

'But....'

'More to the point, if you hadn't interfered, none of this would've happened.'

'No, I'm sorry.'

She slouched into the chair. She began to rub her hands together. Her right palm was reddened by her actions.

Then she burst out crying herself. 'He promised me he'd concreted the passage up. You must've come back through the old chapel in the woods. Right?'

'Yes. Why didn't you go after her yourself?'

Janis stared right through me. Her fingers clenched the arms of the chair. Her nails became embedded in the leather, such was her grip. She began to shudder uncontrollably.

I came up beside her and put an arm on her shoulder. She shrugged me off.

'What d'you know about the cavern down there?' I asked.

'I can't go there. I *really* can't go there!'

'OK.'

'I only came over to see if you could look after E-J for the evening. My childminder's let me down and I've got an important night exercise with corporate clients. I wasn't expecting all this!' She rose and karate-kicked the secret door shut in a fury.

Then she ran out of the Lodge and was soon driving off.

I sat down in the leather chair, in pensive mood. I felt ashamed about E-J. And the terror of my escapade down in the cavern, and what I'd discovered, had caught up with me again.

Some time later, suitably recovered, but still chastened, I went upstairs for a long soak in the bath.

- XXI -

OVER THE NEXT two days, Dylan showed no sign of knowing about my discovery of the cavern. Naturally, I made no mention of it and it didn't seem Janis had disclosed to him, either. He had noticed the state of my fingernails and my knee, but had made no comment. He made few demands on me, in bed or around the house. I was left to my leisure, whilst he occupied his time with his writing. He'd give me broad reports of how many pages he'd completed at the end of the day, but gave no hint of the story line of his new work.

I lounged around, finishing the last of his novels. Taken as a whole, I was very impressed with his literary achievement to date. He was merely continuing in a long line of writers, from Wordsworth, Coleridge, Scott and Ruskin, through to Potter, Wainwright and Bragg, who had sought, and successfully found, their inspiration in the Lakeland landscape.

At midday on the third day, Dylan announced he was going down to the mill, to collect his Land Rover, which had now been repaired. Once Veronica had picked him up in a Vauxhall Cresta, I was left on my own at the Lodge for the first ever time during my stay.

I knew I had to take this opportunity to discover the secrets of the tower. I felt uncomfortable about invading my lover's privacy. Yet my own unravelling of Dylan's past – and the thought of what John would say if I failed to take this opportunity – gave me the impulse to find out more.

The connecting door on the landing was always routinely locked. But I could now enter through the secret door in the library. I made my way through this door and up the unlit steps to the landing I'd discovered on my previous visit. I mounted the wider staircase, coming to a half landing and a large oak door. It was unlocked, so I opened it and crossed the threshold. It turned out to be a bedchamber. A chandelier hung down from an ornately plastered ceiling. Paintings decorated the walls.

All looked very ordered. But something was wrong. It was simply too tidy. Or rather, unlived in.

Closer examination brought clues to solve the mystery. A whole array of cosmetics bottles and hair brushes lay on the bedside dressing table. They were well-known brand products, yet the labels and packaging were a generation old. I found an array of silken lingerie in the drawers and Sixties' teenage fashions hung inside the wardrobes.

Studying the pictures more closely, I recognized a certain style in the brushwork. Brooding landscapes of mountain, crag, tarn and forest.

Nothing here was Dylan's.

Everything was Seraphina's.

He had created a shrine to his dead wife.

It was as if she had never left. Or perhaps it was as if he was sure she'd return one day.

I sat down on the bed, swooning for a while, feeling a greater affinity for Seraphina, yet hemmed in by the room's oppression. Suddenly I could feel her pain. And for Dylan to have created such a place to honour her memory only reinforced my understanding of the way her loss had affected him.

After about half an hour of quiet, yet increasingly claustrophobic introspection, I left the room as I'd found it and proceeded to the next storey. I was met by another similar door.

I didn't know what to make of the room as I entered. Its dimensions were similar to those of the room below. The only piece of furniture was a square sofa in the centre of the room.

The walls were covered in photographs of women. All were in identical frames, which joined together in a mosaic of faces. All the walls had been covered with these pictures, and now the ceiling was in the process of being filled as well. Each photograph had the name of a woman, and a day, month and year below it in gilt lettering. I only understood this must correspond with the date of sexual conquest when I found my own face gazing down at me from above.

Each of the frames contained locks of the women's hair as a form of trophy. I placed my hand on my head and felt the tuft of my own hair which Dylan had surreptitiously cut. Now I understood. I struggled to contain my anger.

I calculated there must have been in the region of five hundred pictures on display.

All the women I'd met in association with Dylan appeared to be represented. A number of other faces were clearly recognizable, household names mostly from the music and entertainment world. One was of Lady Jennifer, the woman Rupert was now pursuing; she had long, chestnut hair and a horsey face. I was struck by the wide variety of women: their differing hair colours, shapes and sizes and levels of attractiveness.

I was flabbergasted. Surely no one could get through that many lovers in only seventeen years!

I'd come here to allay my deepest fears. But now I had the proof: there was indeed something ultimately sick about Dylan, behind his sadness and promiscuity.

His obsession didn't stop there, either. I had entered the chamber from the corner of the eastern wall. As I turned to face this wall, I discovered four built-in video screens, surrounded by more of the pictures. They were relaying and simultaneously recording all that went on in the bedrooms downstairs. It appeared Dylan had installed cameras behind all the mirrors.

Dylan was into voyeurism as well.

Cupboard doors behind the pictures revealed a photograph album and video library. I hunted through the albums. They contained pictures of his lovers in more revealing poses. I even discovered a file on me. I pulled it out and found a couple of shots of me, still asleep, in carefully posed naked display.

I shuddered.

I discarded the file and began a search through the lines of videos, all as neatly labelled and catalogued as the albums had been. Finally, I found one with a faded designation: *Seraphina 1970*.

I trembled as I placed it into one of the video recorders, then sat back on the sofa to watch it. It was an old film reel of deteriorating quality transferred onto the modern video format.

A cavern came onto the screen, after a flickering of blank frames had dissipated. It took me a while to realize it was the chamber under the Lodge. An altar, draped in a white, shroud-like sheet, was at one end of the dark chamber. A circle of naked women were dancing around it in a rabid frenzy. Their limbs cast shadows as they were hit by light emanating from flaming beacons on the walls. Discordant music was being played by several naked male musicians. All the figures were wearing bizarre masks.

A beautiful young girl lay naked on her back on top of the altar. Her open legs were draped over the sides; her long, raven hair fell over the end, almost to the floor.

A masked man stepped forward and began chanting in an indecipherable language. A long, black cape completely shrouded his body. His hands were clasped together in front of him to support an ancient book.

A young man stepped out of the shadows, wearing a goat headdress. Viewing his naked body told me he had to be a youth still in his teens. He strolled purposefully forward, his arms raised above his horns to herald the crowd of followers.

The music, the chanting and the dancing suddenly halted. The goat-man had ascended the steps beside the altar. He stood still. His head bowed to view the spread-eagled maiden from his high vantage. Then he descended on top of the young woman.

The young woman who must surely have been Seraphina!

Immediately, the frenzy of music and dancing recommenced, even more eerily than before. The cameraman focused in on the altar and appeared to be jostled by the dancers as the picture shuddered.

The young woman was crying out as the goat-man corrupted her. Finally, he collapsed onto her. The music ceased once again as the goat-man withdrew from her.

Two masked men came forward from either side of the altar. Each man carried a live chicken (one black and one white), gripped by the neck in their left hands, and a long, curved dagger in their right. I sat, incredulous, as I watched the men dismember the birds over the body of the defiled girl. The blood flowed, coating her breasts and stomach, gradually dripping over the side to soil the white cloth.

As these men departed, four others approached and lifted the girl over their heads. They marched off slowly down the sunken passageway, all the others following on behind.

The picture broke off, probably coming to the end of the original reel. There followed a few seconds of white fuzzy screen with a high-pitched hissing. Then new images materialized.

The crowd of worshippers had congregated inside the nave of the black chapel. Now its former magnificence could be seen. The interior was awash with colour, lit by flaming torches, which accentuated all the weird carvings. The windows, whilst beautifully designed, appeared to have such opaque glass that no reflexions were caught in any of them.

The cameraman framed a shot down the length of the nave. The young woman was now seated upon the black altar. The goat-man sat down next to her and the two of them embraced again. Then the old priest-like man stepped forward and began to dress the two of them in colourful robes and strange jewellery. The woman was given a medallion to wear – surely it had to be the same one I had found under the tree! – and a rod with a golden phallic tip.

She and the goat-man then walked hand-in-hand into the middle of the circle marked out on the floor tiles. Twelve women linked hands around the outer circle.

Men hovered behind. I counted about eighteen people in total, plus the cameraman and the priest-like figure. The goat-man gave the young girl a five-fold kiss: on the knees, genitals and breasts.

The picture started to deteriorate again as the dancers descended to the floor and began an orgy of sexual coupling with each other. The cameraman took an obsessive fascination in these indiscriminate encounters, focusing in on each one in turn. There was certainly a highly charged sexual power which began to stir me. Enhanced, perhaps, by the anonymity of the worshippers, all still hidden behind masks of various primeval animals.

As my interest was deepening further, the picture was lost completely. There were a few more flickering blank frames before the hiss of the modern video tape took over.

So the rumours of devil worship had been correct all along, as I'd gradually come to suppose. Yet even I found it hard to digest that this had extended into Seraphina's generation.

I was left there, staring at the screen, curling up into an upright ball, arms clutching bent knees, trying to take in the import of what I had seen.

I wondered what else could be in store when I ascended to the last storey. The top of the tower was Dylan's retreat, where he came to write and reflect. He'd always told me this; now, at least in this regard, he'd been telling the truth. The room was like the lower bedroom: a perfect square, pure white in decoration. There was an arched window in the middle of all but one of the walls. A custom-made desk encircled the walls beneath these windows, breaking off only for the stairwell leading to the turreted battlements above. Office equipment covered the work surfaces.

My attention was swiftly drawn to the fireplace in the wall without a window. Above the mantelpiece there hung the painting of a beautiful woman. I was in no doubt it had to be the self-portrait Veronica had told me about. It had a maturity beyond the age of the artist.

It was the work of Seraphina, like the pictures downstairs.

Gazing up at the imposing face of the long-haired beauty, I could see why Dylan could have become so captivated by her. And how the memory of her could still haunt him as vividly as the image of this picture fascinated me.

Now I was convinced beyond all doubt that Seraphina had been the young woman in the film.

I paced around the room, noticing how her eyes followed me no matter where I stood. A technique not quite as perfected as in the later portrait of her father. Still, I found it very difficult to break its hypnotic allure.

Eventually, I pulled myself away and climbed up to the battlements above. These were a lot larger, more intricate and higher off the ground than those of the outer gatehouse. The view from here was spectacular. Skiddaw and the Northern massif rose above the green of the forest. I spent ten minutes soaking up this vista, allowing the strong wind to blow back my hair and bite into my face.

I retreated only when I spied Paul Norton sauntering across the lawn. I ducked my head below the parapet, but he didn't look up. Dylan must have let him in through the gates, I supposed, on his own way out.

I was sure he hadn't seen me.

I returned inside and began a more detailed survey of Dylan's workroom. I rifled through the piles of ordered papers on his desk, then through the drawers beneath. I found nothing of any import to my continuing investigation. But I did pick up a few pages of his novel-in-progress.

There was a large, ornately carved chair next to the chimney breast. I walked over to take a seat, so I could study the pages in more comfort. As I approached, I could make out the head of a goat on the central back of the chair. It was similar to the stone carvings over the door of the ruined chapel and above the altar in the cavern. And the medallion and the headdress of the youth on the film.

I sat down. Before I knew what was happening, circular bars had shot out from the arms and the legs of the chair to trap my wrists and ankles firmly in place. I must have set off a mechanism as soon as my bottom had touched the seat.

I went into an unthinkable panic!

I dropped the papers on the floor. I fought to free myself from the chair's clutches. But it was a bulky piece of furniture, made from solid oak. No matter how hard I struggled, the chair itself wouldn't move and the clasps remained rigidly in place.

I cried out, struggling more forcefully. Getting more desperate. My wrists began to chafe, but still I did not desist.

I must have spent over an hour in this fashion, until exhaustion set in.

I leant back in the chair, gazing up at the antique clock on the wall as the hours ticked by. I was consumed with terror. Wracked with guilt. Too much so to fall asleep, even though my body was aching for rest.

I thought I heard a vehicle drawing up in the courtyard below. Then I heard footsteps upon the stairs. Gradually drawing nearer.

I was paralysed with fear.

Dylan's form became framed in the doorway. His countenance went from complete shock, to disgust, then fury.

'Shame on you!'

I bowed my head. I could feel the force of his stare upon me.

Then he was gone.

I looked up. Then I screamed and struggled again.

But he left me there to suffer.

- XXII -

DYLAN REMAINED AWAY for the next two hours, extending my torture and delaying our confrontation. I could make out a lot of commotion downstairs, as he vented his feelings. However, he returned to me in a calm state. He strolled into the room, pulling his swivel chair from underneath his desk, and straddling it back-to-front so he could prop his arms against the backrest. He did all this without any reference to me.

'So, tell me: why have you invaded my private space? I've been very hospitable to you. My only condition was for this tower to remain sacred to me. And you abused that.'

'I'm sorry. There's no excuse. What must you think of me?'

He did not reply, despite my contrition. But his face conveyed the whole story.

'Look, please let me go, I'm bursting for the loo.'

'Should've thought about that before. No, you can stay here till I'm satisfied with your explanation.'

I grimaced. The way the chair had secured me meant there was no way of crossing my legs.

'I came up here to find out more about you.'

Dylan's vexation returned. 'No one's allowed up here.'

'I needed to find out why you were so promiscuous.'

'Why? Can't you just accept I'm a bit of a lady's man?'

'No. When you went with other women you tore me apart. I was falling hopelessly for you.' I tried to make this sound convincing. 'I think few stay long enough to realize something's wrong. Now I've seen the rooms downstairs, I know for certain there is.'

'What rooms?'

'The shrine you've created for Seraphina. And the trophy room.'

'How dare you!'

'You're an obsessive. A voyeur....' I struggled to remember an appropriate term from all those library texts: 'a compulsive satyr!'

Dylan swayed around on the chair from left to right, keeping his eyes fixed firmly on the floor. 'I've never denied my sexual compulsion. No doubt you're gonna come up with some half-cocked explanation for my deviousness.'

'Well, there's no doubt Seraphina's suicide holds the key.'

Dylan stared blankly at me. He couldn't speak.

'I don't believe you've come to terms with the manner of her death. Nor her death itself. Judging by your false cover stories, the room downstairs and her untended grave.'

'You've seen her grave, too?'

'Yes.'

'No one goes there! It's out of bounds!'

'Emily showed me it before she left. And Janis goes there as well. In secret.'

'Damn them!'

'Then, of course, there's your pursuit of Janis and Emily, the sisters so close in looks to Seraphina.'

Dylan shrugged his shoulders as if conceding this point. But it was clear he was becoming increasingly anxious, as I bombarded him with facts he had no inkling I'd discovered before now.

'Then, of course, there's Sir Frederick and the Satanists.'

'How could you know about that?'

'The medallion I found started it off. Then discovering the ruined chapel.'

'I'd've destroyed that place completely, but for the bat people slapping a preservation order on it at the last minute.'

'Then there were the old legends; books in the library – censored by you, no doubt; the cavern under this house; the old painting in the folly.'

'Christ, you have been busy.'

'And now the film in your trophy room.'

'Film?'

'Yes. The one of the satanic ceremony with Seraphina and the goat-man.'

'Goat-man?'

'Don't feign innocence. The goat-man was you, wasn't it?'

Dylan rose and kicked the swivel chair out of his way. He paced the room, distraught, as if suddenly taken back to the event in question. His anger welled and he left the room.

When he returned, he was wearing the goat-mask and came marching towards me.

I let out a yelp when I thought he was about to attack me. My worst fears were being confirmed. I closed my eyes. I felt the thud as his fist hit into the wall above my head.

He staggered backwards, clutching his bloodied knuckles. Then he sat down in an armchair in the alcove near the stairs to the battlements.

'You really think I'm an evil Satanist?....Intent on causing you harm now you know my secrets?'

I nodded, horrified, as plaster dust floated down onto my hair and face from the hole he'd punched in the wall.

He tore off the mask and threw it over his shoulder. It sailed out of the window and thudded onto the roof below. He was laughing. 'You've got me all wrong.'

'Really?'

'Yes. Faversham was the evil Satanist, not me, you idiot!' He was still laughing.

'I see....Will you let me go now?' I was feeling a stabbing pain, as my bladder was close to bursting point.

'No.'

I let out a deep breath in disgust. 'Then why don't you tell me the whole story. You can't keep it all bottled up inside forever.'

Dylan remained silent for a while. Presently, he said: 'OK, you're right. I was the goat-man. The Satanists did exist. I was compelled into that ceremony – the one you saw in the film – against my will. I only did it because Sera wanted me to. I was in love with her. She and Faversham said we were predestined for great things. I went along with it, but despite all his teachings, I never believed in all that junk.'

'No?'

'No. It never stood up to any serious scrutiny. Any more than all that Christian mumbo jumbo my mother forced onto me did. I fundamentally do not believe in the idea of blind faith. Their faith allowed them to create a powerful force with a perverse sense of morality, which I could never share in.'

I nodded, feeling relieved.

'Faversham's blind faith convinced him he was the agent of the Devil. The Circle also had a long history, dating back way before the old Baron. So this was no sudden impulse on Faversham's part. That history gave him a great stature which indoctrinated his followers. And his powerful charisma inspired a deep loyalty and devotion.

'Faversham had a wealth of esoteric knowledge at his disposal, passed down through the generations. I have to say, I've acquired some of this power....For example, I'm an expert mesmerist.'

'Really?'

'Yes. He taught me from a young age. It's helped me to seduce women. It also aided me in persuading an eminent publisher to purchase the rights to my first novel. But it doesn't always work. I never totally mastered the art, not like Faversham, at any rate. I've rejected all the rest of his teachings. I'm not a fundamentally evil person like him, you know.'

'No....Now I don't believe you are.'

'Veronica and my mum'd been part of the Circle for years. Sera and I'd been unwittingly born into it.'

'What about the other children?'

'Well, I never got the chance to speak to Eric about it. Janis has always denied she knew anything beyond the old legends and playing in the ruins as a child. I always thought she knew more than she's let on. But she's very fragile and I've never tried to force her. Anyway, I've been trying to forget it all myself. It's not a subject we've broached often.'

'I see.' I made a mental note to seek out Janis for further questioning later on.

'Sera may've had more idea than me of her father's ultimate purpose. I would never've gone through with it if Sera hadn't insisted. I'd've done anything for her. We were madly in love.'

'I never thought anything different, Dylan.'

'Her father was the real influence in her life. As she was in mine. She found it very difficult to disobey him. But we knew he hadn't long to live. We planned to marry once he'd died.'

'But Janis's told me that's not what actually happened.'

'No. Something about the ceremony and its aftermath deeply disturbed Sera. We ran away to the North Wales coast and were formally married there. She wanted to negate the black rituals we'd taken part in by having a white, Christian wedding.'

'I can see the logic in that.'

'Those brief three months together, away from our families for the first time, was the greatest period of my life. And hers, I hope. But dossing in a beach hut, and making love whenever we felt like it, couldn't possibly last....But then we read Faversham's obituary. It had been in the paper used to wrap up my portion of chips. One of those curious occurrences, that. Faversham was now out of our lives for good and I felt obliged to return. Sera wanted to embark on a simple, anonymous life in London, away from all pressures, so was very reluctant. I should've listened to her, because my decision turned out to be the worst mistake we could've made.'

'Because Seraphina committed suicide very shortly after you came back.'

'Yes.' He paused. 'She went into a deep depression. Must've hidden that medallion you found around that time. She was also working manically on the painting in the folly.'

'A fantastic piece of artwork. She far exceeded her other works with this masterpiece.'

'Agreed....Didn't do her much good, though, did it?'

I shrugged my shoulders.

'Once completed, she went and threw herself off a cliff.'

'And you've felt responsible for her death ever since.'

'Of course! I could've ensured we escaped Faversham's clutches long before the black ceremony actually took place.'

'Why d'you think she killed herself? Did she leave a note?'

'No. I've never understood. She had so much going for her. We should've been so happy. She had such talent. But she also had a delicate constitution. She was prone to bouts of depression and she could get wound up in a tight coil over even the most trivial of things. Her folly painting shows how much anguish she must have been under. Feeling the Devil's curse upon her must've tipped the balance.'

I found it hard to digest. Dylan was talking very matter-of-factly, divorced of all feeling and emotion. Yet I was completely filled up with grief. Maybe even on his behalf?

'What happened after her death?'

'The funeral was awful. I kept staring at the congregation, wondering how many of them could've been part of the Circle. Veronica insisted we buried her in the chapel. I hated the idea, and only managed to force a compromise at the last minute.'

'Burying her outside its walls, you mean.'

'Yes.' He seemed annoyed by my interruption. 'I spent months in grief. I was desperate to join her. Only Janis's love saved me from a similar fate.

'Then I started being cajoled by Veronica into taking on Faversham's mantle. You see, I became the Master after his death. Janis helped me out of my conflicting loyalties and confusion. I used my new position to disband the Circle permanently. I severed all connexions with those evil people. They'd all remained sinister and anonymous to me. I had to get Veronica and my mother to convey the news to the other followers. Veronica was devastated. She carried on cajoling me to change my mind. All that succeeded in doing was pushing me away from her. I hardly spoke to her for months after that.'

'How did the two of you make up, then?'

'Well, deep down I'm a compassionate man. It took ten years, though. We had to get over the hurdle of her selling this place, too. And then me buying the place back and systematically dismantling the chapel and disinterring Faversham. She fell on hard times, so when I bought the mill I installed her as manager. I find it difficult to trust people, so I tend to employ those I've known for a while.'

'And your mother?'

'She was very proud of my actions. But I'm sure Faversham put a curse on her, for she was never the same after that.'

'Maybe she bore the guilt of destroying Seraphina and nearly destroying you?'

'I'm certain she did. She spent years begging for my forgiveness, but we never regained our former closeness. She died shortly before my first novel was published.'

'And Veronica?'

'I'm sure she felt guilty, too; though she's loath to show it.'

'Can you let me go now?'

'It's a useful contraption, isn't it? Built by the old Baron. The chair – apart from the headdress – is the only thing I still keep relating to the Satanists.'

'Look, I'm bursting.' I bobbed up and down with increasing agitation.

'But I thought you wanted to learn everything. I've kept the chair up here precisely to ensnare anyone who dared invade my space. Never thought it'd work so well. In fact, come to think of it, *I never thought it'd ever be used*!'

'Please! Please! You've made your point! Now let me go before I piss myself!'

He came and leaned over me, kissing me once. I was expecting him to release me, but he tucked my hair around my left ear and whispered into it: 'I'm not going to just yet. Let it be your punishment!'

He stepped back a few paces and calmly watched my discomfort.

He didn't take his eyes off me as I wriggled and struggled, grimaced and moaned, for the next five minutes.

When I knew I was defeated, I sank back and stopped all resistance.

'You bastard!' I cried, as I felt the urine filling my knickers.

- XXIII -

WHEN DYLAN RELEASED me, I rushed down to my bedroom. I grabbed the rucksack of clothes from the wardrobe, then continued down the main staircase and out into the courtyard. I made my way over to the old stables and the Austin-Healey.

'That's it, run away!' Dylan screamed from the tower battlements.

I checked myself and looked up. 'You're right. That would be too easy for you, wouldn't it?'

He was too high up for me to gauge his reaction. His form disappeared from view.

I hastened back inside, retrieving a set of keys from the hallway hooks. Then I ran over to the inner gatehouse. I fled up the spiral steps and opened up Yasuko's old quarters. I drew the three strong bolts across the door and hurried to the window.

Dylan had come down into the courtyard. He glimpsed me as I opened the window. 'What're you doing up there?'

'Well, you didn't expect me to stay with you in the main house, did you? Not after what you've just done!'

He cast his eyes to the ground and thrust his hands into his pockets, looking dejected. He kicked out at a loose stone on the cobbles.

I moved over to the wall and pulled out a handful of sado-masochistic gear from the cabinet. Then I cast them out of the window. The whips and canes scattered across the ground in front of him.

'And I won't be needing these. In case you had any ideas!'

Dylan frantically picked up the instruments of Yasuko's torture. He seemed very confused that I knew. He cursed when he discovered one or two of the canes had been damaged. He shouted a few expletives and waved his fists at me. Then he returned inside. He seemed more intent on safely storing these items, than being concerned for me. A case in point, I thought.

I set about a detailed survey of the quarters, making sure there was no other way in. Unfortunately, an arched glass door gave access to a walkway along the top of the inner wall, leading off, with a parapet either side, to a smaller turret fifty feet away. I opened the door and walked across. The door in the turret was unlocked.

I headed down the narrow spiral steps and found myself coming out into a walled garden. This was awash with brilliant colours of roses set against a verdant background of vegetables. There was even a small orchard of fruit trees in one corner and a dovecote.

I stood perplexed in wonderment at this secret haven. I hadn't been shown this on my grand tour and it had been invisible from my bedroom window. It looked to be a treasured private retreat.

Then I remembered what I needed to do. I hunted around the walls for any further sign of entrances. After a speedy search, I found one half camouflaged by rampant honeysuckle. Sure enough, it was open. I shut it and drew across the two bolts.

I relaxed. Now I could discard my soiled clothing and freshen up.

As I remounted the stairs inside the turret, I heard a sudden banging. I stopped, stunned, catching my breath. I peeped through an arrow slit and saw Dylan down below, kicking at the door I'd secured, in his frustration and anger. He must have seen my mad dash along the battlements, for he called out to me. I paid him no attention, not registering what he had said.

Once back inside, I stripped naked, piling the stinking clothes into the washing machine in the kitchenette. Then I tried to run myself a bath. But the water was cold. I searched for the immersion switch and turned it on. I was left for an hour, huddled on the side of the tub, waiting for the water to heat up.

This gave me time for my thoughts and for my anxieties to increase. This, in turn, blanked the past from my mind, until I couldn't remember anything about my life before coming here.

I went into a complete panic. My whole body was gripped by violent spasms.

I steadied myself with the idea I was in too much shock over recent events. I relaxed only after immersing myself in warm bathwater. I found some bubble bath Yasuko had left behind, and its fragrance, and the caressing of the bubbles soothed me further. I stayed there until the bathwater went cold around me and goose pimples began to appear on my arms and breasts.

Later, as I was dressing in new clothes from my rucksack, I found Yasuko had left her kimonos on her bed. They had been ripped to pieces with a knife or a pair of scissors. There were seven of them, all different in colour; only now did I realize there was one for each day of the week. I discarded the garments in the wardrobe.

Then I cooked myself a meal from the assortment of tins in the kitchen cupboard.

I telephoned Janis, conveying what had happened and some of my distress. I wanted her to come straight over. But she told me I'd have to come to her rock-climbing school as she was too busy with clients. And that it was better to wait until morning. I hadn't even realized how late it had become until I gazed through the window and saw night was beginning to fall.

She seemed upset I was bothering her. Yet she did give me detailed directions of how to find her.

Once the phone call was over, I decided to climb up to the gatehouse battlements. The walled garden was clearly in view, with the outer grounds fading away into the enveloping darkness. The courtyard was a long way down from here.

I looked across to the main house. I was at about the same height as the top of the Lodge's roof-line. The central tower swept another three storeys above me. I noticed only the lights in his workroom were on.

The atmosphere felt very close and humid. Sweat began to build under my T-shirt. Dylan had told me convection currents were the predominant meteorological feature in August in these parts. Another thunderstorm was on its way.

I stayed up on my lofty belvedere as the first few spots of rain fell on my head and arms.

Suddenly, lightning filled the sky and a rumble of thunder soon followed. It was forked lightning. Like giant fireworks illuminating the night sky.

I glanced up and saw Dylan was standing motionless on the tower battlements. He was looking in my direction.

It was too far away to make out his expression, but I was certain he was staring at me.

Then the rains came. My instinct was to retreat indoors immediately. I didn't want to be drenched. Nor set myself up as a lightning conductor.

But Dylan remained motionless. Still looking down on me.

I became transfixed by him. Despite my clothes and hair rapidly matting against my skin in the downpour.

I couldn't say how long I remained there. Shivering. Even when I finally withdrew, Dylan remained in position. Hours later, I was sure he was still up there in the heat of the storm, as I gazed upwards from the living-room windows.

I had a very unsettled sleep. When lying awake, I wondered whether Dylan would burst in on me at any moment. When asleep, I re-experienced the episode in the tower in a dream, even down to wetting the bed in memory of that gruesome chair.

I felt very ashamed. I had not done this since earliest childhood. A fleeting memory of that time had come back, at last. I cursed John for sending me here: I had reached my lowest ebb since my arrival at Grimshaw Lodge.

I looked at the clock: it read four. I'd wanted to get up early to avoid Dylan, but not quite this early. I stripped the bed, had another bath, then discarded the saturated sheets in the tub. Then I left.

The night air was cool and refreshing. The front door was locked, so I had to clamber through the lounge window in order to activate the portcullis mechanism from the hallway.

Once back outside, I crept over to the stables and opened the door, trying to be as quiet as I could. I climbed into the Austin-Healey and let off the handbrake. With effort, I managed to start a forward motion with my leg, hanging out of the door. This brought the car into the courtyard. The cobbles were gently cambered towards the inner gatehouse, so the weight of the car was enough to send me down towards it. I guessed at the direction I should steer through the archway, as I daren't put on the headlights. Once I'd negotiated the opening, the drive sloped down and I began to gather speed.

I came to a standstill where the road flattened out at the bridge. I climbed out and looked back towards the Lodge. I listened carefully. No sound came out from the lightening darkness.

I sat back inside, started the engine, put on the headlights and accelerated as fast as I could towards the outer gatehouse. For a moment, my confidence grew as I approached. Then the portcullis began to descend. I applied the brakes and skidded to a halt only a few feet from the spikes.

I crumpled against the steering wheel. There was nothing I could do but head back up the driveway. I walked slowly back, resigned to the likely conflagration I would have with Dylan when I returned.

But Dylan was nowhere to be found in the inner courtyard. I went back inside Yasuko's quarters and headed straight for the phone. After I'd dialled, I could hear a faint ringing from across the courtyard. It was coming from the tower room! I slammed the phone down, realizing I must have inadvertently dialled up the internal system. I fiddled with the phone and redialled, pacing up and down in front of the window.

The line connected. I heard John grumbling and shifting about. 'Who's there? This better be good. Do you know what time it is?'

'It's Freya.'

'Oh.' I could make out bedsprings creaking as he shifted in bed.

I did not give him a chance to wake up fully before I had launched myself into a tirade over what Dylan had done to me with his ghastly chair.

'Calm down. Calm down.'

'No, I won't calm down. You never said I might be exposing myself to danger when I took on this mission!'

'Well, I wasn't to know. Tell me what he told you. He was a Satanist himself?'

I recounted everything Dylan had said.

'He helped to destroy my Seraphina....'

'Why didn't you tell me you were once Sera's boyfriend?'

'I wanted you to keep an open mind....Stay impartial....Dylan's stolen her memory away from me. Just like he stole a lot of my ideas.'

'Eh?'

'Well. I wanted to be a writer, too, once. Sera was fascinated by this. That's why Dylan took it up, I reckon. He got all the glory. And I was left with nothing! Find me the rest of the answers and you will be handsomely rewarded.'

The phone went dead and I collapsed into a chair, exhausted.

I was aroused from sleep by a knock at the door. I was startled, trying to take in my strange surroundings. Morning light streamed in through the window. I consulted my watch. It was nearly half-past nine. I shifted in the chair, finding difficulty in rising to my feet. I stretched my back in response to the pain of being in an unaccustomed position for so long.

I reached the door and opened it before I realized what I was doing. I slumped back in the chair as Dylan entered the room.

'Hi Freya, how are you?' He appeared cheerful and calm.

I didn't respond.

He sat down on the sofa opposite me. 'I thought it best to prevent you from leaving last night. I was worried for your safety.'

'Is that all?'

'No. If you're going to leave, it would be nice to have a proper goodbye.'

'I wasn't trying to leave, you fool. I was going to Janis's.'

'Oh.' He was taken by surprise. He came over and sat on the arm of my chair. He began to stroke my hair. He felt me tense up and immediately stopped.

'Look,' he said, getting to his feet again. 'I'm sorry about what happened yesterday, truly I am. I was so shocked to discover you in the tower. And for you to subject me to such a barrage of questions. And to find out you knew so much.'

'You need help, Dylan. You really do.'

'No, I'll be fine.'

His response didn't augur well.

'Look, I need some space to gather my thoughts. If I

do decide to leave, I will tell you. And I will say a proper farewell. Your recent behaviour doesn't negate your hospitality up till then. Nor the very genuine feelings I've had for you.'

He detected my use of the past tense, and looked perturbed. He wandered around the lounge.

Then our eyes locked and we spent a few seconds duelling across the room with each other.

He came towards me again.

I averted my eyes, breaking his mesmeric stare, just as he was about to lay his hand on me.

'Look, I must go. I'll be back tonight, or tomorrow at the latest.'

I stroked his cheek and felt him kiss my hand. But I didn't let our gazes meet.

Instead, I scrambled out of the door and down the steps. I began my walk down the driveway, back to the Austin-Healey at the outer gatehouse. By the time I reached the car, the portcullis was in its opened position.

I motored through the gates as quickly as I could.

- XXIV -

I HAD NEVER had a great aptitude for navigation, so I struggled to follow Janis's directions to Branthwaite Farm, where her rock-climbing school was based. I travelled out on twisting roads to the very western margin of the mountains. I first became confused around similarly named hamlets, then over the small deciduous woodland which masked the farm from the road. I passed the gateway several times over a twenty minute period, until finally seeing the white hoarding advertising the school and its courses.

I drove down the dirt road, finding a space in the small car park under the trees. Then I meandered up a track between dilapidated outbuildings. The cries of climbers shouting 'That's me!' and 'Climb when ready!' echoed around the confined spaces.

As I entered a cobbled courtyard, the vista spread out over an open field. Two artificial climbing towers were located there, scaffold-and-board structures of around a hundred feet in height. Clients were grouped around the bottom of each one, dressed in readiness for their turn. Instructors on the top platforms were guiding climbers up two of the four faces on each of the towers.

I walked towards them, all the time being reminded of the fearful abseiling off the bridge at the Lodge.

'Stand back, lady!' An instructor had stepped forward, barking the order. He was making a stop sign with his outstretched arm and hand and didn't look amused. 'No one past the gates without a helmet! Can't you read!'

I backed off, suddenly realizing I was abusing the safety code. I went back through the gate, finding the sign I'd not seen on entry in my absent-mindedness. Then I strolled through the courtyard towards the ancient farmhouse, with its rare galleried first floor. There were barns on either side, their doors wedged open to air the interiors, revealing their conversion into dormitories and equipment stores.

I could hear a vacuum cleaner droning out from within, and the wafting smells of food. I felt my stomach groan. It took a while for the young girl hoovering to respond to my knock upon the door. She was in her late teens, with a brown bob secured with a headband. She tried to put on a carefully coached customer-service smile, but it was clear she had not wanted to be disturbed.

I read the name tag on her crop top. 'Hi, Tara. I've come to see Janis.'

'The gov'nor's up at the quarry back yonder,' she motioned over her shoulder. 'She won't be free till lunch.' She looked at her wristwatch. 'At least another two hours.' She held her ground as if hoping this would be enough to send me on my way.

'May I come in and wait? She is expecting me.'

'You're not the new laundry maid, are you?' She had loosened up a little.

'No.'

She hardened again. 'Well, it's really not convenient. I've got the whole ground floor to clean. Then I've got to re-make the beds upstairs. The present guests are leaving this afternoon. It's changeover day.'

When she saw I wasn't going anywhere, she eventually invited me through the building and out onto the terrace at the rear.

I sat down at a picnic table and asked for a drink.

Tara humphed, putting her hands on her hips.

'I'm sorry, I'll make it myself, if you show me where to go.'

She frowned.

'Look, I've come down from the Lodge and I'm feeling rather scorched!'

'Lodge?....Grimshaw Lodge?'

'Why, yes.'

'Well, you should've said so in the first place.' Her whole outlook changed in an instant. 'You'd better come this way.'

She guided me around the side of the building and into a walled garden. One of the converted barns lay to the right, and a lawn sloped down to mature trees and a stream. She led me down towards this, offering me a seat in a wooden summerhouse.

'There's a mini-fridge in the corner. There's iced tea, lemonade or cola in there. Help yourself.'

'You know the Lodge, then?'

'Yes. And that lecherous old bugger Dylan as well. E-J's always ranting and raving about the place, but I never go up there.'

'Why not?'

She gave me a wry grin. 'He flirts with me whenever he comes down here. He's very brash and arrogant. In truth, he disturbs me.'

I kept quiet and tried to avoid eye contact. My reaction made it clear to her I must have been Dylan's latest conquest.

'Make yourself at home. Sorry you'll have to wait, but I believe Janis assumed you were coming after lunch.'

I tried to recall what she'd said on the phone. But I'd been too overwrought at the time to remember now.

Tara began to walk off up the slope. Then she stopped and turned around. 'I take it you know E-J?'

'Yes.'

'Well, if you see her, tell her I'm looking for her. She's been very naughty. I'll be telling Janis if she doesn't come back and apologize to me soon.'

'OK. I'll tell you if she returns.'

I watched her depart through the gate in the low wall, then helped myself to a drink.

'Hello, Auntie Freya. Has she gone?'

The sudden call made me jump and I jerked up in my chair.

E-J giggled.

I looked up to find her wide-brown eyes and freckled face beaming down at me through the window of a tree house in the boughs of a sycamore. Her long, dark-brown hair, as unkempt as ever, dangled down below the sill.

'Hi yea! What're you doing up there?'

'Hiding. Tara's going to tell Mummy. Then Mummy will spank me again.'

'What have you done this time?'

'I threw water bombs at some of the guests from the roof.'

'Oh, that's naughty!' But I couldn't keep a straight face for long. Soon I was consumed with mirth and I'd condoned her poor behaviour once again.

E-J disappeared from the window. In a moment she was climbing down a ladder on the other side of the trunk.

'Careful!' I said, yet knowing she'd be fine. She was such a tomboy.

I furnished her with a drink and she sat down beside me. She guzzled it down and I poured her another. We sat there for some time, talking about all the adventures she'd been up to since we'd last met.

'I know,' she said. 'Let's go for a walk. I'll show you a good place to watch Mummy from.'

'Hadn't I better wait here, like Tara said?'

'Forget Tara. She's a pussycat. I can wind her round my little finger.'

I thought for a moment, then came to the conclusion she probably could. And me as well!

E-J helped me to jump over the little stream and we headed up the field outside the farm's boundary. Then we nipped back through a gap in the dry-stone wall and were lost in a small copse. Her route had obviously been planned to avoid being overseen from the main house.

'E-J!' I puffed as I was struggling to keep up with her. 'You sure we should be doing this?'

''Course not, Auntie Freya. But I'm going to get a spanking anyway, so I might as well enjoy myself till then.'

I chuckled. Some of my own youthful rebelliousness towards my parents was being remembered as we climbed the steepening bank.

Being with E-J also brought out the mothering instinct in me. When I thought this, I was harrowingly brought back to that grim day: lying flat on my back upon a cold hospital operating table, naked legs bound high in stirrups, having my own baby sucked out of me. I stopped and leant against the nearest tree trunk in anguish. Tears welled up and began a slow and guilty descent down my cheeks.

'Come on, Auntie Freya. Faster! Faster! You're nearly as bad as Auntie Amy was. And Auntie Sheila. And Auntie Beth. And Auntie Monique. And Auntie Charlotte. And Auntie Christabel. And Auntie....' She carried on reciting this list of names, with a speed that soon blurred all her words together.

She was some distance ahead now. All I could see were her naked legs below her cutoffs. I hurried after her. The list of names she had reeled off had reinforced Dylan's promiscuity once again. And that I might be as ephemeral in E-J's life as the rest had been. I couldn't help thinking I should have had the foresight and courage to have resisted him, like Tara was doing.

I caught up with E-J at the top of the hill. I regarded the sudden edge and the gaping chasm of the old quarry below with fear. E-J was swinging around on a tree trunk, her outstretched legs hovering over the mighty drop.

I hurled myself towards her and clutched us together tightly against the tree. Then I pulled her away by the hand. We settled down on the grass some way back, but still with a good view of the crater.

'You must be more careful, E-J! One slip and you'd've been over that edge. And I'd never've been able to forgive myself.'

E-J laughed at my sense of melodrama. She didn't seem to have a concept of danger and I was becoming increasingly nervous. But she calmed down and did what she was told, alive to my mood.

'There's Mummy on the crag now.'

There was a group of three men at the foot of the far wall. Some way up the hundred-and-fifty-foot face was a slight figure, moving with cat-like stealth up the rock.

Every now and then, she'd hang off and shout down instructions for certain moves to the men below. Then she'd fiddle with pieces of gear on her harness.

'What's she doing now?' I asked.

'She's putting chocks or friends into the cracks. They come in various shapes and sizes. She'll select the right one. Once in place she'll first check it's stable....yes, look she's doing that now....then she'll put the rope through the karabiner on the end.'

'Why's she need to do that?'

'Well, silly, she's lead climbing. There's no top rope, so she's being belayed from below. If she falls off, the pieces of gear she places in the rock are the only things that'll protect her.'

'What? You'll not see me trust my life to such little bits of metal!'

'The only thing that could go wrong is incorrectly placing them in the cracks. And Mummy knows what she's doing.'

I could see that. Her movements were precise and systematic. She always kept three of the four points of contact with the rock. Every now and then she'd scoop a handful of chalk dust from a little bag on her harness to improve the grip.

E-J's expert commentary filled in all the technical details for me. This enhanced my view of how she'd been steeped in climbing from early childhood. And its pseudo-adult delivery was typical of the precocity of an only child.

Janis was securing herself to a ledge a third of the way up the face. E-J explained she was setting up a belay to bring up the other climbers one at a time on a top rope. 'Watch how the next climber'll take out all the gear on the way up. Then he'll possibly take over the lead for the next pitch. They're on *Trembling Fingers* at the moment.'

'Eh?'

'*Trembling Fingers* – it's the name of the climb. All of them have names. The first pitch was E1, but the later ones are HVS and VS.'

'Sorry, you've lost me again.'

'The later ones aren't as hard. See that great crack above Mummy's head?' She waited for me to acknowledge. 'Well, that's where the route goes next. They'll have to wedge themselves inside it.'

The wealth of detail and the speed of delivery were beginning to give me a headache. Still, we watched as each climber took turns to rise to Janis's level. The second of the three crept upwards with mounting uncertainty.

There was something quite absorbing about watching their ascent. I began to see the fascination the sport held for its exponents, without ever wishing to take part myself. A couple of hours passed before the final climber was nearing the top of the cliff, after four pitches.

'Come on, we better get going.'

I looked at E-J's worried expression. 'Why?'

''Cause Mummy 'n' the men will be passing this point soon and I don't want her to catch me up here.' She was pointing to a dirt trod weaving through the stunted trees around the top of the jagged edge.

I needed no further encouragement to descend rapidly, after remembering Janis's response to the cavern escapade.

Janis found us in the summerhouse. We had played hide-and-seek for an hour and I felt quite exhausted.

I was nearly nodding off and E-J was reading, quiet for once. Only the clinking of the gear on her harness betrayed Janis's approach.

I sat up and smiled as she appeared. She looked angered. I gazed up the lawn to where Tara was stood, arms folded, smiling smugly.

When Janis saw how well-behaved E-J was being her mood lightened. 'Hi, Freya,' she said, undoing and stepping out of her harness, then sitting down on the grass. 'Hope my daughter hasn't been too much of a handful.'

'No, she's been fine.' I was building E-J's defence as best I could, fearing the punishment that might be meted out.

E-J was quivering behind her book.

'Come to me,' was her mother's stern command. 'You may've been good for Freya, but Tara says you've run her ragged all morning. You know she's had a lot to do today.'

'Yes, Mummy.' She climbed to her feet, resigned to her fate, and walked out of the summerhouse and past her mother. She bent herself over a log, which provided seating for a campfire, and began to fumble with her shorts, trembling.

Janis picked up a switch from behind the wooden building in preparation for her daughter's punishment. Then she looked at me. 'I think you're partly to blame for this unruly behaviour. I know you were up on top of the quarry today. She knows not to go up there. And Tara told you to stay here and wait for me.' She handed me the switch. 'I think it only fair – you should punish her today.'

I stared at her, mouth agape in disbelief. Then I flexed the switch and looked at E-J. An expression of betrayal at my treachery was cast across her face.

'Well,' I said, finally summoning the strength to act. 'If I'm in charge of her punishment today, we can do without this.' I broke the switch in half over my knee and threw it into the brook. E-J smiled, watching its progress as it disappeared with the current.

'Stand up, E-J. Don't think you're getting away with it.' I hectored. 'You can spend the rest of the day with Tara, helping her with all the chores.' I called over to the young woman, who was looking on: 'And make sure you give her some of the mucky jobs you hate.'

The scowl, which had appeared on Tara's face when I'd refused the beating, quickly became a broad grin instead. 'Oh, I've got plenty of those.'

'Off you go, then, E-J. Make yourself useful. Mummy won't want to see you till bedtime. And it'll be an early bed at that.'

E-J moaned, kicking at a stone around the scorched earth of the campfire hearth. But she did as she was told and took off towards Tara.

When they were gone, Janis sat down beside me. She didn't look very amused.

'Let's try things my way. See if we get anywhere.'

Janis sighed. 'Well, she hasn't thrown a tantrum, so that's a start.'

'If it doesn't work, spank her later, if you must. But you'll not see me doing something so cruel.' My father used to beat me as a child; I could remember what it was like and couldn't bear to inflict such pain on anyone else.

Janis was quiet for some time; such a contrast from the hours spent with her loquacious daughter. Finally, she poured herself a drink, then took off her rock boots. These were made of rubber and followed the contours of her feet, which aided the grip when climbing.

I noticed she had lost several toes from both feet. I cringed.

She twiddled her remaining toes and this broke her dismal mood. 'Lost them to frostbite. Worth it though, as I nearly bagged the peak. I'd been after a first British-woman ascent of Everest and had to settle for the south summit instead.'

She went down to the stream and bathed her feet, as I reflected upon her bravery. Once seated next to me again, she made me recount what had so disturbed me about Dylan's behaviour to have warranted my emergency phone call.

'You went up to the tower?! No wonder he was angry!' She was cursing me, but underneath I detected her concern at the way Dylan had reacted.

She remained pensive as I charted what I'd found in the tower rooms. Eventually, she acknowledged she was extremely worried about him. 'It also makes my decision all the more difficult. I don't want to leave him like this.'

'Leave him?' I was astonished. 'You said you never would.'

'I know what I said. I only mean temporarily. I've been in talks with one of my climbing pals from the old days, Jeff. He runs a climbing school in Snowdonia. Similar to mine, only bigger, and for summer and winter climbing. He wants a third partner to set up an Alpine climbing centre in Chamonix. Another friend of ours, Jean-Pierre, has an ideal chalet he's presently hiring out to skiers. It'd be a great base for a new centre. Jeff wants us all to merge our ventures together to form one big company. It'll mean placing managers here and in the Welsh centre and living in France for at least the next couple of years.'

'Dylan won't like that, will he?'

'No. I don't think he will. The plan's been in the offing since the beginning of the season. But I've had to wait till I pay off Dylan's loan. The last instalment goes out next week.'

'Feels like you're running away, too.'

'No. Just creating a little space. But I'll be over here regularly enough to see my therapist. And to make sure this place is running smoothly. I've put too much of myself into it to let things slide. And he can visit me whenever he likes. I'll still want a sexual relationship with him. He'll oblige me and on my terms, I know him too well. I'm looking to place E-J in a boarding school over here, so he can have ready access to her, too.'

'You seem to have it all planned.'

'I'm probably going to put pen to paper next week. But I only decided to go ahead with it yesterday. I've put a lot of thought into this. I'm not impetuous like the other two. I had to base it on firm business sense.'

'So the incident with the cavern and my questioning about the Satanists has no bearing on your decision-making?'

Janis tensed up, but she didn't answer.

So I told her about the film I'd found and Dylan's disclosure.

'He and Sera had it easy.'

I endeavoured to entice her to reveal what she knew.

'No, I'm sorry, Freya. You've burrowed into the background of my life – and Dylan's and Sera's – far too much already. Is nothing sacred? What do we know about your past, anyway? It's a blank canvas, compared to what you know about the rest of us. How would you like it if I started forcing you to lay out your own sordid life for me to pick over?'

'I wouldn't. I don't mean to intrude.'

'Good. Then that's settled. I lay myself bare to my therapist. That's where I contain it. And that's where it's going to stay.'

E-J and Tara returned then. The latter detailed all the chores E-J had carried out. Janis wrote out a further list of tasks. 'This should keep you active till bedtime.'

E-J groaned and gazed in my direction.

'It's no good looking to her for sympathy. You're very lucky not to've had a spanking. Think about that when you miss the bonfire tonight.'

'Oh, but Mummy, you know how much I love bonfires! Oh, Freya, please tell her.'

'No. Mummy is right,' I said. 'Let it be a lesson to you.'

'Oh, I hate the lot of you!' she screamed and barged past Tara.

Janis made her excuses. She had to meet with a group of instructors to plan for the next day's activities with the new guests. She left me with instructions to build a bonfire. I spent the next hour wheelbarrowing logs from one of the outbuildings.

Later reports from Tara showed E-J had carried on with her chores as instructed. I now asked E-J to help me build the bonfire, as I felt this would further instil what she'd be missing. She tried to plead with me to let her stay up, but to no avail.

Janis returned long after E-J had retreated to her bedroom. We lit the fire, toasting marshmallows, then laid a grate over the flames to cook a barbecue. As Janis discussed her plans into the evening, I became aware of E-J's face pressed against the glass of a dormer window. I waved at her, but carried on in conversation with her mother. By nine o'clock, E-J had conceded defeat and disappeared from view; into bed, I hoped.

As the night drew in and the dying embers faded, I dismissed Janis's earlier entreaties and began to recount the details of the film I'd viewed in the tower.

'Look, why do you keep on! You're giving me no peace, damn you! I've got plenty more of those reels secreted away. Mother thinks they all got lost in the fire.'

'The mansion-house fire?'

'Yes. I assume she must've told you. Well, they're all locked away in a safe-deposit box. What you want to know's all there. It'll come out only when I think I'm ready. But it will surface one day, mark my words.'

'How did you know to rescue the material? Did Eric warn you he was going to torch the house?'

She stared at me with wild eyes and rocked her head back as she let out a guttural laugh. 'Yes, they all thought it was him, didn't they?'

She nudged me and took a swig from a beer bottle when I remained nonplussed. 'It was me! I did it! I hated them all! Mother and Father and all those horrid people! And Sera! She was the special one. She only had one endurance test. Eric and I had a whole childhood of it!'

She began to pace up and down, tugging at her hair, getting increasingly more hysterical. 'You're dragging it out of me, like you said you wouldn't!'

Something compelled me to continue, when I knew I should've held back. I ran through all the evidence I had uncovered and from what Dylan had said. Then I mentioned my conversations with Paul Norton.

'No! No! I believed him at first as well. But no. He was "Crooked Cock"!'

'What?'

'He turned out to be one of the bastards all along! I didn't realize till my wedding night. He raped me then, just like he'd done to me as a kid!'

She ferociously threw her beer bottle at my head. It narrowly missed as I ducked. Once I recovered, I was lost to know where she had gone. Then I saw the white of her leggings disappearing through the opening in the tree house. She stuck her head out of the window. 'Go away! Leave me alone, you bitch!'

The far-off hum of conversation from the instructors' partying tailed off and several lights came on in the main building.

I climbed up the ladder and hauled myself into the tree house. It was about seven-foot square, with nursery-rhyme murals painted on the walls. Janis was lying in one corner, in a foetal position, sobbing quietly. I went over to her and crouched down beside her. I intuitively held her in my arms from behind as her emotions flooded forth.

When the tears died away, Janis spoke, automaton-like, isolating her feelings from the remembered events: 'I invented names for them all. "Crooked Cock", "Eagle Tattoo", "Three Moles", "Big Tits", "Bad Breath" and so on....Men and women. Twenty, at least....They never spoke to us. Stayed behind their masks like cowards! It only ever happened on eight nights of the year – their blasted "sabbats". I was always consumed with terror, never knowing if they'd come for me or not. I even had to have a hysterectomy shortly after E-J's birth, because of the damage those bastards'd caused me....There were other children, too: Auntie Agnes's triplets and four or five other children of my father's followers. The biggest horror was the waiting as the ceremonies progressed.

Never sure whether you would be abused by your father, your mother, the other followers or even their dogs! As the abuse went on, I learnt to divorce my emotional self from the physical self being violated – "dissociation" my therapist calls it.'

Her suffering at the hands of the Satanists overwhelmed me.

When she had finished, and could cry no more, she nestled up to me. She appeared like an innocent child, wanting succour. And I became a willing surrogate mother. As the morning light pierced through the small aperture to awaken me, I found her still attached to me, sleeping on blissfully.

I smiled, not knowing this would be the last time I'd ever see my friend.

- XXV -

A STRANGE STILLNESS gripped the atmosphere within the library, the room which had given me the most comfort since my arrival here. I sat by the fire, reflecting on the real picture of Dylan Quest, and the wider characters surrounding him, I had developed. I had totally mixed feelings now. He had genuinely cared for me. Yet that hadn't stopped him hurting me through his unfaithfulness and his increasingly erratic behaviour. I was beginning to realize how much my search for the truth by staying with him had taken out of me. I'd learnt so much about the novelist, things which would've shocked even the most seasoned tabloid hacks who'd lampooned him for so long.

Now things were drawing to a conclusion. The fascination he had held for me would wane thereafter, I was sure. And I would be able to leave his depraved world behind and get on with my own life.

The final chapter still had to be told. And the only person I thought capable of telling it was Veronica Faversham.

Dylan was up in his ivory tower, putting the final touches to his novel-in-progress. I was sure he'd not disturb us. I'd called Veronica. Now I was simply awaiting her arrival.

Finally she did turn up, in an immaculate Hillman Super Minx. I met her at the door and led her through into the library. She helped herself to a tumbler of single malt whisky, then sat down in a leather armchair opposite me.

'Your call sounded urgent. I came as fast as I could. What's the matter?'

'Dylan and Janis've told me everything.'

Veronica raised her eyebrow. 'I'm sorry? I don't know what you're talking about.'

'Well, let me spell it out for you: you're a Satanist!'

Veronica looked stunned.

'Dylan has told me all about the satanic circle Sir Frederick ran....'

Veronica tutted.

'....that you, his mother and others were his followers....'

She tutted again and lifted her head towards the ceiling.

'....and that Dylan and Seraphina had been destined to be joined in a despicable and evil union.'

'What rubbish!'

''Fraid not. I've seen an old film of the ceremony.'

Veronica shook her head, non-believing. Yet the first telltale signs of disquiet underpinned her expression.

'Seraphina lost her virginity that night. Dylan was the goat-man who took it from her, just as your husband instructed. I take it he was the priest-like figure?'

'OK. You're right. Dylan must've told you.'

'Yes.'

She went over to the drinks cabinet and poured herself another whisky. 'I admire you, Freya. You must've influenced him greatly. He's been truthful with you, which is unheard of for Dylan. He usually talks in riddles.'

'Believe me, it took a lot of research and piecing together from books, the medallion I found, gossip, Seraphina's folly painting, the ruined chapel, the old film and such like. I only managed to coax it out of Dylan and Janis armed with this evidence.'

'I see.'

'I think I'm the first person who's really tried to find out what lies behind his sexual behaviour.'

'You seem to've been given the full run of this house, too, which is rare.'

'You sound jealous.'

'You're probably right. I've been jealous of all the lovers he's paraded in front of me over the years. And, believe me, there've been plenty of them.'

'Jealous? Why, because all these women were replacing your beloved Seraphina?'

'No. Because I wanted him for myself.'

I couldn't help giggling.

She looked disgruntled. 'I was beautiful, once, you know.'

'Well, let's leave your warped fantasies to one side, shall we,' I said, trying to disguise my mirth but failing badly. 'Dylan's been getting worse, both physically and mentally, even in the short time I've known him. Satanist indoctrination and trauma may account for a lot of this.'

'I don't think so.'

'Care to enlighten me, then?'

'Where's Dylan?'

'Up in the tower. We shouldn't be disturbed, if that's what you're worried about.'

She climbed to her feet and leant against the mantelpiece, picking up a poker to stoke the fire. Then she came over to me and waved the poker in front of my face.

'If I tell you what you want to know, I must swear you to secrecy. If you do tell, no one in the outside world will believe you. But it would destroy Dylan.'

I watched the poker hovering nearer with mounting fear.

'If you tell him, I'll drive you out of his life! And I'll do some damage with this!' – she waved the poker beneath my nose – 'Understood?'

I started to shake and quickly blurted out: 'I swear.'

Veronica retreated and I was glad when she laid down the poker. She sat down again. She had remained calm throughout, despite her threats of violence. And this chilled me to the core.

'Everything you've said about the Satanic Circle is true,' she began, as if nothing untoward had happened. 'I cannot deny my involvement. I was a fervent supporter of my husband's activities. Passed down through generations of von Eschenbachs and Favershams. He was an expert black magician. Renowned throughout European circles. He had plenty of connexions and friendships with other renowned occultists. I don't think you'll ever believe how great my husband's powers were. All you have to know is that his coterie of young maidens became committed to his work.'

'Dastardly work, you mean.'

'I never saw it that way. Dylan's mother and I were two of the twelve selected in my generation. I was further honoured by becoming his wife as well. The Satanists had taken us away from our humble circumstances, educated us, given us belief in ourselves.

'All except Dylan's mother had remained committed to his master plan. She came to loathe Frederick and tried to obstruct our work. She ran off to Wales in an attempt to break away. Turned to evangelical Christianity in a failed bid to block out the dark forces. But she was drawn back here eventually, when her life turned sour. She remained unfaithful. But she couldn't stop Frederick from influencing her son. Dylan simply believed he would become part of the group to which his mother had belonged. He was carefully tutored to take on the role of impregnating Seraphina during a dark ceremony, so that any offspring would obtain the combined powers of Faversham. Once of age, they could take the Circle forward to the next generation.'

'When were they introduced into the Circle?'

'They were educated together by my husband from the age of ten. They were both in awe of Frederick. Dylan, in particular, was very impressionable. Easily manipulated. Yet they were not subject to any induction into the group until the ceremony – the one you say you've seen the film of.'

'Your other children – and the children of the other women – were though.'

'Yes. They weren't special like Dylan and Seraphina.'

'How d'you mean?'

'Well, what he didn't, and still doesn't comprehend, was that roles within the ceremony had been mapped out for both of them since their conception. Sir Frederick had embarked on a six-year programme. Like all the previous Masters had done. Tradition dictated it. All the twelve women were allowed to pair off and breed with other male members of the Circle. But only after each had submitted to Frederick in a specially designed ceremony on the most especial date in the satanic calendar – 30 April. Two of the twelve on that night, each year, until all had submitted.'

'You mean sexually submitted?'

'Why, of course. And as virgins.'

'I see.'

'Dylan and Seraphina were so special because they had been the only children conceived on these dates: Seraphina on 30 April, 1952; Dylan on 30 April, 1953. The twelve women had other children; but they'd been conceived within their own partnerships or during the less important ceremonies.'

'How could you be so sure they were conceived on the night of the ceremony?'

'Because the chosen women were sworn to celibacy between 30 April and the second most important date in our calendar – 31 October. Or Hallowe'en to you.'

'I see....' Then suddenly it struck me. 'Now, hang on a minute. You're telling me Sir Frederick fathered both Dylan and Seraphina?'

'Yes.'

'So they were half-brother and half-sister!'

'Exactly. Seraphina found out about this soon after the ceremony. Then, when she discovered she was carrying Dylan's child, she realized there was a great possibility the baby might turn out to be a monster, because of the close blood ties. That she might, in effect, really become the mother of the Devil's child.'

'And Dylan?'

'Dylan never knew any of this. He was happy that Seraphina loved him; that he loved her; and that his life with her would be everlasting. He was also content with the esoteric powers he'd gleaned from my husband.

'But Seraphina couldn't live with the antagonisms. She'd confided in me several times about the raving thoughts inside her mind before she finally ended it all.

She tried to escape what she called "her father's baleful influence" by running away with Dylan. He arranged for them to have a Christian wedding, which might act as an exorcism.

'She couldn't bring herself to tell him. She'd always been very highly-strung. She loved him, but at the same time, she was ashamed to have committed an incestuous act. Despite our teachings, she'd never really overcome the customs and taboos of wider society....Therefore, she killed herself.'

Veronica bowed her head. She brought out a handkerchief and wiped the tears from her eyes.

'I didn't want to tell Dylan the real reason behind her suicide, for the same reason why Seraphina didn't want to tell him what was troubling her: we didn't want to lose his love and companionship.

'She chose not to tell him. So I, in turn, have adopted her attitude.'

'And between you, you seem to have overladen him with guilt!' I interrupted angrily, a wave of sympathy for him sweeping over me.

'I've suffered, too, you know. I'm sure the Devil's curse was laid upon me and Dylan's mother. I've lost my looks, my husband and my daughter since that ceremony. Anne lost her life to cancer.'

'But look what you've done to Dylan!'

Veronica remained silent.

'So Dylan and Seraphina only entered into these ceremonies once; kept in the dark till that moment. The same can't be said for Janis and Eric, now can it?'

'I don't know what you're talking about.'

'You mean you can't face what you've done to them. That you're culpable in the systematic sexual abuse of both of them! And Agnes's three daughters! And other children as yet unaccounted for!'

'It wasn't like that.'

'How else can you explain it? Little boys and girls being molested, penetrated and raped by grown men, women and even dogs. Some of these perpetrators being their own mothers and fathers – horrific!'

I was becoming increasing frustrated with Veronica's denials of the enormity of what she had been part of. Could this really be the result of Sir Frederick's indoctrination? Or did she have to keep denying it all, in order to survive the horror of what she had done.

'Dylan and Seraphina escaped this. But you've created a line of victims. Some of whom have become sexual monsters themselves. Like your renegade son, Eric. Janis's told me all about his imprisonment for paedophilia.'

'Don't dare mention him!' Veronica was boiling over with rage. She was finally having to face up to her crimes. 'I disowned him long ago. He was always of lowest rank, not even Frederick's son.'

'Conceived during one of those orgies, no doubt.'

'Indeed. He threatened our secrets, you know, spilling them all out through his lewd actions.'

'You tried to gag Janis, too, didn't you? By marrying her off to another of your husband's evil cronies.'

'Yes. She started to pour out all her memories in therapy. Then she'd come to me with her tirades. I thought she needed to be stabilized before she spilled it out to other people. I couldn't let that happen. There's too much at stake.'

'Eh? All this took place years ago.'

'True. But I never retired after my husband's death.' She unbuttoned the top of her blouse and I saw the medallion boldly displayed above her cleavage. 'I spared Emily from all involvement and knowledge, in light of its effects on my other kids. But our Circle still exists; it's simply been relocated since Dylan reneged on his responsibilities.'

'My God! You must tell Dylan the truth! If you don't, then I will. I can't keep this to myself.'

'No! No! No!' she shrieked. 'You swore to me you wouldn't tell!'

She ran over to the hearth and picked up the poker. She thrust it into the fire, then held it aloft in a threatening manner, and walked towards me. Instinctively, I pulled myself to my feet and stood behind the chair as a line of defence.

Suddenly, the false door in the bookcase swung open and Dylan stepped into the room.

Veronica stood still, her body beginning to shake, which made the poker quiver in front of her. Then she dropped it on the floor and tried to make out as if nothing had happened.

But Dylan had evidently overheard everything Veronica had said, from his hiding place behind the mirror. His face revealed his inability to understand why Veronica hadn't told him the real truth before. Why she had allowed him to suffer for seventeen long years in the belief he was to blame for Seraphina's death.

I walked over to Dylan in an effort to comfort him.

Veronica saw the strained and horrified expression on his face. She knew it was all over.

He rushed towards her. He gripped her by the blouse, tearing the fabric as he pushed her against the wall.

'Why! Why!....Why!' he screamed.

It was the first time I'd witnessed his tears flowing.

'I want you out of my life for good! And Janis's and E-J's. You disgust me! I never want to see you again. Pack your bags and leave here. Leave the mill. And leave me alone!'

'But Dylan....Dylan!....Please....'

'Get the hell out of here!'

Dylan hounded Veronica out to her car. I hung onto Dylan's arm in an attempt to stop him from venting his rage further.

We watched the Hillman career off.

Then I returned with Dylan to the hallway. As we arrived there, I was stung on my face by a swipe from the back of his hand.

I fell to the floor, holding my throbbing cheek.

'Look what you've done, you bitch! Why did you have to come here?! Why did you have to meddle in my affairs?!

I cowered at his feet, still stunned from his blow. He'd turned his violence on me. I knew this had to be the end.

'What do I know of your background, now you've delved so deeply into mine? Absolutely nothing!'

'Well, whose fault's that? Not mine. Once you'd got into my knickers you weren't too interested in the back-history.'

Dylan scowled at my cheap gibe. 'Who sent you to haunt me so?'

'Sera's old boyfriend – John.'

'What *are* you on about? You've got that wrong. I've remembered his name now. It was Fairfax....Joshua Fairfax.'

But his puzzled expression soon turned to one more pensive, as if something was beginning to click within his creative mind.

I shook my head, confused, mumbling 'Fairfax? Fairfax?' under my breath. 'John sent me here. John Jones!'

'Now hang on a minute – that's me! The old me!'

And a look of abject terror swept across his face and he hurried out of the house.

- XXVI -

BUT I HADN'T gone outside at all!

Instead, I found myself alone in front of my word processor. I looked around me, caught up in the reality of what I'd tried to disguise in my imagination. My surroundings were familiar. Papers were strewn all around the tower room.

I pulled myself out of my chair, stiff-limbed and aching. I found the door, opened it and walked slowly down the spiral staircase. The Lodge was full of dust. It hadn't been cleaned for weeks. And the building was freezing. The oil to fire the central-heating boilers had dried up long ago.

I became aware of the awful stench emanating from the kitchen. I went inside. Dirty dishes overflowed in the sink. Tins had been left opened and only half eaten. Food was rotting at the foot of the open fridge door.

I walked out of the house. The front door had been left wide open to the ravages of the elements. The hallway was flooded.

The manicured lawns were beginning to overgrow. I turned back to regard my house. All the shutters were drawn over the windows. Only those in the tower remained open.

I scratched my face in bewilderment. It took me a few seconds to notice I'd grown a beard.

Time had moved on. Yet I could remember nothing.

Then I saw Freya, skipping over the main lawn, laughing.

This cheered my mood.

I followed her over the long grass and into the woods. I could hear her ahead. I fought my way through the undergrowth to the yew-tree tunnel, oblivious to the burrs and thorns that bit into my legs. Suddenly I realized I was naked.

Pushing my way frantically through the creepers, I came upon the old folly. I hadn't been here in years. Not since that first time with Emily. I couldn't bear the memory of what I had done to her. I would have retreated had I not heard Freya's soft voice inviting me inside.

I steadied myself, then cautiously entered. Freya stood in front of me, staring at me forlornly. Then I watched her float up into the dome of the ceiling, back whence she had come.

Once again, she became the long-blonde-haired nymph in Sera's exquisite painting.

Now it was Sera's tears I was hearing down the ages, tears she'd shed whilst executing the picture. I turned to her self-portrait, the jet-black-haired maiden being ravished by the Devil. Her head seemed to move, her wild eyes taunting me.

Somewhere in the back of my mind I came to an ultimate realization.

I fought my way back to the courtyard and stumbled over to the old stabling block. I opened the wooden door. Light flooded into the gloomy interior.

And there was Sera's old Fiat 500. A large film of dust covered the tiny car now. All four tyres were flat. It had not been touched since it'd been stored there years before. I rubbed the dust off the window. Sera's old school uniform still lay on the back seat, where she'd discarded it on our journey to a new life in Wales that, as it turned out, was never to be.

All the characters I'd written about – except Freya – had existed in my life, yet they'd been involved in a novel of my own making. And the text saved on my computer upstairs must surely be my last novel!

Freya was as mythical as her name. Sera's angel.

Come back to claim me from my manic flurry of literary endeavour and sexual pursuits that my defences had sustained for so many empty years.

Sexual promiscuity had been such a lonely experience. Mechanical fornication, not genuine lovemaking. Even my longer-term lovers had eventually left me. Even they hadn't been able to overcome my sickness.

And it was a sickness. I was aware of that now.

And I'd driven all my friends and lovers away because of it.

Janis and Emily were not Sera. Nor were all the others I'd conquered. Yet every one of those women had taken on Seraphina's guise when I'd seduced them.

Every one.

But what had I done to them all in the process?!

There'd only ever been one woman for me.

Sera....

Seraph....

Seraphina!

I had to go to her now.

I ran down to the outer gatehouse and picked up the tools I required for the task in hand. Then I made my way across the lawns and battled through the undergrowth to the ruined chapel. The place not visited in so many years.

It must have taken me the whole of the afternoon and evening to dig down into the solid earth. The earth which had remained undisturbed through the seventeen years since Sera had been laid to rest. When my spade hit the lid of the coffin, I was suddenly aware that the sunlight had changed to moonlight.

Once uncovered, the decayed wood fell apart in ruins around my beloved Seraphina.

Then I saw her again.

I'd waited for this moment for so long.

I gazed down upon her beautiful form. She was unclothed, her breasts half-hidden under the silken blanket of her cascading jet-black hair. The dark area at the confluence of her milk-white thighs looked so inviting.

I descended onto her to possess her again at last.

But I felt her ribcage crumbling to dust under my weight.

Something was terribly wrong!

I stared in horror at the whiteness of her skeleton. The sunken voids of her eye sockets looked sadly up at me. Much of her hair was still in evidence, around the skull that had caved in when she'd struck the rocks below Castle Crag all those years ago.

And I screamed!

- Epilogue -

Five years later

THE TAXI PULLED up in the forecourt of the old mill. Janis and her daughter climbed out. Rupert, smiling benevolently, approached them as Janis paid the driver.

She turned to greet him and he stretched out his large hand for her to shake. 'You're a little late. Come inside.'

'Sorry. My flight was delayed. And I had to collect E-J from school on the way up from London. Anyway, I'm here now.'

She had been given Dylan's power of attorney. She'd agonized over what to do with the museum and had gone through a number of failed managers whilst trying to sell the attraction. In the end, it hadn't sold and she'd taken a risk on Rupert. He had come out of a disastrous marriage to Lady Jennifer MacAlistair and several rehabs and had wanted space away from the City. Looking around at all the parked cars and the many visitors, she was pleased with its success and the decisions she had made. It looked like it had done Rupert good, too.

As they walked past the garages, a number of the mechanics and bodywork specialists came out to greet her, staff Rupert had managed to retain. They all seemed pleased to see her after all this time.

After several minutes of re-acquaintance, Rupert led Janis and her daughter into the old mill-owner's house. Janis was taken aback by how different the lounge looked. Rupert had made the place his own, even finding space for a grand piano. All of Dylan's possessions had gone.

Janis was expecting Quasi to come bouncing out to greet them. Then she remembered he'd died here at the mill, pining for his master, only months after Dylan had left.

E-J sat down very calmly and politely. She had grown up a lot in these past few years, Janis thought. She had dyed her long hair blonde, and was a lot taller and more mature. Boarding school had given her independence, and a good set of boundaries for her behaviour which Janis had found so difficult to instil. Not having her around all the time had eased Janis's stress levels and had helped make the holidays so much more special as well. Janis had also worked hard on her parenting skills. She was proud that physical chastisement was no longer a feature of their relationship.

Rupert brought in a tray of tea. E-J offered to pour it out for everyone and he let her do this.

'So, do you want to see the books?'

'No. I trust everything's in order.'

He smiled. 'What are your plans now?'

'I think I'm coming home for good.'

'That's great.'

'I'm not too sure what I'm going to do yet. I've got enough to retire on. My partners and I struck a big deal. The schools in Chamonix, Snowdonia and my original one here are now all under new ownership.'

'Do I detect mixed feelings?'

'Yes. I was happy in Chamonix. I have many friends out there. And winter mountaineering is my real forte. I might be ready for some new Himalayan expeditions. My only responsibility now is to E-J. She's got to be my priority. So maybe I'm dreaming.'

'Look, Mum,' E-J said. 'Don't let me stop you. I'm happy at my school. I don't need you as much as I used to. If you really want to do it, go for it! Life's too short.'

This brought a tear to Janis's eye and she hugged her daughter.

Janis and Rupert spent the next fifteen minutes talking about the museum. Then he gave them a tour around the complex, after which he halted at some garages.

'We've got a little surprise for you,' Rupert said, pointing to Janis's old Citroën, now completely restored.

Janis ran her hand along the wing, opened the door and sat back in the driver's seat. 'It's lovely. You've done a splendid job. I need something of old to help ground me back here.'

'Great. What are your immediate plans? You're welcome to stay here till you get yourself sorted.'

'I'll take you up on that. I need to go and see the Lodge. And I've got an appointment to see Dylan tomorrow.'

E-J heard this and gazed expectantly at her mother.

'I'm sorry, love. You can come to the Lodge if you want. But I need to see Dylan alone. Perhaps you can come next time.'

E-J looked saddened. She bit her lower lip, but said nothing.

Janis and E-J journeyed up to Grimshaw Lodge, after lunch with Rupert and some of the staff. The Citroën felt very smooth as she drove it through the forests. But this couldn't offset her mounting apprehension as they made their approach.

Their upset started when they parked at the front gates. A large security hoarding of wood and barbed wire blocked out the arch of the outer gatehouse. The tree branches had begun to undermine the top of the battlements. A few pieces of masonry had fallen down onto the drive and the grass verge nearby.

They both climbed out for a closer inspection. Janis undid the padlock with the key Rupert had given her. This secured a little door in the hoarding. They passed through this to be met by the portcullis. This had jammed near the bottom, giving only a couple of feet of clearance from the ground. They had to get onto their backs and wriggle underneath the metalwork, careful not to gash themselves on the spikes.

E-J still had a spirit of adventure about her as they brushed the dirt from their clothing. But Janis was overwhelmed by a deep sense of sadness, beginning to get an idea of what to expect.

They walked through the archway and onto the drive, E-J taking the lead. The rooks cawed overhead and their sounds echoed eerily over the deserted grounds. The branches hung down low and the rhododendron bushes encroached onto the sides of the driveway. This left only a narrow passageway for them to walk through. It was evident no vehicles had passed this way in a long time. As the passageway opened out, the outer lawns came into view and they both shuddered. All was a jungle of long grass, with an infiltration of nettles and brambles.

Janis leant against the bridge, thinking back to the abseiling here, so long ago now. And of the plans which had never materialized. She glanced over the parapet.

The ghyll still raged on, but its banks were as overgrown as elsewhere.

Both of them succumbed to tears when they approached the inner gatehouse. Scorch marks around the windows and arrow slits foretold of what they might find. As they walked under the archway, they could look up directly to the sky. Only a few charred beams remained of Yasuko's old quarters. The fire had gutted the whole interior.

Rupert had warned them of the vandalism. But nothing he said could have prepared them for what they were now viewing. They had to hug each other for several minutes, each detecting the other's hesitation about whether to go on or turn back.

Eventually, they crept into the inner courtyard. Weeds were growing out from around the cobblestones. The wisteria on the facade of the main building now covered most of the wall and hid many of the closed upstairs shutters. Extra wooden boarding had been nailed over the ground-floor windows.

E-J ran over to the little door in the side wall. It opened easily into the walled garden. This had been E-J's favourite space. Now she was met by more stinging nettles, blocking out most of the entrance. Some of the rose bushes still clung wildly to the walls. But the flower and vegetable beds had been completely consumed by the overgrowth.

Janis pulled E-J back and they walked around the side of the building to the main ramparted lawns. They fought their way down the old gravel path towards the terrace by the dining hall. They had no sight of the old sloping vista down towards the woods and the yew-tree tunnel.

Bramble thorns bit into the flesh on E-J's legs. This prompted them to retreat. They headed for the front door. Janis undid further padlocks and then placed the heavy door key in the lock. The door creaked open.

Several rats squeaked and shot past them, scuttling away across the courtyard.

Both mother and daughter leapt back in fright. Once recovered, Janis had to coax E-J inside.

The hallway floor was damp. The parquet tiles were beginning to warp and rise. The grand stairway led off into the darkness. Janis looked up and saw the glass dome had several broken panels. Water was pouring in every time it rained.

Janis noticed the portrait of Dylan on the stairwell had been damaged by the water. The paint had run, giving his face a warped appearance, and several droplets gave the impression he was crying.

An air of mustiness filled their nostrils as they went into each room in turn. White sheets shrouded the furniture in the lounge. The door had remained locked here and nothing appeared to have been disturbed. Many of the books had been taken off the shelves in the library. The dining hall was an empty shell. Their shoes clicked on the stone floor and reverberated around the walls and up into the ceiling. Only the head of the white hart remained, skewed on its mounting; casting its eyes mournfully over the desolate scene.

The drawing room had taken a lot of damage. Much of the furniture was missing. Dylan's two Regency globes lay shattered and the grand piano had been upended on the floor. Janis sifted around in the ashes in the marbled fireplace with a poker. There were a couple of charred cabriole legs and pieces of leather bookbinding. Graffiti had been scrawled over the expensive wallpaper and beards and glasses applied to several of the portraits.

Rupert had said they'd had problems with squatters that had taken five months to resolve.

Entering the old conservatory was perhaps the most haunting of all. The pool had been completely drained. Shards of glass from the many panels lay scattered all over the floor. Boarding had been secured over some of the metal latticework of the walls and ceiling. But a lot had been ripped off, either by high winds or by human hand. The elements had begun to destroy the interior fabric here as well.

Janis was plagued by recollections from her childhood. Despite Dylan's best efforts, the Lodge was beginning to slide back into its former ruinous state, because of her absenteeism. A potent symbol of Janis's neglect of Dylan and his legacy.

Upstairs, iron grates had been constructed over all the doors to the bedrooms, without a care for the plasterwork and architraves. Janis opened the padlocks and crept into each bedroom in turn. Two of them had been trashed, almost to the point of non-recognition. The others hadn't been touched. The dustsheets remained intact on the furniture. This strangely gave these rooms added poignancy. Memories came flooding back to Janis, of the many happy nights she'd spent under the covers with the one great love of her life. She'd remained celibate ever since her last time with Dylan, here in this very room.

E-J comforted her as she broke down again.

The door to the tower could be unlocked and opened. But the way ahead had been crudely bricked up. They returned to the library and found their way through the secret door. On the upper levels, nothing had been disturbed. The vandals and squatters hadn't been able to invade this space. The rooms were empty. The contents had been carefully crated up. The wooden containers remained stacked up in the corner of each room.

Up in Dylan's old workroom, the desk remained in place. Janis tried to imagine his last moments up here and shuddered at the thought.

'Don't sit in that!' Janis cried.

E-J was about to sit down in the old carved-oak chair in the corner. She froze, puzzled. Janis came over and put her foot on the seat. The iron prongs shot out around the arms and the legs of the chair.

'Cool!' E-J said, eyes wide in amazement.

Janis started to cry again.

'What's wrong, Mum?'

'Never mind, love. Maybe I'll tell you some day. When you're a little older.'

E-J looked more concerned than intrigued. As if the weight of preceding generations was beginning to fall on her shoulders.

Janis could sense this. She knew she had to increase her resolve to ensure her daughter's future.

Janis pulled open the door and they went up onto the battlements. Now they could really survey the deterioration of the estate from this coign of vantage.

E-J had never been up in the tower. So she was too busy marvelling at her surroundings to detect her mother was in floods of tears again. Until her mother hugged her in a grip too tight for comfort.

'Are you OK, Mum?'

Janis remained silent, thinking. She was about to speak, then paused for further thought. 'I'm upset by what's happened to this place. If only I'd found a buyer.'

'What? Sell this place? Never! Daddy'll be coming back some day....' she looked anxious. '....Won't he?'

'No. I don't think he will, honey.'

Janis gripped her tighter. But E-J did not require consoling. Perhaps she was still too young to understand.

'Selling this place would've secured your future, independent of me. As it is, you'll inherit this place when you turn eighteen.'

'Really?'

'Yes, really. Let's hope there'll be something left of it when the time comes....What would you like me to do?'

'Come home, Mum. Live here.'

Janis relaxed her grip. 'I'm not sure I could ever do that. There are too many demons here.'

'Well, fight them away!' she said vehemently. 'I can see it now. You could set up a new outdoor centre here. Only bigger and better than Branth'et Farm.'

Janis was beginning to grasp her daughter's vision. Ideas flashed through her mind as she viewed the grounds. Abseiling off the bridge....Ghyll-walking underneath....A ropes course in the beech trees. A rifle range in the old chapel....Maybe quad bikes on the outer lawns....Overnight camps in the woods. Orienteering around the whole grounds. Caving in the cavern....It would be easy to add a climbing wall, archery....water sports down on the lake....

'What do you think, Mum? I could join you in the business once I've grown up.'

Janis kissed her on the forehead. 'You know, you may have something there, darling.'

The last vestiges of summer had gone. The leaves had changed colour and were beginning to fall onto the driveway. Janis drove her Citroën into the car park. She stared at the bleak grey walls of the Victorian hospital building.

The doctor was there to greet her. She was a small, slender woman in her early fifties, with short, greying-black hair.

Janis climbed out of the car. She looked reserved, not knowing what the doctor's reaction to her neglect of Dylan would be. She needn't have worried.

'Doctor, it's good to see you at last.'

They shook hands.

'What finally brings you here, Mrs Norton?'

'What you sent me couldn't be ignored.' She pulled off her shoulder bag and opened it enough to show the doctor the dog-eared manuscript inside.

'I see. We're certain it was the last novel he'd been working on. Hadn't even printed it off the machine when they found him.'

'It's very powerful. And so voyeuristic.'

'Yes, it is.'

'It disturbed me so much.' Janis looked unsteady.

'You sure you're up to this?' From their lengthy telephone conversations over the last few years, the doctor was well aware of the amount of therapy Janis had endured in an effort to repair years of ritualistic abuse, never mind the added burden of what had happened to Dylan.

'Yes. I need to see him. That novel is unlike anything he's written as Dylan Quest. Reminds me of the style he had in his early unpublished days, when everyone knew him as John Jones.'

The way the doctor was scribbling down notes made Janis think she must have hit upon something important.

'And the major events are pure autobiography. But sometimes he's taken them out of sequence and he's certainly condensed the time between each event. In reality, they took place over a year, maybe eighteen months.'

'And the other episodes depicted?'

'They seem to have been constructed, with real people being made to act according to their usual character traits. For example, I've never been back to Castle Crag since Sera's death, but the route described was her favourite fell-walk.'

'Right, I see.'

'And Dylan's showering of gifts onto Freya, and his use of outdoor pursuits to woo her, followed a course he often took to seduce his women.'

'Umm. A weaving of fact and fiction. Now that's interesting.' She took down some more notes.

'Emily told me Yasuko had discovered her at the chapel. They'd exchanged their stories, revealing their secrets. I can only assume Yasuko must've used this as ammunition against Dylan when she left. I'm sure Emily wouldn't've said anything to Dylan. His anger would've been too great!'

The doctor nodded and made another note. 'And what of Emily now?'

'Still with the bikers, as far as I know. I get the odd re-directed postcard now and then. And I sent her a sizable sum for drug treatment, but she could've used this to buy more drugs, I really couldn't tell.'

'At least you tried to help her. And Yasuko?'

'Last I heard she was a high-class dominatrix in Soho. Getting her own back, she said, and getting paid for the privilege.'

'Oh.' The doctor seemed taken aback, but recovered quickly. 'And the other events portrayed?'

'Well....let me see....Yasuko had been in the Land Rover crash with Dylan. That's what finally drove Yasuko to leave. E-J found her own way into the cavern, which sent me berserk. Dylan witnessed my punishment of E-J. He was so furious. It led me to disclose my abuse, up in the tree house, as a way of placating him. I burnt the picture of my father. And I discovered the tower and the secret room and got caught in that blasted chair!'

The doctor scribbled away some more. 'And what about the events concerning your mother?'

'Well, the earlier events I knew about. The major dénouement in his text confused me deeply. I had no idea my father was also Dylan's until I read this. I was shocked. It's going to set me back months in my therapy.'

'Oh, I'm sorry to hear that. Maybe I should've heeded my misgivings about sending it out to you. But you were persistent!'

'I know. Don't worry. I've learnt it's better to sit with the truth. I had to fly over specially to visit my mother to get her version of events. She's at an open prison in Kent now. My evidence helped to convict her, my ex-husband, and most of her other cronies.'

'Yes, I took a keen interest in the case. You did very well.'

'Thanks. There were times when I thought I would never find the courage to go through with it. It was like reliving the abuse all over again.'

'So what did you learn from Veronica?' the doctor said, impatiently.

'Well, I had to bully it out of her. She said they had this big argument, more or less as recounted in the manuscript.'

'When he found out the real reason behind Seraphina's suicide?'

'Yes....Except she disclosed directly to Dylan, of course. She reckons this took place on 2 August, 1987.'

'How could she be so precise?'

'It was the anniversary of Sera's death. The tree had fallen down in the storm in the early hours. When he'd found the medallion under its roots later that morning, and realized the significance of the date, it felt like an ill-omen; as if she was calling him from the grave. Apparently, he'd bombarded my mother with anguished questions about why Sera might've killed herself. That's why she finally broached the subject with him.'

'I see.'

'This was also the exact date at which he set Freya's arrival in the story.'

'Oh, now that's very significant.' The doctor paused, deep in thought, scratching her head with the end of her pencil. 'So, come to think of it, is the figure seventeen: Seraphina was seventeen when she died; it was the seventeenth anniversary of her death; and Freya's age was two times seventeen in the story – the age Seraphina would've been had she lived.'

'Yes, of course. In some ways Freya is a projection of what Sera might've become if she'd aborted her child instead of killing herself. A simple life as a secretary would've taken her away from all the stress. But Freya was nothing like Sera beyond that.'

'I see....' She took down some more notes. 'And the date also means he must've been writing at a manic pace.

It could only've taken him two months to complete the manuscript!'

'Well, he was accustomed to locking himself in his tower for days with his writing. Up all night. No sleep. But never that fast. You sure it was only two months?'

'Yes. Positive. Just under two months, in actual fact. It had to be. We sectioned him at the end of September.'

'When my ex-husband found him running naked round the garden?'

'Yes.'

'I hadn't realized it was that early. I was abroad, of course. It took a while for the news to filter through to me.'

The doctor nodded, looking pensive.

'I believe my mother's confession brought on his final collapse.'

'I would agree. Now she has confirmed her part in the manuscript is true. Do you believe her?'

'I have no reason to think she's not telling the truth this time.'

'Even though she's spent most of her life lying to you all?'

'Yes. You see, she's dying. Cancer's eating her away. Just like the fate of Dylan's mother. And our father. She's not got long left.'

'I'm sorry.'

'Don't be. I'm furious with her. She was a terrible mother. It saddens me to say it, but it's the truth. How could she have stood by and let all that abuse happen?'

'Only she can tell you that.'

'She has no answer. There is no defence.' She was spitting the words out like bullets from a machine gun. Anger was still alive deep down within her. Only the responsibility of raising her daughter had kept her from her sister's fate. But she was a survivor.

The doctor guided her to a seat in the foyer. They sat in silence for a long time. After a nurse had brought her the cup of tea the psychiatrist had requested, Janis spoke again:

'I don't regret my relationship with Dylan. Even though he turns out to be my half-brother. It sounds so dirty. Yet he is the only man I've ever really loved. If I'd known the torture he was going through, and the real truth behind Sera's death, I would've condoned his behaviour and tried to get medical help for him sooner. Instead, I ran off to Chamonix, just when he needed me most.'

'Don't punish yourself. Too many people have done that in this case already. Remember, you had enough of your own demons to fight without having to think about other people's. You were too close to help each other. So much of your histories were entwined.'

Janis seemed to hear this. She paused, as if in deep reflexion. 'What makes it even more tragic is realizing Sera need never've taken her own life. And thus Dylan need not've become sick.'

The doctor gave her a quizzical look.

'E-J is Dylan's daughter. She is a perfectly normal child with above-average intelligence. There's no sign of any genetic abnormalities. There's every likelihood Sera's baby wouldn't've turned out any different.'

The doctor put her arm around the visitor's shoulder as Janis began to cry. What Janis had said had not even entered the doctor's own mind at all, even with the evidence of E-J's paternity from the manuscript.

'But what I don't understand is who Freya was? Nor why he joined all those real life events together with her. She was never there.'

'Exactly, Mrs Norton, don't you see?'

'No. It's never explained. The manuscript breaks off.'

'I don't know who or what inspired Freya, but she came straight from his subconscious. A figment of his powerful imagination. A literary device. Freya allowed him to unlock all the traumatic events and emotions he'd kept in separate compartments for so long. Bringing together all the fragments of his own disintegrating personality like some giant jigsaw puzzle.'

Janis looked confused. This was too close to the outskirts of her own "mad bits" for her to swallow.

'My hypothesis,' the doctor continued, 'is that he probably sat down at his desk in a highly delusional state and wrote it as if it was just another novel. Only when he'd finished the book and became its reader did he realize to what purpose he'd constructed the text.'

'And that's when he completely cracked.'

'Yes, I think so.'

Janis looked at the psychiatrist long and hard. And gulped. 'And that's when he....when he....'

'When he dug up Sera's grave. Yes.'

Janis started to cry again. She paused for a while, collecting herself together once more. 'These past five years have slipped by so quickly. Everyone's deserted him. Friends. Lovers. Even the tabloids.'

'Yes, but not his readership.'

'No, true. A "mysterious recluse" is what the publisher's blurb says now. Adds to his cult reputation. Fills up his daughter's bank account with royalties, too. But it doesn't help him, does it?'

'No,' was the doctor's clinically executed response.

'Can I see him now, please?' Janis asked, snivelling and wiping the tears away with the back of her hand. 'I've been dreading this. That's why it's taken me so long to come. But I've got to be brave. I can't run away for ever.'

The doctor was struck by how childlike she looked, belying her forty-one years.

The doctor put her arm around Janis and helped her out of her seat. 'But you've got to realize he's not the Dylan you once knew.' She waited for Janis to acknowledge this fact. 'OK, then, if you're sure. Come this way.'

She guided Janis through the mental institution and out into the walled garden. They walked across the lawn in silence. Now they were upon him.

Two male nurses were escorting Dylan as he took his daily constitutional outside. His hair had been shaved off. His head was bowed and his hunched back was facing towards them.

'Why's he wearing that!' Janis exclaimed, pointing to the straitjacket that bound his upper body.

'I'm afraid we can't take any chances. He's injured three nurses very badly in the last few months alone. Before that, he had a habit of smashing his head against walls. He had to have twenty stitches in his face and lost the sight in one eye when he put his head through a window.'

Janis flinched.

'We thought he'd been trying to destroy his handsome face, in an effort to end the attraction women would have for him. But I was wrong. Quite wrong. His mind's far too gone to know what he's doing.'

Janis remained nonplussed. She couldn't take any of this in.

The doctor tapped Dylan on the shoulder. 'There's someone to see you.'

Dylan turned around, supported by the two burly nurses. He looked up at Janis.

Janis was devastated by his taut, insane expression and drug-fused apathy. And the scars that crisscrossed the right-hand side of his face.

Dylan did not show any kind of recognition as he looked at his half-sister through his one good eye. He broke free from the nurses' grip. He staggered along the lawn by the border of one of the flowerbeds.

As they watched him, they heard him murmur softly: 'Sera....Seraphina.'

They left him in the garden, talking to himself amongst the flowers.

On the way out, Janis took the manuscript from her bag and threw it into the open fire in the hallway. Her eyes widened, as the flames consumed the pages and sent bits of burning paper up the chimney and over the hearth.

The day had finally made clear to Janis that she had lost her best friend. Her half-brother. And her lover. And that his readership had lost their favourite novelist.

Only now could she start to grieve.

THE END

- Author's Note -

Freya's Quest is a work of fiction. Any resemblance of the characters to any person is entirely coincidental. All locations are real, except for the Mill, Branthwaite Farm and Grimshaw Lodge. However, Anthony Salvin (1799-1881) was a Victorian architect, who designed many country houses, including all those described in the text.

- Acknowledgements -

Special thanks:

To everyone at Grosvenor House Publishing

To John Brooks, Geraldine Harris and Jocelyn Ferguson for editorial advice.

To the following people, who all read early drafts of the book and gave me valuable comments: John Wilson, Carole Brooks, Dr Ian Richards, and Karl Elliott. And also to Janet, Ellie, Lindsay and Deniz.

And particular thanks to my fiancée, Hayley Smith, who not only read the book, but has supported me with my writing and has put up with my obsession with getting it into print.

And finally, to my two children, who give me inspiration every day.

Printed in the United Kingdom
by Lightning Source UK Ltd.
132961UK00001B/4-18/P

9 781906 210656